PENGUIN

SHOWERS (

T0247195

Nadia Ayesha is a MA Creative Writing student at LASALLE College of the Arts. She currently teaches English composition at an enrichment centre. From her years of working in the non-profit sector, she learnt the value and meaning in every individual's life story and was inspired to return to writing, her first love as a child. In her leisure time, she enjoys hiking, reading, art, ballet and watching football.

ADVANCE PRAISE FOR *SHOWERS OF LUCK*

'Nadia Ayesha's bold debut *Showers of Luck* is one of those sprawling novels that investigates how we should, and should not, use the same verb, *love*, for family, romance, and country.'

—Professor Darryl Whetter, Inaugural Programme Leader,
MA Creative Writing, LASALLE College of the Arts

'A thoroughly enjoyable read with very relatable characters. A nostalgic love story that will tug at your heartstrings.'

—Eva Wong Nava, author *The House of Little Sisters*

'With an authentic voice and delicate prose, Nadia Ayesha crafts a story full of heart that explores the tribulations of pre-war colonial Singapore, tackling issues such as multiculturalism, colonialism and interracial unions.'

—Joyce Chua, author of *Land of Sand and Song*

Showers of Luck

Nadia Ayesha

PENGUIN BOOKS
An imprint of Penguin Random House

PENGUIN BOOKS

USA | Canada | UK | Ireland | Australia
New Zealand | India | South Africa | China | Southeast Asia

Penguin Books is part of the Penguin Random House group of companies
whose addresses can be found at global.penguinrandomhouse.com

Published by Penguin Random House SEA Pte Ltd
9, Changi South Street 3, Level 08-01,
Singapore 486361

First published in Penguin Books by Penguin Random House SEA 2022

ISBN 9789815017977

Typeset in Garamond by MAP Systems, Bangalore, India

www.penguin.sg

For my parents and grandparents without whom I would not be.

Contents

Part I

Chapter I

15th to 18th January 1939

The shophouse was almost perfect, Lily thought. Its main colour was a tint of light blue, which the patriarch of her home, Pak Kong, thought resembled the sky on a cloudless day. 'Perfect.' Lily remembered hearing him say about the colour when she was a slip of a girl about to turn seven and their home was being repainted. Lily thought that Pak Kong seemed to be a very demanding man and she was glad that she had minimal interactions with him. All she knew about him was that he worked at the Oversea-Chinese Banking Corporation headquarters at Chulia Street. Every time she saw him after work, he looked very serious. She would greet him, 'Selamat pagi, Pak Kong' at the breakfast table where the family had breakfast each day. On the rare occasion, he noticed her, he would reply, 'Selamat pagi, Lily.' But most of the time, he was absorbed in reading the daily newspaper, *The Straits Times*.

As Lily walked through the house sometimes on quiet afternoons when her cousins Charles and Ivy were away at school and her aunt Mak Kong was out playing Cherki, she imagined she was a guest who had been invited to the Kong household. She thought that the guest would sense that the family was a happy and prosperous one. First, the guest would be greeted at the front door by the Chinese couplet that read, 'May your Good Fortune be as Great as the Ocean; your Longevity as

3

High as a Mountain.' Then, she would be greeted by the long reception hall, which housed the ancestral altar, where the statue of Ting Kong, the Jade Emperor, sat against the wall. Lily would observe Mak Kong praying at the altar every morning for the family's good health and longevity. She prayed for every single member of the family, muttering out their names and ending with Lily.

Mak Kong was a distant aunt of Lily's. She knew that Mak Kong tried her best, or so she felt, to accept her as part of her own brood of two children. But it was difficult, and many a time, Mak Kong faltered and showed favouritism. Lily had once overheard her whisper, 'Blood is blood, but it is only natural that children would come before niece,' to herself in the still quiet of dawn, thinking that no one but herself was awake. After Mak Kong was done with her prayers, she would bustle into the kitchen and set about observing the preparation of food for the day. A chicken and potato stew called ayam pongteh and chap chye, a stir-fried vegetable dish, was on the menu for lunch today. As Mak Kong walked into the kitchen, she gave the kitchen a quick look-over with her sharp gaze.

'Good morning, Mak Kong,' Lily and Zhu Jie said together in Baba Malay. Zhu Jie was one of two majies employed by the Kong family. She worked as their domestic helper alongside Leng Jie. Before leaving their home in China, both Zhu Jie and Leng Jie had taken an oath of celibacy as was the norm for majies. Both Zhu Jie and Leng Jie dressed in the same samfu outfit, white mandarin-collar tops and black trousers, and wore their hair in long plaits. After many years of service, they spoke Baba Malay well enough to earn praise from Mak Kong and Pak Kong.

With her chubby elbow, Zhu Jie nudged Leng Jie in the arm. Leng Jie looked up and whispered 'Good morning' without making eye contact with Mak Kong. Mak Kong did not hear Leng Jie, and came up next to her at the counter, where she was peeling potatoes for the ayam pongteh dish. Zhu Jie was pounding shallots and garlic using a mortar and pestle, the ingredients seeming to dance together as their texture was transformed.

At the same time, Lily was chopping a head of white cabbage. She sliced the cabbage crosswise into wide ribbons. As she did so, she imagined eating ayam pongteh, how comforting the potatoes would taste with the saltiness of tau cheo, a fermented soybean paste, and the sweetness of palm sugar that was gula melaka.

'Faster!' Mak Kong barked at Leng Jie, who jumped slightly and then nodded, looking down at her fingernails. Zhu Jie finished her task and walked over to show Ah Huat, the cook. After Ah Huat approved of her paste, Zhu Jie bustled over to Leng Jie and began to help her with the potatoes.

'It should not take two people to peel potatoes,' Mak Kong grumbled. 'Really, Leng Jie, you have to be more efficient.' Again, Leng Jie simply nodded. Lily felt a bit sorry for her as she brought the vegetables to the gas stove for Ah Huat to fry. She joined in the potato peeling, hoping to appease Mak Kong.

'Three people now,' Mak Kong muttered. 'Tachi will be here soon.' Tachi, that's right, Lily thought. Lily always found it difficult to believe that her mousier mother, Mak Wee, was Mak Kong's elder second cousin. For as long as Lily could remember, Mak Wee always made it a point to drop by the Kongs' home every week. These weekly visits were far more frequent than Lily's visits to Mak Wee's home at Joo Chiat Terrace, where she lived with Lily's paternal grandmother, whom she addressed as Mama, and Lily's three uncles and their families. Those visits only happened once a month. Lily cherished the little time she could spend in her mother's midst and so, at the start of every week, Lily would wait as patiently as she could for Mak Wee's visit to the Kong household on Sundays. On most occasions, lunch would have been prepared on time.

However, on the rare occasion that it was not, Lily always knew when Mak Kong was feeling frustrated with her domestic help by three tell-tale signs. The first was sighing and folding her hands on her sarong. The second was clicking her tongue. The third was sniffing repeatedly. This was one of those times. Lily cast a furtive glance at Mak Kong as she sat down at the kitchen table and sighed, folding her hands together on her sarong. A minute later, deciding that prayer would be more useful, Mak Kong made her way to the Kitchen God's altar to ask for his help for the food to be ready on time. The Kitchen God watched over the family and recorded what they did throughout the year. Before Chinese New Year, they would offer him sticky kueh bakul to sweeten his mood and prevent him from making an unfavourable report to the Jade Emperor. The kueh would have to be very sticky and sweet this year, Lily thought as she pondered over the happenings of the past year.

A short while later, Mak Wee arrived, her shoulders slightly bent like she was carrying an invisible weight only she could feel. To Mak Kong's relief, lunch was ready to be served before Mak Wee's arrival. Mak Kong sat at the head of the dining table, and Lily took her usual seat next to Mak Wee, feeling as she always did the desire to reach out and hold her mother's hand. She wondered if Mak Wee felt the same about her. After all, she was her only living child.

Lily thought Mak Wee was a thin long-faced woman who seldom smiled. However, she longed to understand Mak Wee better. She had heard from her grandmother, Mama, just last year that Mak Wee had had a string of miscarriages before her birth which had left her feeling very helpless. Even though Mak Wee had observed all the taboos such as not moving furniture around the house and consuming ubat selusoh, a herbal medicine mixture, from the fifth month of pregnancy onwards, Mama had shared that her five children had slipped away each time in waves of painful cramps and blood.

'Lily sebenarnya anak keenam,' Mama had revealed to her last year while Mak Wee sat solemnly next to her, carefully avoiding Lily's gaze. Lily was supposed to be the youngest of six children, Mama said. The news had hit Lily in a way she found hard to describe. It took her breath away and hurt her heart like someone was squeezing it in her hand.

Anak keenam, she had thought wistfully. I would have been the youngest of six.

Mama said that she and Mak Wee were both determined that the sixth pregnancy would result in a healthy baby, pink with life, a baby whose heartbeat they could feel against their chest.

While pregnant with her, Mak Wee had been forbidden from attending her younger sister's wedding as a pregnant woman was regarded as inauspicious for the couple. Mama made sure that Mak Wee followed all the superstitions to the letter.

To Mama and Mak Wee's utmost relief, Lily was a full-term, healthy baby. Driven by superstition, Mama told Lily that she had advised Mak Wee to let the baby be informally adopted by a relative to save her life.

At this point, Lily had looked at Mak Wee, with pain flashing in her eyes.

Mak Wee still could not meet Lily's gaze but she mumbled, her gaze fixed on a spot on her baju panjang, 'We went to soothsayer. The soothsayer said we must give you away. If not, you won't survive.'

Lily frowned at Mak Wee's recollection. She knew what happened next. A few days later, her father had died in his sleep of a sudden heart attack. He was barely forty.

Lily turned her head to glance over at Mak Kong and then her cousins, Charles and Ivy. Charles was looking eagerly at the spread of food in front of him while Ivy was fiddling with the spoon next to her. After the majies had served the two children and Mak Kong, they served Lily and Mak Wee. Lily tried her best to eat daintily, the way a young nyonya would, pushing rice and chicken into her mouth with her fingertips, though she was very hungry. As usual, Mak Wee did not eat much, moving food around her plate slowly in lacklustre fashion.

'How is the food, Tachi?' Mak Kong asked to be polite. Lily knew how the rest of the conversation would go.

'Good, Adek,' Mak Wee would invariably say. Then Mak Kong would ask her two children what they had learnt in school that week. Lily would often listen intently to each and every detail for she had never had the opportunity to attend school. These conversations were her only glimpse into a world she was denied entry to. In her mind, Lily would build a world of what school was like, based mainly on the stories Ivy shared. Though she paid attention to Charles' anecdotes as well, she was sure that school for him was very different from what school would be like for her.

At fifteen, Charles was just a year younger than Lily. He attended Raffles Institution, which Lily gathered from his stories was a sprawling white building with four wings at Bras Basah Road. One of the wings, Charles had said, housed the Raffles Library and a museum. He once

shared that the rumour going around school was that the only girl who
attended Raffles Institution, a certain Kwa Geok Choo, often spent
her weekday afternoons studying in the library. Geok Choo, Charles
said, had topped the whole of Malaya in the 1936 Senior Cambridge
examinations. Lily remembered how she had wondered for days and
weeks afterward about what this girl looked like, what subjects she
studied and what books she had the privilege of reading.

This year, Charles would take his Standard VI examinations, and
Mak Kong was taking it very seriously. Mak Kong insisted on double
boiling soup for Charles every night so he would be in good health.
Ivy was ten and went to primary school at Singapore Chinese Girls'
School. Lily knew that it was located at No. 37 Emerald Hill because
Mak Kong had mentioned the address several times. She had no idea
what 'emerald' meant but in her mind's eye, she pictured a school
atop a verdant hill surrounded by a lush field. Once or twice, she
felt compelled to ask Ivy to describe what her school looked like
so she could be sure if the image in her mind was accurate. But Lily
restrained herself. Most of the time though, Ivy talked about what she
did in school. That day was not any different.

'Then we made rock buns!' Ivy was thrilled. 'Sedap!' A rock bun?
Lily thought. Does it look like a rock? Lily could not imagine anyone
wanting to eat anything that tasted like a rock, but she gave Ivy an
encouraging nod anyway.

'Can I use the rock bun to throw at your head?' Charles said to his
younger sister. His eyes glinted with a mixture of mischief and affection.
Ivy stuck out her bottom lip, which reminded Lily of a blooming
rosebud. Lily knew that despite the annoyed expression on Ivy's face,
she was actually pleased; she liked it when her elder brother paid her
any attention.

'Charles, don't disturb your sister,' Mak Kong said. She glanced at
Mak Wee, apologising with her eyes before she spoke. 'Maaf, Tachi.'

Mak Wee shook her head with an air of polite indifference.
They were not her children. She was just a guest here and had no
power to speak. Lily wondered in that moment as she had many
moments during different lunches before how her life would have
been different if she had been raised by both her parents. Would she

have had the opportunity to attend school? She pushed the thought away as quickly as it had come to her mind. No point brooding, Lily thought. Tonight, she would at last summon the courage to ask Mak Kong for a tutor. Lily wanted to learn English so she could understand when the Kong family sometimes spoke in English to each other. But more than that, she wanted to learn the language that was the main medium of instruction in Ivy's and Charles' schools. Maybe, just maybe, Lily found herself dreaming, her tutor might even be Khalid. He was already coming to their house once a week to tutor Charles. If Khalid was her tutor, he would finally notice her. A slow, secret smile grew across Lily's face as she took a sip of water, her face hidden behind her glass.

Later that night, Mak Kong reclined on her chair, fanning herself to prevent beads of sweat from collecting at the base of her neck. Lily bit her lip as she looked on. She knew that Mak Kong had to be in a good mood, especially since she had won forty Straits dollars during her Cherki game that afternoon. The three other nyonya ladies had traipsed out of the house, waving their hands at their faces and bemoaning their luck at having lost yet another Cherki game to Mak Kong. Mak Kong had gleefully counted her money and then placed it, note by note, in her safe-keeping box.

'What is it, Lily?' Mak Kong asked, smoothing down her kebaya top as she sat upright in her chair. She must have felt someone looking at her, Lily thought.

'I—I wanted to ask you something.'

'Speak up. I can't hear you,' Mak Kong said, as if she were a teacher who had just called on a student to answer a question in class.

'I wanted to ask you something,' Lily repeated a little louder this time.

'Soalan apa tu?' Mak Kong asked.

Lily took a deep breath before she spoke, the words gushing out of her. 'I want to learn how to read and write English. May I get a tutor?'

'Oh,' Mak Kong said. She looked up at Lily then hesitated.

Standing uncomfortably before her, Lily wondered what Mak Kong was thinking as she seemed to stare into Lily's eyes, a strange expression on her face. Does she feel sorry for me? Lily wondered. Or is she going to say nyonyas don't need to learn to read and write English to get married?

After a few minutes, Mak Kong said, 'Mak Kong will ask Pak Kong, okay?'

Lily nodded, feeling a sense of relief and gratitude wash over her. A discussion was not a refusal.

'Terima kasih,' she said to Mak Kong, pinching herself on her hand as she left the room. For the first time since the idea of asking for a tutor had taken root in her mind around three weeks ago, Lily could feel seeds of hope in her chest. She would learn new words that would become phrases and sentences the way she and the Leng Jie had planted shoots, stalks, and seeds in the garden that grew, day by day, into pandan, lemongrass, and chye sim.

Mr Tan was a balding, bespectacled man who needed the help of a cane to walk. It was a few days later on a balmy Wednesday afternoon when Lily met him for the first time.

Lily's heart sank slowly as she watched Mr Tan exchange pleasantries with Mak Kong. This was the old man who was going to teach her English. Why couldn't it have been Khalid? But Khalid was busy helping Charles with his preparation for the Standard VI examinations. He was known as one of the best tutors in their neighbourhood for the Standard VI examinations with an affordable hourly fee. Maybe he had considered teaching a girl who could barely read and write to be beneath him, Lily thought. Or maybe it had something to do with money. Lily did not know if it was Pak Kong who was paying for her lessons or if Mak Wee had dipped into her savings to fund her daughter's classes. Either way Lily did not want to be ungrateful, so she shrugged off the pang of disappointment and smiled courteously.

'Apa khabair, Lily?' Mr Tan said. 'Nama saya Mr Tan.' How am I? Lily thought. Trying to be grateful, Mr Tan.

'Baek,' Lily heard herself answering, wondering if he was speaking to her in Baba Malay to put her at ease.

The edges of Mr Tan's mouth turned up slightly. 'Baek,' he repeated. 'Mr Tan juga baek. But soon we will be speaking more in English. Today is your first lesson so we will take it slow, okay?'

Not as slowly as the way you walk, I hope, Lily thought. Lily bit her lip and nodded to show deference to Mr Tan.

'Yes, Mr Tan,' Lily said.

'Do you know the alphabet?' Mr Tan asked.

Lily had overheard Mak Kong speaking to her tutor last week on the telephone about her English proficiency. Mak Kong had taught her the alphabet when she was ten years old.

'Yes, she knows the alphabet,' Mak Kong had confirmed. So why is he asking me again? Lily wondered.

'Yes, I do,' Lily thought. She decided then to assume the best of Mr Tan and feel grateful that she had an English tutor. Mr Tan was just being kind and checking that she knew the building blocks of the language.

'Dua puluh enam huruf,' she had said. Twenty-six letters. Just from twenty-six letters, Lily marvelled, a person could form countless words and sentences.

Mr Tan decided to ask her to write all the letters from A to Z in uppercase and then lowercase on lined paper. Lily felt her cheeks grow warm as she wrote the letters down, one by one, with her pencil. She bet even Ivy did not have to do this in school.

For the next hour or so, Mr Tan took great pains to sound out consonants and vowels with Lily. The next week, he taught her what he called 'pronouns': I, you, he, she, we. The following week, they learnt the parts of the face on a drawing he had brought. They practised saying 'eyes', 'nose', 'lips' and 'ears'. Eyes sounded like ice in Malay to Lily. Eyes. Ais. The other words were foreign, and Lily tasted each word with her tongue before she sounded them out. Each week, Mr Tan would ask Lily to write every word she learnt ten times in her exercise book.

'You must practise every day. Every day,' Mr Tan would intone to Lily in Baba Malay.

'I will,' Lily would reply, her rounded jaw set in determination. She started to appreciate Mr Tan and his kindly ways by the end of the third lesson.

While she did her sewing chores in the afternoon, Lily would silently spell out the words she had learnt to herself. One word for each stitch.

At the end of her third lesson, Mr Tan presented Lily with a book.

'Lily boleh baca buku ini,' he said, his eyes twinkling, soft and sympathetic. Lily gasped as she looked at the book in front of her.

Lily could not read the words on the cover but the illustration of the tree and river took her breath away. There was a world out there for her to discover someday, Lily thought. Someday in the future, she promised herself that she would walk along a riverbank and breathe in the fresh air of freedom.

'Reading, Comprehension and Language Practice Textbook, Book 1,' Mr Tan said slowly. Lily had a handful of English children's books from Mak Wee. *Bambi* by Felix Salten and *The Velveteen Rabbit* by Margery Williams were her favourites. She greatly admired their illustrations but could not really read any of them. But this was the first time in her life she had an English textbook. Lily could hardly believe it. She pressed her fingers to the cover. After a moment, she looked at Mr Tan, too moved with emotion to speak.

Mr Tan's wrinkled skin creased into a smile.

'Terima Kasih,' Lily said after a while to Mr Tan in a soft voice.

Mr Tan replied, 'Sama sama.'

That afternoon, after her class with Mr Tan, Lily sat on the step of the five-foot way, stroking the family terrier, Little, on his white furry head as he ate his dry meat. She thought that life for Little seemed to be so straightforward compared to life for a human being. Little probably never had to think about what the future would hold whereas Lily thought and occasionally worried about the future from time to time. When awake, she could never quite fully picture what would happen but in her dreams the future seemed so real to her she could feel her way around. She would have a family and a home of her own someday. Little lapped up his last scrap of food then barked as if asking for more. Lily giggled, her laugh a light tinkle like a wind chime. 'In a minute, Little,' she said, rubbing his right ear. As Little watched her, she got up and looked around for a fallen twig. When she had found one, Lily used the twig to scratch out her name in the sand, and then just beneath it, she wrote 'K-H-A-L-I-D'.

Chapter II

27th January 1939

Khalid parked his bicycle in the front yard, and grabbed the *Straits Times* and the *Malaya Tribune* newspapers out of his basket. His father, Pak Ambi, spent ten cents in total on these daily newspapers. It was important to Pak Ambi that his two sons, Ibrahim and Khalid, keep up-to-date with world events. Moreover, he believed that reading the newspapers would help them improve their English. At twenty-one, Ibrahim was two years older than Khalid and working as a clerk with The Oriental Telephone and Electric Company. Meanwhile, Khalid would be taking his Senior Cambridge examinations towards the end of the year and then his working life would begin. He was three years older than many of his peers due to his years spent in Telok Kurau Malay School. Khalid did not mind this as he had enjoyed his years at the Malay School very much. Now, in his nineteenth year of life, Khalid was eager to enter the working world so he could contribute money to his father and perhaps to his mother, Mak Aisha, too. He had not seen Mak Aisha in so long. As he walked up the stairs to his room, he made a mental note that he would have to visit her soon.

'Hai anak jerung!' his neighbour, Samad, called out as Khalid walked past his room. Khalid closed his eyes and grimaced internally. He did not like the unfortunate nickname of baby shark just because he was his father's child. But in life, sometimes one had no choice but to accept the names others have chosen for you. Unlike Khalid, Pak Ambi was rather proud that he had been dubbed Tambi Jerung in the neighbourhood for walking around with the swagger of a loan shark. Khalid did not know if that swagger had come from his father's involvement as a bet collector for the illegal lottery, chap ji kee, or from his father's confident, sometimes bordering on arrogant, personality. He had decided that it was probably a combination of both. A few weeks ago, Ibrahim had tried to imitate their father's swagger, which made Khalid burst out into laughter. Thinking of the memory now, Khalid turned around to face Samad with a hint of a smile on his face.

'Hi Samad,' Khalid said.

'Nak main bola?' Samad asked as he advanced towards the door eagerly.

'Maybe later, okay?' Khalid said, noting Samad's eagerness. He fancied a game of 1v1 soccer training with Samad. 'I have to finish my homework first and read the papers.'

Samad frowned, leaning against the door frame. 'You promised we'd play today,' he said.

Khalid felt pricks of mild irritation creep up on him. He did not remember promising Samad that they would play soccer that day. Just two days ago, Samad had pleaded, 'Please play with me, Khalid. I'm not as lucky as you. Alsagoff Arab School doesn't even have a soccer team!'

'So, we can play later?' Samad asked as Khalid made a movement to walk away from the door.

'I'll try my best, Samad,' Khalid said. 'If I complete my homework, then we can play, okay?'

Samad made a tsking sound with his tongue and shrugged. Khalid bid him farewell and made his way to his room. As Khalid reached his room, he found his father sitting on his wooden chair, flipping through his accounts book for chap ji kee. Pak Ambi's 6-foot frame looked imposing as always as if it threatened to break the chair.

'Oh Pak Ambi, how come you're at home?' he asked, though he dreaded to hear the answer. He knew it was highly likely that his father had been fired or had quit another job.

'That Mr Lim is so unreasonable. I was only late by a few minutes,' Pak Ambi said. Khalid knew that it was more likely that he had been more than thirty minutes late.

'I see,' Khalid said.

'He got angry at me so I quit,' Pak Ambi said with a shrug. Khalid raised an eyebrow but kept silent. He knew the truth was probably that Pak Ambi had exposed his hot temper, resulting in an immediate dismissal by his boss.

'Anyway, don't worry, many driving jobs out there,' Pak Ambi said, glancing out the window. He yawned widely without closing his mouth.

'Yes,' Khalid said though he did not quite agree. Pak Ambi seemed to implicitly trust in the world's ability to provide for him even in the midst of the Great Depression.

'So how was school today?' Pak Ambi asked.

'Good,' Khalid said. He had especially enjoyed Mr Shepherd's class where they worked on answering comprehension questions based on a passage on the life of Albert Einstein. Khalid had been impressed by Albert Einstein's clear view of the problems of physics and the determination to solve them.

'Good . . . my hopes are on you. Remember to read all the pages of the newspapers today. All the pages, okay?' Pak Ambi said before clapping a firm hand on Khalid's shoulder. Khalid felt his father's expectations weighing on him. Before he could say anything, Pak Ambi announced loudly, 'I'm going out to look for a job.'

'Okay,' Khalid said. He thought it was far more likely that Pak Ambi was going to drink kopi with his friends at the nearby coffee shop. Pak Ambi stalked out of the room, closing the door behind him quietly.

Left alone, Khalid flipped the *Straits Times* open and continued reading the article, 'Britain and Empire are Invincible, Says Minister'.

'Referring to the invincibility of Britain and the Empire, the British economic system stood the strain of the recent crisis better than any other system in the world,' Khalid read aloud. He relished in those words, taking great pride in the reported strength of the British.

'Sir Samuel Hoare condemned scaremongers who talked of the inevitability of war.' Khalid shook his head. War to him seemed like a distant possibility. It might very well come true, but he could not think about that. He had to study for his Senior Cambridge exams, war or no war. With that, he closed the paper and took his copy of *The Oxford English Dictionary* off the shelf above him. It was just where he had left it, next to his copy of Pearl S. Buck's *The Good Earth* that his English teacher, Mr Shepherd, had gifted to him last year.

It's time to get started on my homework, Khalid thought. Focus on the task at hand.

Later that evening, Khalid and Samad played their one-on-one game of soccer in the courtyard. After about an hour, they called an end to their game. While Samad continued to kick the soccer ball about, Khalid sat on the ground, lost in his own thoughts. His childhood memories of learning to play soccer when he was five, running barefoot on Kallang Road, played like scenes from an old movie in his mind. With the other boys from his neighbourhood, he had used a tennis ball in place of a soccer ball, kicking it around on the cement ground that they turned into their soccer pitch. Khalid remembered the land seemed paper-white. Above him, the sun was scorching, and his bare feet had felt like burnt toast. Now he had a proper soccer ball and soccer shoes. With an unwelcome prick of guilt, he realized that if he had stayed with his mother, he might still be kicking a tennis ball around barefooted. After all, Mak Aisha still worked as a washerwoman. Khalid had lived with her for six peaceful years, just the two of them, before he almost met with an accident at the age of seven. He was walking up the hill to get home when he saw a car rolling down the slope towards him. He remembered how he froze in horror before a man had shrieked at him to get out of the way. 'Kereta!' Khalid had frozen, rooted to the spot, before the man dashed over to push Khalid out of the way. Khalid escaped relatively unscathed, with only a scraped right elbow.

But as news travelled from one house to another about Khalid's accident, the story evolved as the severity of Khalid's injury was embellished. By the time it reached Pak Ambi, he heard Khalid had a broken arm. He arrived in a storm of fury and kidnapped Khalid while

Mak Aisha was away at work. A few days later, a frightened Mak Aisha made her way down to Telok Kurau Malay School to visit Khalid. Through the spaces in the bars of the school gate, she passed Khalid a gleaming 10-cent coin so he could take a bus home to her. Khalid was very glad to see his mother again and he slipped the coin into his pocket. That day was nothing but a foggy memory with blurred edges now to Khalid but, looking back and knowing what he knew now, he wondered how much courage it had taken Mak Aisha to visit him. She must have been afraid to take him home herself but driven by maternal protectiveness and love, she had taken that trip down to his school anyway. Khalid knew his younger self would never have been able to see if there was any fear in Mak Aisha's eyes, if she was trembling as she stood outside the school gate, if Pak Ambi would suddenly show up and lay a hand on her like he did in those dreadful whispers he had heard from Pak Ambi in recent years, confessing his guilt when he returned home drunk.

Mak Aisha and Pak Ambi had divorced when Khalid was still growing in her womb because of all the times he treated her like a slave, beating her into submission. But Khalid always knew that despite Mak Aisha's short stature, she possessed a fighting spirit buried deep in her, and he believed this even more when she told him that one day, she summoned all her courage and used her legs to kick Pak Ambi hard. After that incident, it was impossible for them to stay married.

Khalid never returned home to his mother. At his mother's place, it had just been him and her, and two was a peaceful but lonely number. At a house at Ceylon Road, he met Ibrahim, the brother he had only heard of through his mother's stories, his stepmother Khadijah, whom he addressed as Mak Jah, and his two giggling half-sisters, Leha and Fatimah. There was sweet milk to drink and crispy prata as big as plates. His father's sisters would come visit with their families, carrying food in tiffin carriers. Sometimes, they would bring richly spiced curries and tangy mango chutneys. Other times, it was fragrant briyani with raita. Khalid had wondered why Pak Ambi had chosen, a few years ago, to move with him and his brother to a small, cramped room instead of continuing to live in the spacious house with his stepmother's family. He gradually realised that his father would rather be king of their rented room than live anywhere else where he would have to watch what he said or did. But Khalid liked being at his stepmother's house, not just for the food but for the feeling of being part of an extended family.

Had he really left his mother alone just so he could have a better life? Khalid wondered. What did that say about his character? Now he only saw his mother once a month, if even that. He would make it up to her once he had a real job, Khalid promised himself just then. He tried to shake off the picture he had in his mind of her sitting at home, eating an early dinner by herself in a dark kitchen.

'Oi,' Samad said, interrupting Khalid's train of thought. He kicked the soccer ball in Khalid's direction, some of the dirt on the ball coming off in the process. 'Thinking of girls ah?

Khalid shook his head, but Samad did not seem to notice. 'You know both of us are handsome,' Samad continued. 'We could have any girl we want. So many pretty girls around, Malay, Indian, Chinese, Eurasian. But I think the young nyonyas are the best, in their kebaya . . . ' Samad moved his hands excitedly to trace an hourglass shape in front of him and whistled.

Khalid laughed. He did think that young nyonyas looked very beautiful in their sarong kebaya. But he had a girl fancied in mind, a tall Eurasian girl named Dorothy Clarke, who attended Raffles Girls' School. He seldom took the bus to and from school but when he did, Dorothy would be so delighted to see him that she would politely request whoever was sitting next to her to get up so Khalid could sit next to her. Khalid always felt glad to be sitting down next to Dorothy because more often than not, she smelled like scented powder. He was sure that if they stood up next to each other, they would be the same height. That made him feel short, but Dorothy didn't seem to mind. Looking over at Samad, Khalid was glad that he never saw Dorothy walking with him. She always got down two stops before Khalid did.

Samad seemed to be in a dreamy daze. Khalid shoved him lightly, eliciting a moan from Samad.

'Sexy!' Samad exclaimed as if a young nyonya stood in front of him and Khalid. 'Am I right?'

Khalid could not disagree. 'Yes,' he said.

'Maybe you stand a chance with them,' Samad said. 'You're Peranakan too.'

'But Indian and Muslim,' Khalid replied.

'Yes, but Indian Muslim,' Samad said as if the thought had just occurred to him. 'So, I guess it's different.'

Khalid shrugged. His paternal grandmother had Arab blood, and his paternal grandfather was from Pondicherry in South India. 'We are Jawi Peranakan,' his father had told him and Ibrahim many times over the years. To Khalid, it just meant that he was a Straits-born Muslim of mixed Indian and Malay parentage but to Pak Ambi, being Jawi Peranakan seemed to carry with it much pride as if it was an elite group. Khalid thought only the British could truly claim to be elite in Singapore. They rolled through town in their shiny cars and fancy limousines, luxuriated in seaside villas and shopped at Cold Storage, a completely different supermarket from the locals. He heard that they even used different lavatories in government offices like the Municipal Building. Khalid knew anti-colonial sentiment was spreading among Singaporeans the way neighbours murmured about the British acting like they were better than the locals, but he ignored it. In his opinion, the British Empire was the greatest empire in the world.

Chapter III

6th March 1939

The deserted streets below the house were bathed in the soft glow of moonlight. Lily lay in her bed, listening to the sound of silence that she found so comforting. She wondered if tomorrow would bring rain, and with it, good luck and prosperity into the house. She turned over on her side and prayed to the Gods for rain. The prayer went out into the world like a whisper.

Earlier that day, when she was sure no one was looking, Lily had snuck a look at one of Ivy's storybooks. She had flipped the brown pages, inhaling the scent of paper that she liked so much, and had stopped at a page with a drawing of a sun. Though it was in black and white, Lily thought the drawing was beautiful. She had clutched the book to her chest and imagined it was hers.

As she turned on her back, Lily found herself wishing that time would skip ahead to the afternoon when she was sure she would see Khalid again. He always walked or rode his bicycle past her house on his way home from school. Lily knew Khalid stayed at Everitt Road too, but she did not know the exact house number. She thought Khalid was someone who seemed to be on the cusp of great things. Why did men have the opportunities for education to better themselves while women were only educated to be worthy of their future husbands?

It did not seem fair to Lily. She shuddered to think she might someday be married off to a man she did not love and have to sleep with him and serve him.

Can we fight our fate? Lily thought as her head found its comfortable spot on her pillow. She had been taught the concept of wu wei by Mak Kong, which meant going with the flow of her life like flowing water in the koi pond in their home's airwell. A person had to be calm, humble, non-striving and passive. Although going against the Tao did not sit well with her, the idea of not planning for her future was one that Lily could scarcely accept. Lily closed her eyes and breathed in and out. As a yawn escaped her lips, she gently placed her hand over her mouth. In a few minutes, she was soundly asleep.

As the next morning dawned, the rooster next door crowed. Lily smiled to herself; she thought the rooster's sunrise song was a lovely way to start each day. As she got up quickly from her bed, her half-opened eyes took in the light filtering in through her window. She arranged her sheets neatly before taking her bath by the big dragon water urn. As she washed the tender skin underneath her breasts and let the water trail down her body, she found her thoughts wandering to Khalid. She wondered what it would be like if he were to touch her. A thrill went down Lily's spine then just as quickly, she chided herself. No proper nyonya would have such thoughts. Or was it just part of growing up? After all, she was turning sixteen in June. She did not know her exact birthdate, so she had chosen the first of the month as her birthday. She would be sixteen; she would be a real woman.

Lily dried herself off with a towel and put on her undershirt, long-sleeved blouse and sarong bottom. Then facing the mirror, she combed her waist-length hair into a long plait. When that was done, Lily wound her waist-length hair up into a tightly coiled bun that she held in place with three silver hairpins. She knew that the younger nyonyas including her next-door neighbour, May Geok, were starting to follow the latest Western fashion trends, but in the Kong household, not having your hair in a bun was simply not acceptable. Mak Kong had cautioned her a few times that if she wanted a good relationship with her future mother-in-law, she would never be seen without her hair pins or worse, having her hair undone.

'Undone hair is a sign of mourning,' Mak Kong had said. 'Very inauspicious.' Lily received this piece of advice very solemnly each time it was delivered to her. As much as she liked how she looked with her bun, shaped like a seashell on her head, she still wondered what she would look like with a modern short crop or a perm.

'Kus semangat!' she imagined Mak Kong saying in surprise if she dared to cut her hair. Lily stole a last look at herself in the mirror and poked at the small mole just below her left cheek. Oh, the mole that she had pinched, squeezed and tried to remove with bedak sejuk. The cooling powder might have refreshed her skin and unclogged her pores, but it did little to remove her mole. There the stubborn mole still sat on her face, resilient in the face of its owner's struggles against it. Despite her mole, Lily assured herself that she was still pleasant to look at. After all, she often found Teck Soon, her neighbour who was a year older than her, staring at her when she was outside with Little. If he was staring, does it mean he finds me attractive? Lily wondered. But there was no time for her to wonder about this. She hurried off to the kitchen to start her day's work.

* * *

The Raffles Institution principal, Mr D.W. McLeod, was giving his morning assembly address as he did every Monday. As a prefect, Khalid stood in front of his class, listening carefully to every word.

'Tyrone Power,' Khalid's classmate behind him snickered. In spite of himself, Khalid smiled. Ever since he and his friends had watched Marie Antoinette in the cinema two months ago, they had joked that their principal's thick eyebrows looked just like Tyrone Power's. For some of his friends, it might have been a jab at Mr McLeod because they bore some resentment towards their tough taskmaster. But Khalid secretly thought that they were unknowingly paying Mr McLeod a high compliment. He would have loved it if any of his peers compared him to a famous Hollywood actor, especially one that had the good fortune to passionately kiss the glamourous Norma Shearer.

'It's been two years since I urged the curriculum of the school to be extended to include the direct study of public affairs. I can now confidently say that our students of today have a general knowledge of the duties of true citizenship,' Mr McLeod was saying.

True citizenship, Khalid thought. He could not think of his duties to Singapore when he had not even properly performed his duty as a filial son to his parents. He turned his head slightly and saw his schoolmate and former classmate, Harry Lee, in the row next to him. Harry was to take his Senior Cambridge examination this year too. If not for my typhoid fever in Standard VI, would I have performed better in the Standard VI examinations last year? Khalid thought. Pak Ambi had convinced Khalid that the fever had come about from eating too much mee siam for breakfast from a street vendor. But more importantly, he had told his son that the fever had also stolen some of his God-given brilliance away. So, the special distinction of first in the Standard VI exam had gone to Harry. Harry had also won two scholarships, the Raffles Institution and Tan Jiak Kim scholarships, together yielding him a sum of 350 Straits dollars. He had used some of the scholarship money to buy a shiny new Raleigh bicycle with a three-speed gear and an encased chain box. When he parked his bicycle every morning, other students, including Khalid, would look on in envy.

'Probably Harry is already thinking about true citizenship,' Khalid thought. If he was being honest with himself, Khalid knew soccer games and thoughts of Dorothy took up more space in his mind than it should. Just as that thought entered his mind, another thought followed. But Harry had been mischievous and playful. When they had been in the same class in Standard VI, Khalid would see Harry scribbling notes to fellow students or mimicking some teacher's strange movements. Had Harry grown up? Khalid wondered. Maybe Harry is just very smart and determined. Like Geok Choo. Where do I stand in comparison to the two of them?

Then again, Harry isn't good at soccer nor is he a prefect like me, Khalid thought. That's why he has more time to spend studying. This thought consoled him a little bit. Standing up a bit straighter, Khalid continued listening to Mr McLeod.

During tiffin hour later, as hungry students streamed out of their classes towards the canteen where hawkers were waiting with their delicious offerings, Khalid and his classmate Ravinder were among the group headed to the canteen. A few street vendors stood outside the school compound with their carts to peddle their food and drinks. There was warm tea and buns, delectable, deep-fried curry puffs and perhaps, most popular of all, the ice ball drizzled with colourful syrup.

'The moment school is out, I'm getting an iced ball,' Khalid said, an impish glint in his eye. 'Maybe two.'

'Sounds good,' Ravinder said. He licked his lips. 'I'm so hungry!' He rubbed his hand over his stomach.

'You're always hungry, Rav! Maybe I'll get one with condensed milk,' Khalid said, picturing the cold treat in his mind. 'I can taste it now.'

'Stop, you're making me hungry, K!' Ravinder said, slinging his arm over Khalid's shoulder. 'Let's get some food.' Together they made their way to the noodles stall which had a long queue. When it was his turn, Khalid quickly placed his order for a plate of mee goreng. Ravinder took his time to decide while the noodle stall vendor ticked her tongue impatiently before he settled for a bowl of mee siam.

'No mee siam for you ever again, Khalid,' Ravinder said, his hands cupped over the warm bowl. The two friends laughed together as they made their way to a table where their good friend Roy and some of their other classmates were seated. As Khalid put one spoonful of mee goreng after another into his mouth, he mentally prepared for his lesson with Charles later that day.

He tried hard to think about how he could help Charles improve. In his opinion, Charles was smart but lazy. He reminded Khalid of his own behaviour at his age. He hoped that Charles might become more hard-working as his Standard VI examinations approached. That was the way it was for me when I was his age, Khalid thought. Sometimes, the anxiety of a looming examination was all it took for someone to buckle down and start studying.

By the end of the school day, Khalid was mentally tired. He had spent the whole day trying to take good notes in one class after another.

He had especially struggled in Mr Menon's Additional Mathematics class. Khalid thought that Mr Menon was a genius at Mathematics, and it was a painful slog for Khalid to try to keep up with his brisk mental processes.

'Bye. See you tomorrow!' Khalid said to his friends as he placed his hands on the bicycle handlebars to push his bicycle out of school. Ravinder and Roy waved in return while the rest shouted their goodbyes. Khalid parked his bicycle by the side of the road and rushed to join the queue for ice balls, feeling excited at the prospect of finally fulfilling his craving.

He watched as the ice ball cart vendor, Mr Bala, placed a block of ice on the blade of a wooden shaver. Using both his hands, he slid the block back and forth. Watching the movement of the block, Khalid's eyes moved to the bowl below that caught the ice shavings. Mr Bala moulded the shavings into a sphere, topped it off with a generous lashing of milk and placed the ice ball into Khalid's eager hands.

'Thank you,' Khalid said. Mr Bala merely nodded and placed two of Khalid's 1 cent coins in his coin bowl before turning back to the shaver.

Khalid saw a few of his friends standing under the shade of the banyan tree next to the school's tuckshop. Wishing he had the time to join them, he stood alone on the street, eating his ice ball. The ice ball quenched his thirst and made him feel refreshed. After he had finished it, Khalid wiped his mouth with the back of his hand. Then he pushed up the kick stand of his bicycle. It was time to head to 49 Everitt Road where Charles was waiting for him for their English lesson.

* * *

Lily sat in the sewing room of her home, bent over a wooden frame. She was practising her beadwork, which entailed sewing tiny glass-cut beads on a gridded fabric. This task required steady hands, which Lily had and a great deal of patience, which she was trying to work on. Lily worked from the centre outwards and on three rows of beads at a time. She picked up a yellow bead with the needle she was holding and threaded it through the fabric.

Mak Kong had told her someday when her design was complete, they would be sent to the shoemaker and fashioned into kasut manek, a beaded slipper. 'A good kasut manek would make a good marriage,' Mak Kong had said earlier that year. 'Do you understand, Lily?'

Lily had nodded though she was not sure what good shoes had to do with marriage. As if reading her mind, Mak Kong continued, 'Kasut manek shows a girl's virtue, patience and sincerity to her prospective groom. It was the same way when I was a young girl.' Now although Lily understood a little better what Mak Kong had meant, she still thought that a couple in love who chose to commit to each other every day was more important than well-made shoes for the success of a marriage. Mak Kong and Pak Kong were committed to each other, she knew. And they appeared to love each other. How did Mak Kong's vast variety of beaded slippers affect their marriage? Lily wondered.

She threaded another yellow bead on the frame. Then she heard Khalid's voice through the partition which separated the sewing room from the main hall. A quiver of excitement ran through Lily as she put the needle down on the table. It was Zhu Jie's duty to serve drinks to guests. She knew soon Zhu Jie would be bringing a tray of pineapple tarts, two glasses of water and a kamcheng, a covered container for refills, out to the main hall.

'Good afternoon, Mrs Kong and Charles,' Khalid was saying.

'Good afternoon, Khalid. Khalid sudah makan?' Mak Kong asked with a sniff.

Khalid replied that he had taken his lunch and thanked Mak Kong for enquiring. Lily slowly stood up and peeked through the slits of the screen to see what was happening. She saw Khalid sitting down across from Charles. Khalid's handsome side profile was facing her. She knew that Mak Kong would be going out soon to visit a friend. The women were likely to chew betel nut together and share the latest gossip about the happenings in the neighbourhood. Lily turned around and stared at the yellow beads on the small plate before her. They looked like little warm jewels of light. She wished the beads would somehow just form a peony flower on their own. But that was not possible. Beadwork required hard work, patience and determination. Exhaling softly to herself, she sat down. Shaking her head lightly to remind herself to focus on the task at hand, Lily saw that her right hand did not look as steady as it usually did as she picked up the needle. It's because Khalid is nearby, Lily thought, holding her right hand in her left palm to steady it. Focus on the task at hand, Lily reminded herself. It is easy, not difficult. The beading she was doing would be a dainty pair of kasut manek of her own, her very first. She always enjoyed watching Mak Kong leave the house dressed in a different sarong kebaya with a different pair of kasut manek each time, with patterns that seemed to dance in the light as she glided out, accompanied by Pak Kong who looked more sedate in his batik shirt and pants in muted colours. Mak Kong had so many shoes and functions to attend. Lily invariably felt a tinge of envy whenever she watched Mak Kong and Pak Kong leaving the house.

Thirty minutes later, Lily paused to admire her handiwork. Sitting neatly in place on the fabric, the beads looked nowhere close to becoming a peony. Lily wondered how many hours it would take before this piece would be complete. She made her way to the kitchen where Zhu Jie was preparing a tray of kueh lapis, a rainbow-coloured steamed cake. Zhu Jie gave Lily a knowing look. She was perhaps the only person in the household who had any inkling of Lily's fledgling fondness for Khalid.

'Thank you, Zhu Jie,' Lily said as she stood next to Zhu Jie. Zhu Jie placed her pudgy hand over Lily's smaller one for a moment and patted it.

'Go on,' Zhu Jie said. 'Maybe your future husband out there. I cannot get married. I want to see you married, you know, happy.' Lily looked at Zhu Jie, feeling grateful for her friendship. She was at a loss for words. It was the first time anyone had ever said that they wanted to see her happy. She felt very touched that her happiness seemed to matter to Zhu Jie.

'Go,' Zhu Jie repeated. Lily picked up the tray and carried it out to the main hall, trying her best to steady her hands. As she approached the table where Khalid and Charles were studying, she saw that they looked very focused on the books before them.

He's not going to notice me, Lily thought with a pang.

'Read the passage again,' Khalid was saying to Charles whose head was bent over a textbook. Lily carefully averted her eyes though she wanted to look at Khalid. Then Khalid turned to Lily and said, 'Thank you.' A blush crept up on Lily's cheeks as she placed the plate of kueh lapis on the table. She nervously lifted her eyes and met his. It was just for a fleeting second, but that moment stayed with Lily throughout the day. Before she went to bed that night, Lily made sure to tuck the memory away for safekeeping as if it was a precious piece of cloth she placed in her drawer.

Later as he bid goodbye to Charles, Khalid thought that maybe Lily Wee was growing up to become the second prettiest girl in the neighbourhood. Not the first, for that distinction would surely go to Chong May Geok of 47 Everitt Road. Though both Lily and May Geok had oval-shaped faces, May Geok's face was smaller, more like a melon seed, and her skin was fairer, almost like white jade. Still Lily seems more interesting, Khalid thought. Maybe one day we will be friends.

Chapter IV

7th to 11th April 1939

Lily watched as Ivy lifted some sand and patted it between her palms. Ivy dipped her fingers in a small blue pail to sprinkle water over the sand. It was Good Friday, and they were at Tanjong Katong Beach with Pak Kong and Mak Kong. Charles had been invited to a Good Friday lunch at the house of his best friend's family and thus had been given special permission by Pak Kong to be excused from the Kong family outing.

'What are you making?' Lily asked, smiling at Ivy.

Ivy shrugged, poking a lump of sand with her finger. 'I don't know,' she brooded, pushing her lower lip out. 'I don't know how to make anything,' she said.

'How about a turtle?' Lily suggested. She pointed to the piles of sand that Ivy had dug up with a spade. 'You could combine all of this sand into a big shell.'

'Shell?' Ivy brightened up, looking at Lily. 'Let's look for seashells.'

'Okay,' Lily said. She stood up and Ivy slipped her hand in hers. This is nice, Lily thought. A rare moment where I get to hold Ivy's hand. Hand in hand, Lily and Ivy walked down the beach, their long skirts billowing in the breeze and the soft sand crunching beneath their sandals.

Life seemed much bigger outdoors. Without the walls of the house, Lily found herself less inhibited. She could blend into the background and be part of the crowd or talk a little bit louder and maybe no one would notice. She did not understand why young unmarried women could not be allowed out of the house more often. Once a nyonya turned twelve, she would be confined to the house. She knew that May Geok felt the same way and would beg her mother, Mrs Chong, to allow her to go shopping. When she was outside the house with Little, she would see May Geok sometimes and they would chat, occasionally commiserating over their similar feelings of being trapped in a house that did not often feel like a home.

Lily glanced over at where Mak Kong and Pak Kong sat on a picnic mat near a row of palm trees. From where Lily stood, they appeared like small and unintimidating figures. She knew that Pak Kong must be reading the same book she had seen him reading a few days in the main hall. What was it again? Count of Mon . . . something? She could never quite understand the title, but it was all she heard him talk about recently.

'An English classic that my Straits Chinese Reading Club chose as book of the month,' she recollected him saying to Mak Kong.

Lily looked as Mak Kong's eyes were trained on Ivy, tracking her movements. Lily knew Mak Kong was watching Ivy all the time when she was outdoors to make sure she was safe. Lily felt a pang of longing for an enduringly protective maternal love. She wanted to experience it with Mak Wee and give it to children of her own someday. This yearning that she could not explain for a love she had never experienced, a love so strong that she would care more about the other person than she did for herself. Is that why she sometimes felt like she looked for love everywhere she could find it, in Zhu Jie's exuberant teasing, in holding Ivy's small hand, in smelling Little's fur? The reason she had a developed a liking for Khalid? I mean what did she know about him, apart from the fact that she thought he was smart, good-looking and well-mannered? Lily shook her head to stop overthinking.

How hungry she was, Lily mused as she spotted a white shell that lay amidst a bit of debris in the sand, for moments that she could keep inside of her to make herself feel full. Abundance is a gift, Lily thought. Having more than the average person. But is having less also a gift? Maybe some of us have been given the gift of less, Lily thought. A box that might look relatively empty to the rest of the world still had gifts in it for its receiver.

What are my gifts? Lily mused as she stopped to pick the shell up. It was a fan-shaped seashell adorned with ridges but it was chipped. She threw it back into the sand.

'Don't pick the broken ones!' she called out to Ivy who was squatting in the sand front of her.

Ivy turned around to look at her, her brows creasing together. 'Why?'

'Just pick the whole ones. The broken ones could hurt your fingers,' Lily warned.

Ivy picked up a shell from the red pail that she was holding. 'But look at this one, it's broken but it's so pretty!' she chirped.

'Broken and beautiful,' Ivy said. She skipped around in a circle in front of Lily, kicking up some sand in the process. Lily let out a giggle that felt lighter than air. She wanted to do the same as Ivy but not while Mak Kong and Pak Kong were watching. In front of them, she had to act as demurely as possible.

Before Lily could reply, she heard Mak Kong's voice. Lost in her own thoughts, she had not realised that Mak Kong was standing behind them.

'Jangan amek yang kotor-kotor!' Mak Kong called out in a firm voice. I know that I shouldn't pick the dirty ones, Mak Kong, Lily thought.

'We could wash them,' Lily replied, turning around to look at Mak Kong who moved closer to stand right next to Lily. We're almost the same height now, Lily realised as their shoulders almost touched.

Mak Kong wrinkled her nose at Lily, but Ivy piped up, looking at Mak Kong with eager eyes. 'Yes, we will wash them!'

Mak Kong threw Lily a look that plainly said to her that she made the suggestion so she would have to be responsible for washing them. Mak Kong sniffed and folded her arms across her chest.

At that moment, out of the corner of her eye, Lily saw a tall Caucasian man approaching them. She had seen him near the palm

trees, touching a tree's trunk as if he was talking to it and writing in a
notebook. He's probably in his thirties, Lily thought, like Mak Kong.

'Good morning,' he said in a crisp accent that Lily recognised
as British.

'Good morning,' Mak Kong replied. She smoothed down her dress
and touched her hair, without looking at the man in the eye.

'My name is John Corner,' the man said. He adjusted his spectacles
with his right hand then scratched his temple.

Lily noticed that he was stumbling over his words in a stutter but
she did not know what he was saying. John seemed to avoid Mak Kong's
gaze as he stared at the sand in front of him. He gestured with his hands
to the seashells in Ivy's pail. Lily could not understand what the man
said as he stammered but she gathered that he had informed Mak Kong
that they should stop picking seashells.

Mak Kong's head bobbed up and down reminiscent of a life buoy
in the water. 'Oh yes, Sir. We won't . . . won't pick the shells,' Lily
heard her saying as she bowed her head low to John Connor. Lily found
herself wondering why white men were treated as superior. She looked
up at the sky and thought of how every man should be equal. Is that
even possible on earth? Lily mused. She felt a twinge in her heart. There
was so much she did not understand about human nature. Perhaps if I
have a chance to attend school like this British man, Lily mused as she
looked up at John Corner.

John Corner nodded once and tipped his hat at them before striding
away, his long legs carrying him quickly away from them.

'Better not to pick especially large shells. Removal of shells could
damage the coastal ecosystem and endanger organisms that need shells
for their survival,' Mak Kong said in Baba Malay to Lily and Ivy.

Beside Lily, Ivy groaned in dismay. She kicked the sand beneath her
feet in a fit of petulance. 'Nooo,' Ivy whined. She stomped her right foot,
angry that she could not bring the shells home.

'Buang semua ini balik ke pasir,' Mak Kong said, ignoring Ivy's
whining. She gestured with her arms to the shells in the pail.

Lily felt a surge of anger rise up within her. She gathered that
John Corner had asked them to put the shells back. Why do British

people think they know it all?, she thought. Why do we have to put the shells back?

Pak Kong called out to them just then, saying it was time to head home.

'But Mak, why?' Ivy asked, dragging out each syllable.

'The nice British man said so,' Mak Kong replied. 'Not wise to pick the shells, okay?'

Mak Kong gestured to Lily again. 'Make sure you put the shells back.'

She then made her way back to her picnic mat where Pak Kong was already beginning to pack up. Lily watched and exhaled deeply to calm herself.

'Do we have to?' Ivy asked, looking up at Lily, a questioning look in her eyes.

'How about you pick your favourite shell? We can keep one each,' Lily said gently. She thought there could not be any harm in picking a small shell. The shells were empty because the animals in them had died.

'Okay,' Ivy said, still sounding reluctant to part with all the pretty shells she had put in her pail. She picked a spiral snail shell and Lily chose a cockle that looked like a heart. They both slipped their chosen shell into their pockets, scattering all the other shells they had collected onto the sand.

'Goodbye,' Ivy said with a solemn expression on her face. She waved to the shells they had left behind.

'Maybe these shells belong on the beach,' Lily said as she poured water from a bottle over Ivy's hands to wash the sand off.

'Like we belong at home,' Ivy said after a minute.

Lily smiled a little, though she knew she was not truly a part of Ivy's family and home. 'Yes,' she said. 'We belong at home.'

* * *

Khalid and Ibrahim were cycling past Rochor River. Across the river were kampong dwellings, shophouses, factories and warehouses, overshadowed by the colonial buildings rising behind them. In the river, bumboats floated, crammed with bales, boxes and sacks. Coolies were working hard to transport goods off the bumboats. Walking on thin wooden planks that bridged river and land, some carried heavy materials in buckets on poles balanced on their shoulders while others hoisted large gunny sacks. It was back-breaking work. Sweat streamed off the tanned faces of the coolies as they laboured under the tropical heat. As they peddled past, Khalid looked up and spotted a pineapple factory which canned pineapples to help preserve the fresh fruit. These canned pineapples were then exported to faraway countries. When the tide of the river was at its highest, young boys would delight in swimming in the river, making sure to keep their heads above water because of the unfortunate stench the river carried of rubbish, animal and human waste.

By the time they arrived at their mother's house, Khalid and Ibrahim had worked up an appetite for lunch. They walked past the row of wooden attap houses, first the house where the landlord and his family stayed and then their maternal uncle's house before reaching the little house their mother stayed in alone. It was a safe little place, Khalid thought.

'Remember to say Assalamualaikum before you enter,' Khalid said, referring to the Islamic greeting of peace exchanged when two Muslims meet.

Ibrahim tilted his head slightly towards Khalid as he stifled a yawn. Khalid looked up at his brother, noting the bored expression on his face.

'And be nice,' Khalid reminded him, thinking of how he had had to persuade Ibrahim to accept their mother's invitation for lunch.

Ibrahim let out a deep laugh. 'I'm supposed to be the elder brother. I know how to behave.'

True to his word, he was civil to Mak Aisha. Khalid thought that he could hardly expect him to be warm towards her when he had lived with Pak Ambi since the age of two. They ate quietly, chewing on the nasi goreng that Mak Aisha had cooked. It seemed to Khalid like his mother wanted to say something to him and his brother the way she studied their faces carefully while they ate. Or perhaps she just misses us, Khalid thought. When they were almost done with lunch, Mak Aisha's landlady, Mrs Ong, dropped by with a big plate of freshly cut mangoes.

She beamed when she saw Khalid, her eyes crinkling with pleasure. Khalid knew she was likely to engage in a telling of his birth story. He had heard the story many times throughout his childhood. His mother had been writhing in pain after her water broke. She experienced intense contraction after contraction, starting from her sides and working its way to the middle of her stomach, but no baby came. Around 8 p.m., Mrs Ong had taken pity on Mak Aisha. She invited her to come and stay in her house for the night.

'Salmah asked me to prepare a basin of steaming water and cloth,' Mrs Ong said in Malay, referring to the Malay midwife who had been called upon to deliver Khalid. 'Oh, I was so scared. Thought the baby was going to come while I was boiling water! I remember she asked Aisha to lie in the south direction. South because that was where the heat of the prevailing wind was coming from. It was right below Guan Yin!'

Mak Aisha nodded slowly, her smile a shy shadow. 'Yes.'

Khalid had wondered before what his mother, a fairly devout Muslim, had thought of bringing a child into the world with the Ongs' statue of the Goddess of Mercy presiding over her outstretched body. He himself thought it was rather fitting as Mrs Ong had told him in a previous iteration of his birth story that Guan Yin was the goddess of childbirth.

'Salmah rubbed lime paste on Aisha's stomach,' Mrs Ong continued. 'Then she tied a rolled-up sarong on the stomach, just below the womb. Finally, at 4 a.m., the baby came. So brown and small but crying loudly! Thank heavens!'

Ibrahim wore an expression of mild amusement on his face. Khalid knew he would probably be in for a round of teasing later, this being the first time Ibrahim had heard this story. Mrs Ong continued to chatter on, asking Khalid questions about school and his plans after his examinations, and for Ibrahim, questions about his job and whether he had a girlfriend.

'Where's your father today?' Mrs Ong asked the brothers.

'He's visiting my step-mother,' Khalid said.

Ibrahim bit into a slice of juicy mango. Khalid's eyes flickered in the familiarity of the scene before him: Ibrahim's eyes closing, blissfully partaking in the sweet creaminess of his favourite fruit. Whenever Pak Ambi brought home mangoes to eat, it was highly likely that Ibrahim would be in a good mood for the rest of the day.

'Mmm,' Ibrahim said.

'Funny man. Why he doesn't want to stay with his wife?' Mrs Ong said to Mak Aisha whose lips thinned at the mention of her ex-husband.

When Mrs Ong left after they had satiated themselves by finishing all the mangoes on the plate, Khalid felt rather relieved. He had been enjoying the time spent with his mother and brother.

'We'll help you wash the plates,' Khalid said.

Mak Aisha waved her hand in front of her face. 'No need,' she said.

'Okay,' Ibrahim said. 'Maybe we should go then.' He gestured with a slight head tilt to the doorway. Khalid felt himself bristle. We should help Mak wash up, he wanted to say. But at the same time, he did not want to upset Ibrahim by suggesting they help with a chore which might make it less likely that Ibrahim agree to a visit to Mak Aisha's home in the future. As he was contemplating what to say next, Ibrahim spoke up, 'Thank you Mak for having us for lunch.'

Khaid exhaled. 'We will visit again,' Khalid added.

'Wait,' Mak Aisha burst out. 'I have something to say.'

Ibrahim raised his right eyebrow. 'What is it?'

'Please,' Mak Aisha said, gesturing to the chairs in front of her. 'Please sit.'

Khalid sat down and Ibrahim followed suit. Khalid's eyes took in his mother with her faded baju kurung and serkup, which covered all her hair.

Mak Aisha clasped her hands in front of her. 'I—I am getting married soon,' she said.

Khalid and Ibrahim exchanged looks of surprise. Khalid frowned, his brows creasing with confusion. When did this happen? He thought. Mak is getting married? To whom?

As if Mak Aisha knew what Khalid was thinking, she answered, 'He's widower. I think, a good man.'

Khalid did not know what to say. He hoped that Mak Aisha was indeed going to marry a good man. He looked over at Ibrahim, hoping that his brother would say something, but Ibrahim stayed silent, covered his face with his hand and looked away from the table.

'What does he do for work?' Khalid asked after a few seconds.

'He has family business . . . a restaurant. Amin Restaurant,' Mak Aisha said.

'Where is that?' Khalid asked.

'North Bridge Road, same place near Zam Zam and Victory,' Mak Aisha said.

'Never heard of it,' Ibrahim interjected with a raised eyebrow.

'We go there together for lunch,' Mak Aisha offered. 'Or dinner. When you are free.'

Khalid nodded, eager to please Mak Aisha. 'Yes, we could.'

'We'll see,' Ibrahim said.

'Both of you meet him before we get married?' Mak Aisha asked.

'When is the wedding?' Khalid asked.

'Five months from now,' Mak Aisha said. 'Then I move in with his family. Their house at Beach Road.'

'I see,' Khalid said. There were more questions he wanted answers to but he did not expect that they would be answered anytime soon.

Later as they wheeled their bicycles out of the courtyard, Khalid turned to Ibrahim and whispered, 'Why do you have to be so cold towards her? She's our mother.'

'Yes, she is but she let Pak Ambi take me away. She let him take you back,' Ibrahim hissed. The forcefulness in his voice did not take Khalid by surprise but it hurt him.

'She couldn't help it,' Khalid said, biting his lips.

Ibrahim shook his head as he raked his fingers through his hair. 'She's weak. Some women are.'

Khalid opened his mouth to speak but no words came out. While he had compassion for his mother and the struggles she had gone through as a wife and mother, Ibrahim had resentment and contempt. Perhaps his disdain stemmed from the fact that his mother had arranged a marriage for him two years ago with Pak Ambi's agreement.

'To a cousin!' Ibrahim had shouted when he was alone with Khalid in their room.

'I don't think Mak Aisha is weak,' Khalid said finally.

Ibrahim shrugged as he let out a snigger. 'I hope not or this new husband will bully her,' he said. 'Let's head home.'

He pushed his bicycle forward, hopped on and started peddling out onto the main road. Khalid turned back for a moment to look at his mother's house before he hopped on his bicycle, following behind Ibrahim.

Chapter V

1st June 1939

The Kong family were each holding their own suitcase as they stood in the main hall of the house. They were waiting for a taxi to Tanjong Pagar Railway Station where they would take the morning train to Malacca to visit Pak Kong's parents and siblings. Since Pak Kong's parents did not like to travel, Lily had only met them once when they came over to Singapore for a visit. Since she could remember, Lily had been taught to address them as Kong Kong and Mama, as if they were her biological grandparents. Kong Kong and Mama were now in their fifties but seemed much older to Lily. Kong Kong was reticent. Mak Kong's stories about him revolved around how he acted like his living children were a disappointment and how he spent his days longing to join the dead members of the family. Mama, on the other hand, took an immediate dislike to Lily for reasons she could not fathom. She criticised the dishes Lily made and complained about the shoulder massages she had commanded Lily to give her every evening. Lily was glad she would probably never have to see the old couple again.

'Remember to place the chap ji kee bet tomorrow,' Mak Kong said.

'Of course, Mak Kong,' Zhu Jie replied.

'Take care of the house,' Pak Kong reminded.

'We will,' Zhu Jie said. Leng Jie, who was standing next to her, nodded meekly.

The Kongs left after exchanging goodbyes. Zhu Jie gestured excitedly to Lily to follow her to the kitchen. Her round face was pink with pleasure.

'Come, I have something to give you,' Zhu Jie whispered, beckoning Lily over with a wave of her hand.

'Okay,' Lily said.

Zhu Jie bustled into the kitchen, her pillowy arms swinging beside her.

Lily followed behind Zhu Jie, her heart rising with each step. She had a feeling that Zhu Jie was going to surprise her.

Zhu Jie put her hand in her black trousers' pocket and took out a silver comb.

'For you, Lily,' Zhu Jie said. 'Your birthday today.'

In an instant, Lily felt her eyes well up. She looked down at the comb in her hand.

'What's wrong?' Zhu Jie asked. 'You don't like? I know you already have one from Mak Wee but that is gold. This is different, you see, silver.'

Lily looked up into Zhu Jie's eyes that were warm and inviting like a bowl of chicken soup.

'Thank you, Zhu Jie,' she managed to say.

Zhu Jie placed her hand over Lily's. 'You deserve good thing. You are good girl.'

Lily felt her face grow warm. Zhu Jie thought she deserved good things and that she was a good girl. 'Thank you, Zhu Jie,' she said.

She held out her palms and Zhu Jie placed the comb on it. Lily stared at the silver comb as it lay in her hands like a precious butterfly had landed on it. How precious, Lily thought. Butterflies are a symbol of joy and beauty, romance and dreams.

Leng Jie cleared her throat a little as she walked past them, a mopey, melancholic look on her face.

Zhu Jie glanced over at her and wiggled her eyebrows. 'Asking me to go do work. You think she be happy, day off from following little mistress around.'

Lily giggled and looked down at her hands as the image of the butterfly disappeared. She slid the comb into her hair and wondered if Khalid would notice her new comb when he visited them next week. How could he? Lily thought. He's always in the main hall, and I'm always in the sewing room with a partition separating us.

Later that night, Lily looked out her window as Zhu Jie left the house. All of a sudden, like many times before, Lily felt a sudden impulse to follow her.

I just have to, Lily thought. But I can't. Or can I? She swallowed her saliva and dug her fingernails into her palm. Taking a deep breath, Lily decided she would sneak out of the house at that very minute. Knowing Leng Jie would be in her room behind the kitchen, she ran down the stairs, feeling a rush of renewed rebellion. Haven't I stood at my window many times before and watched Zhu Jie leave the house? Lily's mind went on as she slipped her feet into her clogs. I wanted to follow her but I did not. It's today or never. Who knows when Pak Kong and Mak Kong will be out of the house again? Lily's guilt pricked at her and she felt her dinner of chicken porridge rise up from her stomach. She hurried down the street, thanking the heavens that Zhu Jie walked at a leisurely pace.

Should I approach Zhu Jie? Lily wondered. Or just continue to follow her from behind?

Lily pushed all thoughts aside and grabbed onto her sarong. I have to do this now, Lily decided at that moment. She raced up to Zhu Jie. When she reached her, she tapped her on the shoulder. Zhu Jie whipped her long ponytail around and her eyes widened in shock. She firmly grabbed Lily by the arm.

'What you doing outside the house this hour?' Zhu Jie asked, her face ablaze with anger. 'You cannot here.'

The force in Zhu Jie's voice took Lily by surprise.

'Zhu Jie . . . jie,' she stammered.

Zhu Jie sighed. 'You know that you cannot. Cannot allow out of house.'

Lily cast her eyes downwards and in the silence that stretched out between them, Zhu Jie knew that what she was about to do next, she might pay dearly for the rest of her employed life with the Kongs.

'So much trouble if anyone find out,' Zhu Jie said.

'I just didn't think,' Lily said. 'I'm sorry. I'll . . . '

'Come with me,' Zhu Jie said, muttering under her breath. 'We go to my friend's house first.'

Lily nodded, not daring to ask any questions.

Zhu Jie looped her arm through Lily's and Lily looked at her rounded face and felt her soft arm through her baju, like a cushion she could hold onto for security.

'You're going to dress like majie. You understand?' Zhu Jie continued. 'You walk down the main street like this, many people look at you.'

Lily nodded again as Zhu Jie sighed and started mumbling in Cantonese to herself.

They threaded through dimly lit alleys until they stood in front of a compound house at Ceylon Road.

'Wait here,' Zhu Jie commanded, pointing to the pavement outside the house.

Lily felt foolish from nodding so much. She watched as Zhu Jie made her way to the back of the house. Lily turned her head up to the sky and bit her lip, wondering what insanity had possessed her. Why did I do this? Lily wondered. What is Zhu Jie doing for me? Her thoughts continued in an endless stream until she once again took a deep breath and told herself to just enjoy the evening air. It was a warm evening, with only a few stars dotting the night sky. Lily promised herself at that moment that one day she would see what the sky looked like in another country, Malaya perhaps.

After Lily had counted the number of plants in this mysterious house's garden, Zhu Jie appeared from the back of the house and gestured to Lily.

'Come,' she waved Lily over. 'Come here.'

Lily hesitated for a moment, then followed Zhu Jie.

A dubious face of an older majie greeted her. This majie was taller than Lily, and very slim. She was wearing the samfu like Zhu Jie and

Leng Jie did, but her hair was done up in a tight bun. She passed Lily a samfu set.

'Go change,' the majie said. She pointed to a restroom in front of her.

Lily gulped and looked at Zhu Jie as if to ask for permission.

'Lily,' Zhu Jie said. 'This Khau Jie. You understand what happening? You dress as majie.'

Lily was about to nod then she stopped herself. 'Yes.'

Khau Jie and Zhu Jie exchanged a few words in Hokkien as Lily picked up the samfu and black shoes. Lily's hands shook as she undressed and put on the white top and black trousers. She came out of the restroom holding her kebaya top and skirt.

'Thank you, Khau Jie,' Lily said. She bit her lip, feeling uncertain about what to do next.

'Let's go,' Zhu Jie said with authority. 'Don't want to be late.' She embraced Khau Jie. There was a pleading look of longing in Khau Jie's eyes that Lily noticed but did not understand. After a moment, Zhu Jie tore her eyes away from Khau Jie's and then grabbed Lily's hand.

Anyone looking at her would think she was a majie, Lily thought as she and Zhu Jie hurried along the street. How easily she had slipped out of her kebaya and assumed a new identity. It was just a piece of clothing but it changed everything. Now she could walk freely.

'Where are we going?' Lily asked, looking over at Zhu Jie, who was muttering under her breath.

'Chinatown,' Zhu Jie replied. 'Where I stay. You sleep tonight. Tomorrow we wake up 4:30 a.m. go back Everitt Road.'

In spite of herself, Lily grinned gleefully. 'A young nyonya can have an adventure. Why should it just be the boys and men who get to have fun?'

Zhu Jie laughed. 'Nothing fun about going to my coolie fong room. You see.'

They reached the bus stop and sat down.

'Bus come soon,' Zhu Jie said. 'When sky getting darker, bus come.'

Lily placed her palms on her lap and leaned forward in anticipation. She had never taken a bus before. They sat in silence for a while, watching the colours of the sky change to welcome the night.

'Oh no, I forgot to change my shoes!' Lily said suddenly, as she looked down at her peep-toe beaded slippers. It was one of her favourites, a white base with blue flowers and green flowers. She had five pairs of beaded shoes and nowhere to go, she had found herself thinking wistfully the day before as she looked at the shoes sitting in a neat row in room. But now she was about to actually go somewhere and with Zhu Jie, her friend, at that.

Zhu Jie gasped. 'I never check.'

She smacked her palm lightly against her eyes and sighed. 'Maybe no one notice.'

'Hope so,' Lily said, as she pinched herself on the left arm. They fell into a companionable silence.

After a few minutes, Zhu Jie spoke. 'May Geok getting married. Next year,' she said. 'Majies next door told me.'

'Oh,' Lily said. 'Wow.' May Geok had told her that her parents were looking for a match for her but she was dreading marriage. 'Why would I want to marry a man I barely know?' May Geok said. 'At least your parents care enough to look for a match for you,' Lily had wanted to reply as she thought of Mak Wee.

'Did you ever want to get married?' Lily asked.

Zhu Jie looked thoughtful before she spoke. 'Yes. But not my destiny. Maybe one day, I adopt a daughter.'

Lily turned her head upwards slightly, taking in Zhu Jie's pensive look. She tried to figure out what to say in response but could not decide what was the right thing to say. A short while later, the trolley bus came chugging down the road. Lily watched, her eyes widening a little, at the trolley poles that seemed to hold the bus back and its wheels which propelled it forward.

Zhu Jie whipped out her coin purse and jiggled it about. She handed Lily a single 5-cent coin and took out five 1-cent coins for herself. Lily's lips quivered as she took the first step to board the bus. The tips of her kasut manek peeked out from under her trousers, the last vestige of her nyonya skin. Zhu Jie put her hand on Lily's back as if to guide her up the steps.

As they sat down, Lily pointed to her feet. Zhu Jie grimaced and started chuckling silently to herself. Lily stared at her for a moment then let out a small giggle that expanded to fill the space in front of her. A middle-aged male commuter in the seat in front of her turned to look at Lily. Lily averted her eyes and stared at her hands. Zhu Jie pursed her lips and patted Lily on the hand to reassure her.

'Look, bus is moving,' Zhu Jie said. Lily drew in a breath and looked out of the window as the trolleybus glided down the road. She glanced from the shophouses and cars to a man walking with a stooped back, weariness clouding his expression. Everything was bathed in soft moonlight. Suddenly, the traffic lights seemed a bit too bright. She closed her eyes for a moment and ended up dozing off. The next thing Lily knew, Zhu Jie was gently shaking her awake.

'We here,' Zhu Jie said. She looped her arm through Lily's. Barely able to believe that she was about to see where Zhu Jie stayed, Lily pinched her left hand. As they alighted from the bus and the warm air embraced her, Lily stood in front of the shophouse and stared.

The shophouse could have passed for any other she had seen on Everitt Road. Decorated with plaster and tile, it was the same two-storey building with three timber windows on the upper storey façade to allow for good ventilation.

'What you staring at?' Zhu Jie asked. 'Never see a shophouse before?'

Lily giggled. 'Not yours.'

'If this my shophouse, I won't work for Kongs anymore,' Zhu Jie joked, winking at Lily.

Zhu Jie bustled into the entryway. Lily hesitated before taking one brave step forward to follow her. Lily took in the room in front of her. There was a round table and a small chair where a young majie sat, her long hair cascading down her back. She balanced a cigarette between her fingers as she twirled her hair around her fingers. She took a puff from the cigarette and started coughing.

'Lui, last week you say no more smoking,' Zhu Jie rushed over and patted her on the back.

'I-I-I can't help it. Help me relax,' Lui Jie stammered. She wheezed and wiped away some saliva at the side of her mouth.

Lily hung back, not knowing what to do or say. A nyonya would never smoke. But she was curious what it would be like to try a cigarette. I might be staying over at Zhu Jie's tonight but I'm still a nyonya. Act like

one, Lily told herself. At once, she reproached herself. Did she believe
that a nyonya conducted herself better than a majie? Were people not all
the same at the end of the day? A nyonya was not better than a majie,
Lily thought. At that moment, she wondered what Zhu Jie's monthly
wage was. All she knew was that both Zhu Jie and Leng Jie received two
pairs of wooden clogs a year from the Kongs.

Lui Jie put her cigarette out on the ashtray in front of her and
cracked a sheepish smile.

'Who are you? Never see you here before,' Lui Jie said. She stared at
Lily with wide, round eyes that seemed to bore a hole into her soul. Lily
found herself shivering. She put her arms around herself.

'Long story. Rui Jie staying with me tonight,' Zhu Jie said, her eyes
darting to the direction of Lily's feet.

'Your employer kick you out? What you do?' Lui Jie said, her eyes
glinting in gleeful delight. She stood up and peered closely at Lily.

Lily cast an uncertain glance at Zhu Jie and kept mum.

'Too long story to explain,' Zhu Jie said, putting her hand on Lily's
elbow. 'We going up. Tired.'

Lui Jie shrugged, a look of nonchalance crossing her face. As quickly
as Lily's story appeared to have piqued her interest, she had dropped it
now that Zhu Jie refused to share more. She skipped back to her chair
and picked up her cigarette.

Zhu Jie glared at her. With a grimace, Lui Jie put the cigarette back
down obediently.

'Just one more puff,' Lui Jie pleaded.

'No,' Zhu Jie said. She shook her head and continued staring
at Lui Jie.

'Remember what I said,' Zhu Jie intoned. Standing behind Zhu Jie
with her hands clasped together, Lily thought it seemed likely that Lui
Jie would resume smoking once Zhu Jie was out of the room.

Lui Jie sighed with a petulant air and folded her arms across
her chest.

Zhu Jie beckoned Lily to follow her up the rickety stairs. Zhu Jie's
soft black shoes barely made a squeak but Lily felt the thud of her kasut
manek on each step, just as loud, she thought, as her beating heart that
only she could hear.

They walked past two rooms with the doors closed before Lily entered a narrow room with four beds. One majie was asleep in bed, snoring softly and curled up in foetal position.

'All is mine,' Zhu Jie announced, waving her hand across her bed. Lily felt a rush of empathy layered with pity for Zhu Jie as she looked at the thin bedspread and the tiny bed with its flat pillow. So, this is where Zhu Jie lays her head every night after working for more than fifteen hours with the Kongs, Lily thought. Hers was a life of scrimping and saving money to send back home. Lily felt guilt coalesce to form a dark spot in her mind. She had heard Zhu Jie and Leng Jie speak once about death houses at Sago Lane but she did not ask more. What would happen to Zhu Jie once she left the employment of the Kongs?' Lily wondered.

'Tonight, you sleep here,' Zhu Jie said. 'On bed.'

Lily bit her lip slightly and turned her head to look Zhu Jie. 'What about you, Zhu Jie?'

Zhu Jie pointed to the ground and cracked a half-smile. 'Sleeping on ground is good for back.'

'Is it?' Lily asked with genuine curiosity.

'I think so,' Zhu Jie said. 'Ground good for back.'

'I should sleep on the ground,' Lily said, her eyes fixated on a spot on the ground.

'Don't think you can,' Zhu Jie said. She patted Lily's hand. 'You want bathe again or sleep?'

'Sleep,' Lily said as a yawn escaped her mouth. 'So tired.'

'Okay, I bathe again,' Zhu Jie said. 'Good night, Lily.'

'Good night, Zhu Jie,' Lily said. She sat down on Zhu Jie's bed and stretched her feet out. How different Zhu Jie's life is from mine. How did I ever feel sorry for myself that I stay with the Kongs'? I have a comfortable life. Feeling a new sense of appreciation for the home she had and a renewed rush of affection for Zhu Jie, Lily fell asleep.

Lily waited with her hands in her lap, her head bent over her embroidery frame. She moved the beads around its box with her finger. Green beads, blue beads, yellow beads, pink beads—they were all different colours and beautiful in their own way, Lily mused. Soon she thought she would hear Khalid's steady voice.

A few minutes later, she heard Charles greeting Khalid. Lily smiled to herself.

Khalid could be a teacher in future, Lily mused as she heard Khalid ask Charles how he was doing today.

'Okay, I suppose,' Charles replied, his voice coming out small and tired like he wished to be anywhere else but at the tuition lesson.

Lily sensed Charles' sadness immediately. She wondered if Khalid would notice too. She held her breath, put down the needle in her hand and listened intently through the partition.

'What's the matter?' Khalid asked. Though she was not in the room, she felt the concern flooding his voice. She wanted to be enveloped in his voice and listen to his eloquence for the next hour. But she had to focus on her beadwork. Lily heaved a small sigh in spite of herself.

Maybe I could serve the tea again, she thought. Yes, I will ask Zhu Jie later.

Lily decided to try her best to tune out Khalid's and Charles' voices and focus on her beadwork. As she threaded a green bead through her needle, she pictured leaves of the fig tree at the air well swaying slightly in the wind the way they always did when it was about to rain. Bead by bead, she whispered to herself. At that moment, she heard Khalid's voice.

'Day by day,' he said.

'Okay,' Charles replied.

Lily turned her head to listen, struck by what Khalid had said. She pressed her palm on the table. Yes, she thought. Bead by bead. That was how she would complete her beadwork. And day by day. That was how a person should live life.

Thirty minutes later, Lily was carrying out the tray of tea and ang ku kueh from the kitchen. Zhu Jie had wiggled her eyebrows when Lily came into the kitchen. Her hands trembled as she carried the tray. She would be seeing Khalid again. How she had longed for this moment, Lily mused, as her heart fluttered in her chest.

'Okay, let's move on to the next comprehension question,' Khalid was saying as Lily approached the table.

Charles nodded. Lily bent down and placed the tray on the table, hoping that Khalid would say something to her. It would not befit a nyonya to speak directly to a man though she wanted to say something, anything, to Khalid. Perhaps she could start at the very beginning with a greeting, 'Apa khabair?' or 'Hello', both of which she had been practising writing.

'Thank you, Lily,' Khalid said. Lily could feel Khalid's eyes on her but she did not look up to meet his glance this time. She simply bowed her head and left the main hall. I have to be a good nyonya, she thought. Besides I already have the memory of the first time I looked at Khalid in the eye.

Through the partition Lily went, back to her sewing room. Oh, Lily thought. I have to find a way to become friends with Khalid. What could she do? I can't very well speak to him, especially in front of Charles. My actions would be reported to Mak Kong.

Lily took a deep breath and tried to relax. The answer will come, she thought. In good time.

Chapter VI

5th June 1939

Ibrahim took a long puff from his cigarette and blew out a wisp of smoke.

'Ahh . . . ' he sighed. 'Want to try?' Khalid shook his head, his eyes drawn to the cigarette in Ibrahim's hand. He was certainly curious about it but he did not think today was the right day to try.

'Maybe one day,' he whispered.

'You say that all the time but one day never comes. I'm offering it to you now because you look nervous.'

'I'm not . . . nervous,' Khalid said, the lie edging its way out of his mouth.

'You're a bad liar. Remember: be prepared to run if the police come,' Ibrahim said, puffing on his cigarette. 'Through the backdoor.'

'I know,' Khalid said. 'Pak Ambi warned us.'

Ibrahim put his hand on Khalid's shoulder. 'Just reminding you.'

They arrived at a dimly lit back alley at East Coast Road and Ibrahim strolled in through a backdoor like he had been to the house before. Khalid lingered outside, staring at the house. It seemed old with some of its paint peeling but held a certain kind of grandeur with its baroque style windows. It had two backdoors, both of which were open. A young, skinny boy, perhaps no older than seventeen, stood in front of him, guarding one of the entrances. He was flanked by a taller, older and muscular boy whose eyes darted about frantically on the lookout for the police. Khalid raised an eyebrow at him by way of a greeting. As he entered the house, he saw Pak Ambi standing in the middle of the room and talking loudly. He threw his head back and laughed. Ibrahim stood in a corner with his arms folded. Khalid caught Ibrahim's eye and walked up to him.

'I didn't even want to be here,' Ibrahim said as he scratched his chin. 'You know I had a date tonight?'

'Oh?' Khalid asked, raising an eyebrow. 'With whom?'

'Some girl,' Ibrahim replied.

'Some girl,' Khalid repeated. 'Does she have a name?'

Khalid wondered why Ibrahim was still dating when he was betrothed to their cousin Sara. Perhaps it was an act of rebellion, simply a way to do what he wanted before his marriage. Or perhaps he really likes the girl he is dating, Khalid thought, staring at the ground.

Pak Ambi saw Ibrahim and beckoned him over with a wave of his hand. Khalid thought, 'He will never notice me first.' Ibrahim was not only older; he was half a head taller and more confident. Khalid thought his presence in a roomful of adults could more easily be overlooked not only by Pak Ambi but by any other stranger. The only way I can beat Ibrahim is in my studies, Khalid told himself. Ibrahim might work harder than me but I'm smarter than him.

Pak Ambi clapped his meat-like hand on Khalid's shoulder. He approached him and the man he was standing with, who was short and stocky with a crooked smile.

'Ibrahim, Khalid, meet Mr Chua,' Pak Ambi said. Mr Chua shook hands with Ibrahim first. Khalid extended his hand out and made sure he gripped Mr Chua's hand firmly. A handshake of confidence.

'This tall, skinny boy is Ibrahim,' Pak Ambi said to Mr Chua. 'My older son. And this darker, shorter one is my younger son, Khalid.'

Ibrahim's eyes twinkled in amusement as he looked down his nose at Khalid, a smug expression on his face. Khalid gave him a sidelong glance, his eyes narrowing. He did not like being shorter than Ibrahim or Pak Ambi. He crossed his arms in front of his chest.

'Almost time for the chap ji kee draw,' Mr Chua said, gesturing to the front of the room.

Khalid looked beyond the gaps between the men and boys standing in front of him. A man in his forties with streaks of grey hair sat at a mahogany table with six red and six black Chinese Chess playing pieces laid out. The pieces were engraved with Chinese characters that Khalid could not read. Khalid watched as the man picked a card from a bag containing twelve cards and placed the chosen card into a small wooden box.

The man looked around the room, grinning widely and then opened the box a little, drawing sharp, eager breaths from a few members of the crowd gathered at the front. He closed it just as quickly, teasing the group.

Pak Ambi groaned loudly. 'Come on!' he shouted, waving his fist in the air.

'What do you think the first number is going to be?' the man called out.

Khalid listened intently as the crowd shouted different numbers. 'Two! Four! Seven!'

The man grinned, a manic glint in his eye. 'The first number is six!'

Some of the men cursed while a few of them whooped in the air for joy. Khalid frowned as he watched a gangly man spit on the floor.

'Second number is four!' the man announced like it was his own personal triumph. Khalid looked up at Pak Ambi and could almost see the wheels of his brain turning, thinking about how much money he would earn tonight. Like the other collectors of chap ji kee bets, Pak Ambi earned a ten per cent commission on every winning stake. Money, Khalid thought. Mr Shepherd had said just last week that the love of money is the root of all kinds of evil.

Khalid wished that Pak Ambi had a steady job instead of being a collector for chap ji kee. Pak Ambi loved money but he loved lazing around more. Being a chap ji kee collector was his only steady source of income. What would happen to them when the police stopped chap ji kee operations in Singapore? Khalid worried.

Khalid hoped by then that he would have a job himself so he could support his family. The crowd dispersed quickly and moved out of the back door after the winning numbers were read out. Ibrahim slung his arm over Khalid's shoulder before they left the room together. Pak Ambi stormed out behind them, grinning widely. Khalid could see he was in a mood to celebrate.

'Going to see Mak Jah,' Pak Ambi said. 'Staying with her tonight.'

His sons nodded. Once Pak Ambi had left, Ibrahim stuck his index finger and thumb out and brought it to his mouth.

'Yes. What else?' Khalid said. They both knew Pak Ambi would be out drinking with his friends. The brothers fell in step with each other as they made their way home.

As they wended their way through the back streets that led to home, Ibrahim put his arm on Khalid's shoulder and asked, 'Want to hear a ghost story tonight, K?'

Khalid raised his eyebrows in surprise. It had been a few years since Ibrahim had told him a ghost story. Khalid shrugged; he was not a fan of ghost stories. Ibrahim knows this but still he wants to subject me to this torture, Khalid thought as he shook his head.

'Just heard a scary one from my friend,' Ibrahim said.

'Okay,' Khalid said.

'So want to hear it or not?' Ibrahim asked. 'Or are you too chicken?'

Refusing to take his brother's bait, Khalid shrugged again. 'If you want to tell me . . . '

'Yes,' Ibrahim said, nodding his head. 'I do. Maybe you'll cry.' He let out a throaty laugh.

Khalid rolled his eyes. 'I've never cried during one of your stories.'

'I'm sure you did at least once or twice,' Ibrahim insisted, pushing Khalid on the shoulder.

'Your stories aren't as scary as you'd like to think,' Khalid said.

'Okay, let's see tonight,' Ibrahim said, rubbing his hands together in glee.

When Khalid was in bed that night, Ibrahim tiptoed over and shook his shoulder.

'Khalid,' Ibrahim said. 'Don't fall asleep yet.'

'Okay,' Khalid said. 'I'm awake, Ib.'

'Ready to hear the story?' Ibrahim asked.

'Okay,' Khalid agreed, hoping to get this over with as quickly as possible so he could go to sleep. He sat up in his bed and put his pillow behind his head.

'Last year, a woman went missing in her hometown,' Ibrahim said in a quiet voice.

'Where?' Khalid asked. He had learnt that by asking questions, he could break the spell of horror Ibrahim tried to weave with his low, eerie voice.

Ibrahim paused for a moment. 'Her hometown,' he repeated. 'Singapore.'

Khalid laughed. 'Seems like you didn't know where this hometown is until I asked. Just made it up.'

'Just be quiet and listen,' Ibrahim said. 'I'm going to start over.'

Khalid groaned as he shifted his pillow slightly.

'Last year, a woman went missing in Singapore,' Ibrahim said. 'For days, her family searched for her. But to no avail.'

'Is she married?' Khalid asked.

Ibrahim ignored him. 'The police had no leads. It was like she had just vanished into thin air.'

'Not possible,' Khalid said.

'Her mother prayed every night that she would come home, safe and sound. But day after day passed, and the woman did not return,' Ibrahim said, his voice low.

'What's her name?' Khalid asked, scratching his eyebrow.

Ibrahim ignored him. 'The woman did not return. The days turned into years. The years turned into decades. Her mother continued praying until one night, she heard a small voice speak to her very softly.'

Khalid shuddered in spite of himself and pulled his bedsheet up to his chin.

'Scared already, right?' Ibrahim chuckled, his head bent.

'No,' Khalid said.

'This small voice sounded a lot like her daughter's. But it was sad.'

At that moment, the door opened and Khalid sighed in relief. Pak Ambi was home earlier than expected. Maybe now Ibrahim would stop, Khalid hoped as he watched Pak Ambi stagger into the room.

But Ibrahim did not turn his head around. He continued to relate the story.

The sad voice said, 'Help me, Mama . . . ' Ibrahim continued as Khalid's eyes followed Pak Ambi staggering to his bed. He fell into bed with a heavy thud.

'Help me, Mama,' Ibrahim repeated. 'The mother turned around and saw her little girl. She could see through her.'

Distracted by Pak Ambi and wondering if he would start confessing more of his secrets or fall asleep immediately, Khalid was only half-listening to Ibrahim's story.

'Pak's drunk, Ib,' Khalid said, peering at his father's form on his bed.

Ibrahim put a firm hand on Khalid's shoulder. 'I don't know, K. Don't interrupt me anymore, please?' Ibrahim said.

'Sorry,' Khalid said. He kept his eyes focused on Pak Ambi, watching his stomach rise and fall.

'Mary,' Pak Ambi muttered.

Khalid tried to keep his attention focused on Ibrahim but he could not help wondering who Mary was. He had never heard Pak Ambi mention her name before. An old girlfriend perhaps, Khalid mused.

He turned his attention to Ibrahim, sure he had missed a bit of the ghost story.

'The mother tried to hug her but she couldn't feel her. She was as light as air. The next minute, she was gone. Every night after that, the mother continued to be visited by the spirit of her daughter,' Ibrahim continued.

Pak Ambi started to snore and Khalid continued to stare at his father's body sprawled on his bed.

'No one believed the mother. The father tried to tell her to accept that her daughter was gone,' Ibrahim was saying. 'One day, the police visited to inform the parents that they had found their daughter's body.'

Khalid sighed heavily as he pulled the covers over himself. 'Can we continue this tomorrow?' he asked.

'Almost done,' Ibrahim snapped, frowning.

'Leave it for tomorrow then, Ib,' Khalid said.

Ibrahim groaned loudly. 'Tomorrow night, I'll tell the whole story again. Don't think you were really listening,' Ibrahim said. He stood up and strode to his bed.

Finally, Khalid thought with relief. He turned to watch Pak Ambi sleeping in his bed.

I'll think of some other reason not to hear the ghost story tomorrow, he thought as he listened to the symphony of Pak Ambi's loud snores.

Chapter VII

12th July 1939 to 25th August 1939

Lily hid behind the carved wooden screen as she saw the dark, shadowy figure of a man coming closer and closer to her. Her pulse quickened but she stood there to see who it was. The edges of the man became clear to her as he stumbled into the reception hall. His eyes were glossed over and he drifted into the room with his jaw hung open slightly. So, this is what Mak Kong meant, Lily thought. It was Pak Kong's younger brother, Chuan He.

Every day, Mak Kong had been complaining about Chuan He, the surprise guest who had come home with the Kong family the month before. When sober, he was friendly and full of stories of faraway lands and beautiful women. He was polite to the domestic help, the cook and Lily. He pretended it was hard to find Ivy during hide-and-seek, when she had only two favourite hiding spots she used: one under her bed and the other behind the red-and-brown cabinet in the hallway.

'Chek Chuan will bring you to Happy World,' he promised Ivy once after she had emerged, sneezing from behind the cabinet.

'Much too old to be playing hide-and-seek,' Charles snorted as he walked past, not looking up from his book.

'Happy World!' Ivy squealed, clapping her hands together.

Lily had thought Chek Chuan was a friendly, harmless man. Then the drinking started, or rather resumed according to the murmurings from Pak Kong and Mak Kong.

'A layabout,' Mak Kong had scoffed to the majies when Pak Kong was at work. 'Good-for-nothing. Only knows how to drink and gamble.'

He was supposed to stay a week but his stay had stretched to two weeks and then three. Soon a full month had passed.

Lily stared as Chek Chuan tried to slump into the armchair but ended up sprawled across the floor instead.

'Dayung sampan,' he spluttered as a spot of drool foamed out of his mouth. 'Dayung-dayung sampan.'

Should I let someone know? But whom? Lily wondered. Everyone was asleep. She pictured the tiredness and anger that would travel its way across Pak Kong's features when he found his brother's sleeping body, maybe in a foetal position or with legs and arms wide open, the next morning.

She stared as Chek Chuan continued mumbling bits of 'Dayung Sampan' before he fell silent and started snoring. Her curiosity satisfied, Lily felt a prick of guilt as if she had witnessed something that was meant to be private. She took a step back from the screen and sat down on the sofa to compose herself. After a few minutes, she climbed the stairs to her bedroom, feeling sleepy all of a sudden.

She wound up the alarm clock on her dresser table to set the alarm for five-thirty in the morning. As Lily lay down on her bed, she thought about how Mak Kong would be angry the next morning and in a sour mood the rest of the day, a mood that would permeate throughout the rest of the household the way dirty water from the night soil bucket spread across the ground.

Lily woke up with a start and glanced at the clock. It was only a few minutes past four in the morning. For the second time this week, she had the same dream about her parents reciting a pantun as she worked on beadwork in the next room. Her dreams seemed so real like they were a solid doorway to a warm and welcoming home she could walk into any time she wanted. Her parents would be there, beaming at her.

Her mother embraced her and her father started reciting a pantun on good deeds one night and hope and faith the next.

It wasn't real, Lily thought. She pinched her arm as her eyes started to well up with tears. Focusing on her breath, she drifted off to sleep again, hoping she would dream of Khalid instead. When she woke up next, it was to the sound of the alarm going off. A peaceful, dreamless sleep. But I will see Khalid today, Lily told herself. She untangled her legs from beneath her blanket and stretched out her arms, ready to embrace the day.

When she reached the kitchen, she saw Zhu Jie and Leng Jie seated at the round table, eating their breakfast. Zhu Jie was talking in hushed tones while Leng Jie looked grim, her face set in a strange sulk that Lily did not want to spend time deciphering. Ah Huat was unwrapping the pork belly trotters for their lunch of babi pongteh, braised pork in fermented soybean sauce.

'Good morning, Zhu Jie. Good morning, Leng Jie,' Lily chirped as she approached the table. Leng Jie's thin lips curved upwards slightly as if she could not decide whether to smile or not. Without looking at Lily, she took a sip from her cup of Milo. It's ironic that it's Leng Jie who cares for Ivy all these years, Lily thought. Zhu Jie would be better suited. But even then, she knew how much Leng Jie loved Ivy. Even when her face did not show it, her actions of spending time with Ivy did.

'Good morning, Lily,' Zhu Jie replied. 'Good mood today. I know why.' Zhu Jie giggled. The sound of her soft but hearty laughter rang in Lily's ear. Had Lily been feeling down, it would have been a balm for her spirits.

In the silence that followed, they munched on bread and butter. Lily watched as bits of kaya, a custard coconut jam, oozed out of Zhu Jie's sandwich that she brought to her lips with glee. All of a sudden, they could hear Mak Kong's murmurs from the ancestral table.

'She early today,' Zhu Jie whispered. 'Praying to Tian Gong that Master Chuan go, go home to Malacca.' Lily stifled a giggle. A short while later, Mak Kong strode into the kitchen. The trio at the table stood up immediately and busied themselves with taking the ingredients for babi pongteh out of the cabinets.

'Pak Kong will be back for lunch today,' Mak Kong barked. 'So agak-agak lunch for seven, dinner for eight. No wastage.' Lily started peeling the shallots while Leng Jie rinsed the garlic cloves in the sink.

'Master Chuan not eating?' Zhu Jie asked.

'Do you think he'll be awake in time for lunch?' Mak Kong snapped. She smoothed down the front of her kebaya and glared at Zhu Jie, her eyebrows, thin lines of anger. Lily admired Zhu Jie for daring to ask questions that she knew the answer to, simply to elicit a reaction from Mak Kong.

'No, mistress. You right,' Zhu Jie replied, sliding back into the dutiful maid role. Sighing softly as if placated, Mak Kong marched over to sit at the table, keeping an eye on Ah Huat as he chopped up the pork.

* * *

'Remind me that I have to go to Good Books later to get a book for my dad,' Roy said as he took his jersey from his bag. Khalid and his soccer teammates were in the dressing room, sweating under the August heat as they got ready for their soccer semi-final against St. Joseph's Institution.

'Who are you talking to?' Barker asked, laughing as he tucked his shirt into his shorts.

'Anyone who is listening,' Roy replied.

'I'll remind you, Roy boy,' Khalid offered. He tied the laces on his soccer boots and cracked a friendly grin at Roy. Roy was one of his best friends.

'Thanks!' Roy exclaimed. 'Now let's go crush them.'

'Barker will score another eight goals,' Zaid predicted. 'I'm still waiting for a repeat of that friendly against St. Andrew's.'

'Amen,' Barker said, lifting his hands up in the air. With Barker's charisma and athleticism, he was Head Prefect and soccer team captain. Khalid had much affection and admiration for Barker's gifts, talents and but most of all, his morally upright character.

'Ameen,' Rahman echoed, resting his arm on Barker's broad shoulder. 'Double hat-trick. Remember the *Straits Times* said it was a splendid display.'

'Splendid!' Zaid said. 'Of course, it's Captain Barker we're talking about. On the rare occasions that St. Andrew's attacked, their attempts were well-saved by Bala.' He turned away from his locker and met the eye of the team's goalkeeper, Balakrishnan, who let out a hum of approval.

'Let's not get carried away though,' Zaid said.

'SJI is a different opponent. Much stronger,' Khalid intoned to his teammates. 'They are not going to be easy to beat.'

'We know, Vice-Captain K,' Noor said. 'Don't worry. You've said this so many times.'

'If we beat SJI, we go to the finals!' Rahman said, pumping his fist in the air. He linked arms with Noor and they bobbed their shoulders together from side to side like it was the day before in the locker room when they were listening to Bob Crosby's 'Whispers in the Dark'.

'Okay, everyone ready?' Barker asked, looking around at Khalid and the other boys who chorused their replies with gusto.

Khalid knew that neither he nor Barker had dared to dream that they could bring home the coveted champions' cup for Raffles Institution but it was all a few of their other teammates could talk about in the run-up of matches to the National School Games' soccer semi-finals.

'Let's go!' Khalid cheered, though his stomach was churning with trepidation. 'We got this! Do our best!' He did not want his teammates to see how nervous he was to face the St. Joseph's Institution soccer team. The boys strode out of the dressing room in a single file towards the soccer pitch where Coach Choo was waiting for them, a determined look emblazoned on his face. Khalid tried to keep his mind focused on Coach Choo's pep talk, which was more passionate than usual, and the 3-2-2-3 formation. Out of the corner of his eye, he saw St. Joseph's institution goalkeeper, Guan Hong, taking a casual swig from his bottle of water. He was sure he saw Guan Hong smirk as he proceeded to stretch his long limbs.

Ignore him, Khalid reassured himself though Guan Hong's tall and lanky frame cut an intimidating figure. He looks just as tall as Pak Ambi, Khalid thought. Will we be able to score at all?

'The gap in the centre of our formation between our wing-halves, Noor and Rahman, and our inside forwards, Khalid and Roy, will allow for an effective counter-attack,' Coach Choo was saying, his face scrunched up in focus as he pointed at the circles he had drawn on paper. He held the clipboard in his hand firmly. Khalid could sense the tension radiating from Coach Choo though he tried hard to look relaxed and optimistic about the prospect of a win for Raffles Institution.

'We've trained hard and had a great warm-up earlier!' Coach Choo said, fervour pulsating through his voice. 'Now go out there and bring us to finals! I believe in you, my Rafflesians!' He brought the team in for their customary huddle. Khalid stood in between their goalkeeper, Balakrishnan, and his fellow inside forward, Roy. Although his left arm could not reach Balakrishnan's shoulders, his right arm easily found a place on Roy's shoulder.

As Barker gave his motivational speech, Khalid reflected on how he had been playing with most of this group for four years. For four years, through countless trainings, banter and music in the changing room, several deep conversations after matches about their plans once they graduated, and even one ugly brawl with an opposition team that resulted in a few bloodied noses and concussions on both sides, they forged the unbreakable bonds of brotherhood. With a lump in his throat that he found hard to swallow, he realised this might be the last competitive match he ever played in.

Let this motivate you, Khalid said to himself as the thought repeated in his mind. Let it motivate you. Do your very best for the team. He allowed that thought to run its course from his mind to his heart. With a deep breath, he cleared his mind to focus on the task at hand, the match and only the match. At that moment, the image of Mak Aisha came unbidden to his mind. She looked diminutive and nervous in his imagination; he knew that she very much wanted Khalid's team to win. Last Sunday, she had brought some rice and chicken curry for Khalid and Ibrahim to eat for lunch. He knew that she would be in the stands today and he wanted her to be proud of him. Pak Ambi could not attend because he had started a new driving job while Ibrahim was at work. Khalid was determined to make the only loved one he had in attendance at the stands proud of him.

'Let's go, Raffles, let's go!' Barker shouted, pumping both fists in the air. He was cheering with a confidence that inspired Khalid. Then Barker exchanged a knowing wink with Khalid. They clapped their hands together in a handshake of solidarity. Khalid looked on as Barker took long, decisive steps towards the referee, a middle-aged man named Mr Retnam. Mr Retnam took a coin out of his shorts' pocket and placed it in between his thumb and forefinger. Then he gestured at Barker to make the call.

'Heads,' Khalid heard Barker saying. Khalid looked on as Moses, the St. Joseph's Institution captain, a lanky boy whom Khalid realised was half a head taller than him, smiled broadly at Barker. Smiling like a rotten cockle, Khalid thought rather petulantly.

Khalid held his breath as Mr Retnam threw the coin in the air and deftly caught it in his palm.

'Heads it is!' Mr Retnam declared. 'RI kick off first.'

With his hands on his hips, Khalid smirked a little as Barker and Moses shook hands with each other quickly. Then Barker spun around on his heel and gave Khalid a thumbs up. Moses' smile seemed to slide off his face. Khalid thought the tiny victory of the coin toss was a good omen for the game. He looked up into the stands where his mother sat with the other parents. She seemed to glance heavenwards as her eyes widened as she waved wildly at Khalid, who gave her a small wave back by lifting his hand up. I can't be seen waving excitedly, Khalid thought although he wanted to give her a big wave in return and shout 'Mak!' It would not be manly so Khalid stood up a little taller and turned back to face Mr Retnam.

Here we go, Khalid thought, taking a deep breath. Standing in the middle of the pitch, he waited for Mr Retnam's whistle, with his hands on his hips. He watched as Moses spit out some saliva out onto the grass. When Mr Retnam blew on the whistle, Khalid immediately kicked the ball to Roy, who passed it in a swift motion along to their right winger, Zaid. Up the pitch the ball was stroked to Barker who tried to loop it over one of the opponent's full backs. The full-back intercepted the ball and launched a cross-field pass to his fellow full-back. In spite of himself, Khalid found himself admiring the way the St. Joseph Institution players traded passes and the fluidity of their movement.

Such talent, Khalid thought as he chased after their half-back like a hungry tiger who had spotted its unwitting prey. The half-back had the ball at his feet and he tried to go in for a tackle. The quick-footed half-back darted away from him as he passed the ball to his team's winger. The winger's low diagonal drive through a thicket of legs found his centre-forward. Khalid held his breath as the centre-forward took a shot at goal. Thankfully, Balakrishnan was quick off his line. He dived to the left to stop the ball going into the net with his body.

Phew! Khalid thought, exhaling in a wave of relief that flooded his body. We can't let them score first.

Both sides had several attempts to score a goal but neither side could find a breakthrough as half-time approached. When Mr Retnam blew the whistle, Khalid exchanged a look with Barker as they walked quickly to their team's bench together.

'We have to do better in the second half, K,' Barker said, glancing at his watch.

'Yeah, Barker,' Khalid said, nodding his head vigorously. 'We will.'

Twenty minutes after the second half started, Khalid watched as Zaid went in for a last-ditch tackle but the St. Joseph's Institution centre forward evaded him. The ball soared into the top right corner of the net. The goal scorer curled his fists and screamed. He ran to his teammates, who were cheering loudly. Khalid kicked at the blades of grass in front of him, releasing his frustration as the St. Joseph's boys exchanged high-fives. As play resumed, Khalid ran after the ball as if his life depended on it, his body high on adrenaline and driven by unyielding determination to get his team back into the game. His eyes followed Zaid as he intercepted a pass from Moses and passed the ball onwards to Noor, who received it well then hiked it up the pitch to Roy. Roy kicked it to Khalid and on the ball rolled to another Raffles player till it reached Barker. As Barker leapt high in the air to meet the volley with a header aimed straight at the goal, Khalid willed, with all his might, for the ball to go in. Guan Hong jumped up and caught the ball with his gloved hands.

Cursing under his breath quietly, Khalid tried to rally his team.

'Come on, boys!' he shouted. He dived harder into every tackle; he ran with the ball traveling into any open space on the pitch at top speed. Get the ball to Barker, he kept thinking. Barker will score two goals.

But it was not meant to be. As hard as they tried, the Raffles soccer team could not find a way past Guan Hong. His heart sinking into his stomach, Khalid barely heard the referee blow the whistle at full-time, signalling the end of the match. In spite of himself, Khalid felt his eyes start to well up. He grabbed his jersey, which was streaked with mud, and rubbed his face on it as if he was simply trying to remove sweat from his brow. He would not let his teammates see him cry or give the St. Joseph's boys the satisfaction of knowing how much this defeat affected him. At that moment, he felt a firm but unfamiliar hand on his shoulder. Khalid turned around and looking up, to his surprise, he found himself eye-to-eye with Moses.

'Good game,' Moses said, his eyes soft with encouragement.

'Good game,' Khalid echoed, hoping he had the sincerest smile he could have on his face though his insides were writhing with disappointment and anger. Moses nodded a little, an empathetic nod from the winner that somehow made Khalid feel worse. Khalid was about to turn away when he noticed Moses still standing there, as if hoping for more. Khalid leaned his weight on one foot, wondering what Moses wanted to say or hoped to hear. He just wanted to be left alone.

Khalid bit his tongue and took a breath. Then he extended his hand out to Moses and said, 'Congratulations, Moses!'

Moses smiled earnestly. 'Thank you, Khalid.'

The rivals shook hands. Then Moses strode off the pitch, leaving Khalid to his own ruminations.

He saw Roy sitting on the pitch with his face in his hands. At the goalpost, Barker was deep in conversation with Balakrishnan. A captain's job is never done, he thought. And what an amazing captain Barker is. Khalid knew that it was likely that Barker was offering words of motivation to Balakrishnan, who had a tendency to be hard on himself. He pushed away the sad thought of the headline in the Sports section of the *Straits Times* now: 'St. Joseph's Institution defeats Raffles Institution by a single goal in semi-final.'

Feeling dazed, he stumbled over to Roy and sat down next to him without saying a word. He could hear Roy's quick and shallow breaths. Khalid put his hand on Roy's back and said, 'We tried our best, Roy.' Roy did not look up.

Khalid did not verbalise the thought that appeared next in his mind.

'I know how you're feeling, Roy boy,' he wanted to say. All Khalid wanted to do at that moment was take a long bath and cry. But he continued sitting next to Roy and as he felt Roy's body start to tremble next to his, Khalid's eyes closed as a single tear rolled down his cheek.

Chapter VIII

30th August to 2nd September 1939

Chek Chuan had declared that he was going to quit drinking last week, his pale face ablaze with the fervour of someone who believed in the goal he had set for himself. Lily overheard a conversation between Mak Kong and Pak Kong that Pak Kong had brought him to see a soothsayer who gravely informed him that he would die young if he continued drinking. At the dinner table, in Chek Chuan's absence, Mak Kong had sniffed then laughed when she heard this piece of news from Pak Kong. Lily looked from Mak Kong to Pak Kong, as confusion set into her mind, and she wondered whether they were hoping that Chek Chuan quit drinking or hoping he did not so that their perception of him would be proven right.

'Common sense,' Mak Kong said to Pak Kong, as she scratched her nose.

'Hopefully he will quit,' Pak Kong had said. 'If he doesn't, well, I will have to have another serious discussion with him.'

That day, Lily watched as Chek Chuan left home early with Pak Kong, determined to look for a job. She had overheard that he had one interview lined up at the bank where Pak Kong worked. Mak Kong appeared to encourage him but once he was out of earshot, she mocked his newfound desire to work while fanning herself in the kitchen.

'Even if he finds a job, he won't last long,' she said with a sniff. Lily turned her head slightly to watch Leng Jie's head moving up and down slowly as if she agreed with Mak Kong. They were frying a pomfret fish and a crispy chincalok omelette for lunch that day. Lily broke four eggs into a bowl and whipped them together with the chincalok seasoning. She did hope that Chek Chuan would get a job so he could spend his time more fruitfully. She glanced over at Zhu Jie who was adding light soy sauce to the fish marinade. When the marinade was ready, Zhu Jie brought it to Ah Huat who skilfully mixed the fish with it and then set it aside. They left the fish to sit and soak in its marinade for around two hours. At noon, Ah Huat deep-fried the fish. He was lifting the fish, all golden brown, out of the wok when Lily caught an inviting whiff of durians.

Chek Chuan was walking into the kitchen carrying two bags, one unmistakably containing the spiky fruit. Mak Kong frowned when she saw the other bag. It was a clear plastic bag with a fish swimming inside it.

'Durians and ikan betok,' Chek Chuan said cheerfully. 'One to eat, and one to keep.'

'Why did you buy a fish?' Mak Kong asked, raising an eyebrow at the plastic bag. 'Little will put his paw inside and try to disturb the fish.'

Chek Chuan shrugged and smiled before opening his mouth to yawn a little. 'Just felt like it. Besides, Little already tries to disturb the koi.'

Lily observed that one side of Mak Kong's mouth was pulled upwards. Lily was familiar with this expression of Mak Kong's; it was a subtle one of contempt and disapproval but Chek Chuan seemed not to notice.

Lily wondered if Chek Chuan truly did not care to gain Mak Kong's approval or pretended not to. Apa yang dalam hati manusia, she thought. Tuhan sahaja yang tahu. She had overheard Chek Chuan sharing that a Muslim friend of his had said that to Pak Kong. What is in the heart of Man, only God knows. She did not know what the context was but Lily liked the saying very much. It was comforting to know that no one except Zhu Jie knew about her romantic feelings for Khalid.

'We can eat the durians after dinner,' Chek Chuan said, handing the bag of durians to Leng Jie, whose body seemed to sink with the weight of the bag as she took it from him.

Mak Kong was still staring at the fish. 'Are you going to feed the fish?'

'Yes,' Chek Chuan said. 'Charles and Ivy can feed it too.'

Mak Kong jerked her head slightly which Lily understood to mean she did not agree but which Chek Chuan seemed to interpret as acquiescence.

'I'll ask Charles and Ivy what they want to name the fish,' Chek Chuan said, striding out of the kitchen, fish in tow. He started singing 'Ikan kekek' loudly as he swivelled his hips, dancing his way out of the kitchen.

Zhu Jie was grinning broadly. Looking over at Zhu Jie, Lily stifled the urge to laugh herself. She pinched her arm slightly.

'Doesn't say a word about his interview but comes home with a fish!' Mak Kong said. 'I'm going to see where he is going to keep this fish.' She bustled out of the kitchen. Lily glanced at the durians sitting on the kitchen cabinet as she was looking forward to eating them. She loved the sweet, custard-like flesh of durians. It was her favourite fruit.

When Ivy came home from school, she brandished a toy airplane she had won from the tikam tikam stall. Once a week, she spent one cent to spin a wheel to see if she could win a prize. Last week, she had returned home, disappointed with the sweet she had gotten as a consolation prize.

'I finally won the airplane!' she said.

Charles sniggered as he put his backpack down. 'Only babies play tikam tikam.'

Ivy ignored him as she bobbed the white airplane up and down. The paint was peeling a little but it did not seem to bother Ivy.

Lily wondered if Ivy would let her hold the toy airplane but felt too embarrassed to ask.

'Come see the fish Chek Chuan bought,' Chek Chuan said.

'It's so cute!' Ivy said, her hands on her knees, as she peered at the fish swimming around in a large earthen jar at the air well.

'What should we name it?' she asked Lily.

'Hmm,' Lily said. 'Let's think about it.'

Lily turned around and looked at the koi pond. It was calming just to be near it.

Poor fish, Lily thought. You have no friends unlike the koi, all swimming together like a family. For about a week after, the fish went nameless until Charles christened it with the name, Thunder.

While they ate durians that night, Mak Kong made sure Little was leashed and stayed away from Thunder. Lily wondered how long Thunder would survive before he was eaten by Little or cooked for dinner. She related to Thunder, more than she did to the koi. Thunder, like her, was trapped.

Mr Tan looked unusually pale in the afternoon during Lily's lesson with him. He spoke even slower than usual, as if the mere act of speaking was a great effort. Lily wanted to ask if he was sick but stopped herself. It was painfully obvious to her that Mr Tan should be resting at home. Lily thought that perhaps it was better if she did not remind him. She admired his work ethic and his dedication to tutoring her. In that way, he was like Khalid who had never once missed a lesson with Charles, Lily thought.

'Today, we—we will look—look at —' Mr Tan said, his eyes closing with each word he enunciated slowly.

Lily nodded and waited for him to complete his sentence.

'Less-lesson 15,' Mr Tan said after a minute.

Lily looked at the page in front of her. 'Lesson 15,' she read out. There were three pictures of sticks at the very top of the page. Lily studied each stick carefully.

Mr Tan tapped his finger once on the first stick. 'A . . . stick,' he said.

'A stick,' Lily repeated. She stared at the other two sticks. The first stick was the longest stick of the three. Her eyes wandered to the picture of the boy and the dog below the lines of text. The dog looked nothing like Little; it had a sleek, muscular body with dark spots on white. But somehow it reminded her of him anyway. She giggled to herself and looked up at Mr Tan. He nodded at her, a slow nod as if he was about to fall asleep. Lily furrowed her brow in concern. Maybe he has a fever, Lily thought.

'Yes, a stick,' Mr Tan said. 'Write—write . . . it.'

Carefully, Lily copied each letter on the page of her notebook. After she was done, she leaned back to admire the two words on paper. Copying words was not satisfying as cooking or as strenuous as beadwork and embroidery, but nonetheless, Lily took pride in her work. She turned to look at Mr Tan. To her surprise, his eyes were closed. Lily wondered if she should say something. She looked at the cup of tea in front of him. He had not touched it at all, let alone the ang ku kueh in front of him. She took a sip of water. It would be polite to keep quiet and just wait, she decided.

The next second, Lily heard the joyous laughter of children from the street outside. She let the sound move around in her ears as if it was music. Mr Tan still did not open his eyes. If only the stick on the page was real, she could gently prod him with it. She admonished herself as soon as the thought left her mind. It would be most unbecoming of a young nyonya to do anything of the sort. She took a deep breath as another thought came to her mind. She stood up abruptly from her chair and peered at Mr Tan's belly; she could see it rise and fall. But he was not opening his eyes. An icy cold sensation came over her as she froze, unsure what to do next. Lily trembled, feeling tears well up in her eyes. Then she realised she had to do something to save Mr Tan. Standing up, she shouted as loudly as she could, 'Help! Help, please!'

Zhu Jie was the first to arrive on the scene. She dashed into the room, wearing a concerned expression on her plump face.

'What happened?' Zhu Jie asked. She took one look at Mr Tan whose jaw was now open and body slumped in the chair. Lily gasped, her hand on her mouth. She did not realise Ah Huat was behind her. He grabbed Mr Tan's left wrist and held it between his thumb and index finger.

'Dead,' Ah Huat proclaimed, exhaling sharply. He quickly let go of Mr Tan's wrist.

'How?' Zhu Jie asked, wringing her hands. 'Call ambulance?'

'Yes, go,' Ah Huat commanded in an authoritative voice. Lily watched as he dragged Mr Tan's limp body out of its chair and placed him face-down on the floor. He placed both his hands on his upper back and pressed down then lifted his arms up. He did this repeatedly but there was no movement at all from Mr Tan. Lily felt her eyes well up with the certainty that her English tutor was gone. She put her arms around herself, closed her eyes and breathed in and out slowly to calm herself down.

By the time, Mak Kong arrived home from her Cherki game, the ambulance had arrived and taken Mr Tan away. That night, over dinner, Pak Kong said he was a widower and lived alone so there was no family to inform. Was she the only one who felt a bit sad that he was gone? Lily thought to herself as she tried her best to eat. Did he have friends that would mourn him? It was her first encounter with death. Death was meant to just be a transition from a living world to an afterlife but Lily thought there had to be more to it than that. She wanted there to be a heaven, full of light and love, a blooming garden of paradise where good people rested. In this heaven, she could finally meet her father, where he would feel more real to her than in her dreams. He would give her a tight hug and tell her he was exceedingly proud of her and extremely glad to finally meet her. Now she added Mr Tan to the list of people she wanted to reunite with in the afterlife. She hoped with all her heart she would see her dedicated tutor again in heaven.

* * *

Khalid's stepfather-to-be, Karim, was a stout man. The first time they had met a few months ago was over lunch at Amin Restaurant and the conversation had been stilted. They made polite conversation about his restaurant business and how Khalid was coping with studying for the Senior Cambridge examinations. Mak Aisha had tried to fill the silences that stretched between the trio by sharing stories of Khalid as a boy. Khalid was glad that Ibrahim had decided not to join or he would have been teased endlessly after lunch.

'Khalid—good at sports,' Mak Aisha had said, which Khalid thought was as much about her pride for him as it was about cheering him up after the soccer finals. 'First in 75-yard race, potato race and wheelbarrow race at Telok Kurau Sports Day,' she had beamed at him as if the son who sat before her was still that gangly primary school boy. 'And now always scoring goals in soccer matches.'

'Not always,' Khalid had replied.

If he was honest with himself, the defeat against St. Joseph's Institution still stung and no reminder of past sporting victories would erase that. He did not win anything in the annual sports meet this year either. Barker had emerged with the most individual honours. Even as he felt a pinch of envy, Khalid knew his teammate deserved it. He was a gifted sportsman who also represented the school in badminton, cricket, rugby and hockey.

Barker is the best athlete. Harry is the best student. Khalid thought with an unwelcome pang of self-pity. What am I best at?

He was pulled out of his thoughts by his mother calling his name. Khalid had never thought that his mother was beautiful but, on her wedding day, her joy added a glowing quality to her features.

'Eat more,' Mak Aisha said in Malay. 'You are skinny.'

Khalid managed a smile and stuffed a spoonful of mutton briyani into his mouth.

At the long table in his home, Karim was talking and laughing with his brothers. Their wives were mostly silent, engaging in polite small talk about the curry and raita while their children ate hungrily.

Khalid hoped that this would be a better marriage for his mother than the one with his father. This was not Karim's first marriage as he was a widower so surely he must know how to properly treat a wife, Khalid thought.

'Khalid is taking his Senior Cambridge exam,' Mak Aisha was saying. This was met with a soft chorus of acknowledgement from her three sisters-in-law, Khadijah, Siti and Mardiah.

'Pandai,' Cik Khadijah said.

Siti, seated diagonally opposite Khalid, murmured, 'If my sons will go to RI one day.'

'How old are your sons, Cik Siti?' Khalid asked, looking at the three young boys ensconced between her and her husband. The smallest one smiled hesitantly at Khalid as he tugged on his mother's sleeve.

'Six, eight and nine,' Siti said before she turned to her youngest son and nodded, giving him permission to play. Khalid watched as the boy scooted off his chair and ran into the house alone.

Maybe Mak will have more children, Khalid thought. Maybe he would never be the best athlete or best student, but he could endeavour to be the best son and brother. Comforted at that thought, Khalid looked around the table, feeling thankful and blessed all of a sudden to be present at the wedding reception and spend time with family. He took a huge bite of the piece of mutton on his fork and grinned at his mother.

'The briyani is good, Mak,' he said.

'Yes,' Mak Aisha replied. 'So eat more.'

'Of course, it's good!' Karim said. 'Made with love.' He winked at Mak Aisha and patted her small hand with his much larger one. Khalid watched, feeling a bit uncomfortable. Mak Aisha is married now, he reminded himself.

'Bring some home for Ibrahim later,' Mak Aisha said. 'Hope he okay by evening.'

Khalid nodded as he thought of his brother, probably at the movie cinema with a date, and felt a sudden urge to tell his mother that he had lied to spare her feelings; Ibrahim was not sick at home. The thought rolled around in his mind. He remembered his promise to be the best son and brother. As much as he believed in telling the truth, what good was it if it would hurt others? It was a white lie. He thought of his former English teacher, a kind Englishman, in Standard VI who explained that the term could be traced back to a 14th century letter. The colour white was associated with being morally or spiritually pure. So the intentions behind a white lie, Khalid believed, were actually good.

After lunch, Khalid hugged his mother goodbye and then jumped onto his bicycle. It was September now and his Senior Cambridge examinations were three months away. There was no time to waste on anything else but his studies.

Chapter IX

4th September to 30th September 1939

'This is bad, K,' Ibrahim said, as he breathed out and threw a copy of the *Malaya Tribune* newspaper on Khalid's opened *Essentials of World Geography* textbook. The headline read 'BRITAIN AND FRANCE DECLARE WAR IN GERMANY'.

'Soon, the war will come to Singapore,' Ibrahim said, flopping to his bed. Two days ago, the newspapers had reported that German troops had crossed into Poland, annexing Danzig and bombing Warsaw. Khalid read through the article. Part of Winston Churchill's speech was in bold: 'We must expect many disappointments, many unpleasant surprises, but we may be sure that the task which we have freely accepted is one not beyond the strength of the British Empire and the French Republic.' Khalid felt a strange feeling of unease in the pit of his stomach. Then he heard soft snores coming from his brother's bed. It was not unusual for Ibrahim to catch a quick nap before dinner. Khalid carefully put the paper in front of him and continued reading his textbook. He used his ruler to underline the important points he wanted to remember.

He could hear Pak Ambi's loud voice down the hallway.

'War is coming!' he shouted.

For weeks, he had been regaling his sons and their neighbours with his vivid recollections of the 1915 Singapore Mutiny. Half of a regiment

75

of Indian Muslim sepoys had mutinied against the British in Singapore
during the First World War.

'You see, in India, the sepoys always eating goat meat and milk.
But here, they eat chicken and not enough milk.' Pak Ambi had said
last week. 'Of course, not happy.' When Ibrahim and Khalid had
looked unimpressed, he continued to talk about the deaths and public
executions, waiting for some reaction from his sons. Khalid was sure
that Pak Ambi had exaggerated the numbers. He did not understand
why people relished in recounting gruesome details. He leaned back
in his chair. Now he could hear Pak Ambi talking to Mr Rashid,
Samad's father.

'You see I told you—prepare for war,' Pak Ambi said. Khalid could
not hear Mr Rashid murmuring his reply, but he was certain that it
would be a dua, a prayer of supplication to Allah for his assistance and
protection. He tried to shut out the murmurs he heard and turned his
focus back to his textbook.

Over dinner, Pak Ambi helped himself to third helpings of ayam
ros, chicken slow-cooked in a rosy-hued sauce made from red onions
and tomato.

'Good eh?' he asked. 'Mak Jah is a good cook.' He said it every so
often whenever they visited Mak Jah and her children. Khalid nodded
in affirmation, his mouth full of chicken. At that moment, he wondered
how much longer Ibrahim would stay there with them. Ibrahim was
turning twenty-one soon. It is very likely he will get married next year,
Khalid thought. Is he going to go through with his engagement? Though
he and his brother did not always get along, Khalid felt an ache, as if his
body anticipated what it would feel without his brother around to tease
him or talk to.

'China and Japan are at war. Now Britain, France and Germany,' Pak
Ambi said, shaking his head. 'That Adolf Hitler is a real troublemaker.'

'Mmm,' Ibrahim mumbled over his plate. 'You're right, Pak.'

'Do you think the war will come to Singapore?' Khalid asked,
looking from Pak Ambi to Ibrahim. He tried to gulp down his worry
that was mingling with the ayam ros in his throat.

Ibrahim swallowed his mouthful of food. 'Yes, war will come to
Singapore,' he said.

'Why? We are a small island.' Khalid said, biting the inside of his lip.

'Don't be naïve, K,' Ibrahim said, sniggering at Khalid. He tossed his head back and laughed.

Khalid felt his cheeks burn with indignation. 'You don't know what you're talking about, Ib. Anyway, we have a strong defence. The British have made sure of that.'

Ibrahim snorted into his glass of water before he composed himself to speak. 'Yes, if attacked from the sea. But what about if attacked from land? We are an important British military base and economic port. If they want to hurt the British, they will attack us.'

Pak Ambi nodded solemnly. Khalid looked away from Ibrahim and stared at his plate of food, feeling a mixture of curiosity and embarrassment. How does Ibrahim know so much? Khalid wondered. He rarely saw Ibrahim reading the newspapers at home after all. Maybe he had heard his British superiors at work talking about the probability of war coming to Singapore.

'Don't worry, Khalid,' Pak Ambi said in a low, encouraging voice. 'Just focus on your exams.'

Ibrahim sniggered as he smirked at Khalid. 'Yeah Khalid, you're lucky that Current Affairs isn't a subject.'

'Be quiet, Ibrahim,' Khalid said. Ibrahim looked amused as he stretched his long legs out then stood up. Khalid shot a glare at Ibrahim's back as he made his way out of the room, carrying his empty plate.

Later that night, Khalid read the article closely. He knew war was coming to Singapore; it was only a matter of time. But he still found himself wishing it would not. No one knew when it would happen. The uncertainty of it all made his stomach lurch. When he closed his eyes that night, he saw bombs exploding. He dreamt that everyone he knew died and he was left alone, walking through the wreckage left behind. He woke up, sweating, and quickly looked around for his father and brother. Both were sound asleep in their beds. He had never felt more relief to hear Pak Ambi snoring so loudly. But Khalid stayed awake for close to an hour afterwards, convinced that if he closed his eyes, more dreams of war would follow.

* * *

A month had passed since the funeral. Lily had counted off each day on her calendar with a cross, waiting patiently for the day that she could ask Mak Kong for a new tutor. She was certain that today would be the right day to ask Mak Kong for a new tutor. Lily stared at the white cloth covering the mirror in the living room, feeling a painful ache in her heart. Mak Kong had instructed the majies to cover all the mirrors in the house with white clothes to prevent deflecting Mr Tan's recently departed soul since he had died in their home. From time to time, Lily felt a sense of deep sadness that Mr Tan was gone but she tried to comfort herself by letting herself believe that Mr Tan had ascended to heaven.

'Bila jantan mati, mata busok dulu,' Mak Kong had said the day after Mr Tan's death. When a man dies, it is his eyes that rot first. Lily did not understand why. Mak Kong had continued to explain as she fanned herself in the kitchen. Zhu Jie explained it to her later when Mak Kong left the house to play Cherki. Lily had been uncomfortable at the thought of Mr Tan's eyes rotting. Mr Tan had never acted in a lascivious manner in front of her and it made her feel a bit sad to think of men staring at women other than their wives.

Am I naïve? Lily wondered. Teck Soon stares at me and I'm not his wife. He must stare at other women too when he's out of the house.

Mak Kong seemed to be in a good enough mood; her Cherki winnings that afternoon were not her all-time high but fairly respectable. She was sitting in the living room on her favourite rosewood chair and fanning herself with a turquoise paper fan, looking fairly content. Lily hesitated for a few minutes, practicing in her mind what she would say, before she summoned up the courage to approach Mak Kong.

'Mak Kong?'

'Yes?'

'I was wondering if I could have a new tutor, please?' And if it could be Khalid, please? She pleaded silently. That would be a dream come true, to have Khalid as my tutor.

'Oh,' Mak Kong said. She whipped the fan back towards herself and stopped as if to consider Lily's request. 'I will have to ask Pak Kong.'

'Of course, Mak Kong,' Lily said, trying to arrange her features into the most sincerely grateful expression she could manage. 'Thank you.'

'Good night, Lily,' Mak Kong said as she started fanning herself again. Lily watched as the fan swished back and forth. She found herself bowing her head in respect before she left the room.

'Good night, Mak Kong,' Lily said, feeling a prick of annoyance. She resented how she felt she had to act with Mak Kong; formal and ingratiating. As Lily made her way up the stairs, she prayed that she would get a new tutor, whether it was Khalid or not. Her English Language education could not stop after Mr Tan's death. She decided then that if she did not get a new tutor, she would try her best to learn the language on her own. She would read Ivy's books at night when everyone else had gone to bed or try to ask Charles questions about anything she was unsure of. Whatever it took, Lily was resolute in her purpose and determined not to give up.

In bed, Lily tried to get comfortable as she turned from her back to her side and then to her back again. She curled up with her pillow in a foetal position. She thought of Mr Tan yet again and how he had died in front of her. Was Mr Tan in the same place as her father? Life and death were each other's companions. We are of the Tao when we live and of the Tao when we die, Lily thought although she did not really know what that meant. She had just heard Mak Kong murmuring it in prayer several times before the ancestral altar.

The next afternoon, as Lily was about to sit down for a beadwork session, Mak Kong entered the room. She inspected the four blossoming peony flowers on the fabric stretched over the wooden frame.

'You should be able to complete this today,' Mak Kong said with a sniff.

'Yes, Mak Kong.' Should I ask about the tutor? Lily wondered.

Lily heard Khalid's voice filtering through the partition and her face softened. She bit her lip, careful not to let Mak Kong notice.

'Ah, Khalid is early today,' Mak Kong said, sniffing again. Lily supposed Mak Kong might be coming down with a cold.

Mak Kong walked out of the room, leaving Lily to her beadwork. Lily sat down and looked at the four peony flowers, two a warm yellow and two blush pink in colour. It had taken her forty-nine days, once a week, two hours each time. If Mak Kong was right, today would be last beadwork session for the kasut manek. All she had to do today was complete the lush green background. One day, Lily thought, she would have her own garden.

She threaded a green bead onto the fabric. Bead by bead—that was how she was growing her patience. After Lily was done with her first row of beads, she stopped, put down her needle and listened intently to what Khalid was saying to Charles.

'You keep spelling this word wrong, Charles,' Khalid said. 'Did you notice?'

'Oops,' Charles said. 'Just noticed.'

What word? Lily wondered. She thought that she would probably spell it wrong as well. How could she get Khalid to notice her? It felt like an impossible task to Lily. Every week, they were separated by a partition. Since the first time she had served him food, Mak Kong had been home every week, making it difficult for Lily to see Khalid. Lily sighed as she arranged the beads on the plate into a small heart.

Then she heard Chek Chuan singing. She stood up and clasped her hands together.

It was a beautiful ballad about eternal love. Chek Chuan's passion came through in his voice. He must have been in love before, Lily thought. Maybe more than once. But he is not married. I wonder why. Lily lifted up her sarong a little and tried to move the way she had seen Chek Chuan dance, his hips swivelling and his arms waving up and down in the air, in alternate fashion, as his quick feet moved forwards and backwards. She had no idea how a woman might dance to dondang sayang. Mak Kong did not dance, at least not in front of her. Giggling to herself, she was sure she looked silly. What did she know about dancing? Lily took a deep breath to compose herself. She patted her flushed cheeks, sat down on her chair and threaded another bead onto the needle. It would be better if she focused on what was needed to be completed.

Two hours later, Lily was done with her beadwork. Pleased with herself, she ran her finger across the two patterns. As she moved the wooden frame, sunlight caught the beads and they glinted, bright with the promise of tomorrow. Mak Kong came into the room just then. Wordless with pride, Lily showed her the finished product. Mak Kong inspected the fabric with her fingers, sniffing as she did so. She turned it this way and that, as if inspecting each and every bead.

Finally, she put the wooden frame down on the table and said, 'Baek, Lily.' Lily smiled, her eyes crinkling a little as she basked in Mak Kong's praise. Now would be a good time to ask about the tutor, she thought. As Mak Kong turned to leave the room, the words got stuck somewhere in Lily's throat. Lily swallowed them. Maybe it would be better to be patient and wait for Mak Kong to bring up the subject. Lily started to put the leftover beads back in their box. Out of the corner of her eye, she saw Mak Kong re-enter the room.

'Oh yes, I remember,' Mak Kong began. 'Pak Kong said no need for another tutor . . . '

A rush of indignation came over Lily but she could not speak.

'You've learnt all the English that you'll need as a young nyonya,' Mak Kong continued. Lily opened her mouth to say something to plead with Mak Kong. She wanted to say she had not learnt nearly enough. They had stopped at Lesson 15 of her precious English textbook. There had to be more English books and many more lessons in her future.

'Don't worry,' Mak Kong said. 'We'll find you a good husband.' Still, Lily said nothing. A husband? she thought, anger shooting up in her. I don't want to be matchmade. All I'm asking for is another English tutor. Is that too much to ask for, Mak Kong? Her eyes fixated on a spot on Mak Kong's baju panjang as Mak Kong glided out of the room. Lily dug her fingernails into her palm, willing herself to calm down. Warm tears came unbidden to her eyes. She frowned as she looked at the wooden frame in front of her. How helpless she felt, not being able to say or do anything to change Mak Kong and Pak Kong's mind.

Lily pinched herself to stop the tears. Stop, she told herself. She thought that she just had to accept that life was not fair and try to make the very best of her situation. She knew that there were others out there who were suffering far more than she was. Lily said to herself, 'Be grateful.' She would find some way, no matter what, to learn English on her own.

* * *

Khalid and Ravinder were walking along the streets of Sungei Road on their way to the Thieves Market. Most of the goods sold at the market were cheap and acquired by illegitimate means. Khalid's eyes passed over a braised duck hawker, his eyes shielded from the sun by a wide hat. He had a shallow bamboo basket in front of him with two braised ducks in it. There was also a half-covered large bowl with three dice in it. Khalid recognised this was actually a stall for gambling of some sort.

'Braised duck?' he asked Ravinder, with a small smirk on his face.

'No thanks,' Ravinder said. 'I don't like duck.'

Khalid leaned in and whispered. 'It's not really a braised duck stall.'

'Oh?' Ravinder asked. His eyes wandered from a duck leg to the dice surreptitiously hidden in the bowl.

'For people to gamble,' Khalid said.

'Oh,' Ravinder replied. 'No wonder there are dice.'

I'm more street smart than Ravinder, Khalid thought. Thanks to Pak Ambi.

Khalid spotted an older British couple just then. The woman was wearing a pristine white dress and a straw hat; the man was more casually dressed in shirt and slacks. They stood out against the backdrop of suntanned hawkers crouched on the grey cement roads and weathered buildings with grimy paint. He wondered what it was like to live in a country that was not his own. Would most things seem like a pleasant surprise or a rude shock? He supposed it depended on the person looking at the scene. Mr Shepherd had said the same thing could be seen so differently by two different people. What was delightful to one person could be odious to another. Khalid tried to imagine looking at Singapore from the perspective of a foreigner and traveler, but he could not quite manage it.

I'm Singaporean, he thought. Will always be. My first loyalty is to my family and then to Singapore.

'Ah finally,' Ravinder said as they reached the entrance of the Thieves Market. They were greeted by the sights of many locals and some British soldiers trawling through the stalls and haggling for bargains. Some hawkers had spread out a canvas sheet on the ground to display their items while other stalls had a foldable table and chair to fill up the 1 metre by 1 metre space each hawker was allotted.

'Army goods here!' a skinny man at a nearby table stall called out. 'Parachutes, knapsacks, boots!'

'Maybe you can buy something to woo Dorothy, the girl you like,' Ravinder said.

Khalid's eyes scanned over the different items from raincoats to magazines to pottery. Somehow, the girl that came to his mind just then was Lily. He did not understand why. Was he taken by her beauty and demure ways? He had not seen her since she had served tea to him the other day but he knew that he hoped to see her again.

'I don't think I can find something here,' Khalid said as he turned to Ravinder with a dry smile on his face.

'Is she from a rich family?' Ravinder asked, his face alert with curiosity.

'Well . . . yes,' Khalid said after a few seconds. As he looked into Ravinder's face, he wondered whether Ravinder fancied Dorothy.

Ravinder chortled. 'Yes, then you can't find something here. Rich people know when something is cheap.'

'You're including yourself in that, right?' Khalid asked.

'Yes, of course.' Ravinder stopped at a stall with a selection of comic books next to several dough figurines. He picked up a copy of *The Adventures of Tintin*. 'Do you still read comics?'

'Not really,' Khalid said.

'I still do,' Ravinder said as he flipped through the pages of the Tintin comic. 'Reminds me of a simpler time.'

'A time where you didn't have to worry about Senior Cambridge?' Khalid asked.

'Sure,' Ravinder said as he fished out a 20-cent coin and a 10-cent coin for his new copy of Tintin.

They walked to the next stall which had an array of beauty products. The middle-aged balding hawker, who was selling the products, beckoned them over.

'Looking for something for your girl?' he asked, as his eyes darted from Ravinder to Khalid.

'My sister always asks me to buy her Two Girls brand face powder,' Ravinder said.

'Isn't she twelve?' Khalid asked.

'Yes,' Ravinder said, laughing. 'Already so vain.'

'Why doesn't she ask your parents to buy for her from an actual store?' Khalid asked.

'I don't think they'd approve,' Ravinder said. He picked up the vibrantly coloured square box containing the Two Girls powder inside.

'One dollar,' the hawker said, raising an eyebrow at Ravinder as he looked him up and down.

'Okay,' Ravinder said, handing him a dollar note. Khalid noticed that Ravinder never bothered to haggle with the hawkers but when Pak Ambi brought Khalid and Ibrahim to Thieves Market, he was always insisting on getting a better bargain, occasionally to the ire of the hawker.

'She uses her pocket money to buy and I'm her errand boy,' Ravinder said. 'I should start charging her for buying her things.'

'What else do you have to get for her?' Khalid asked.

Ravinder pretended to consult a list in his hand. 'Some hairband thing and a watch,' he said. Khalid gestured to Ravinder to follow him. They wove through the stalls to find what they needed. By the end of their visit, they heard the sound of the Ting Ting candy man, striking his bowl-shaped bell.

Ravinder turned and grinned at Khalid. 'It's the Ting Ting man,' he said.

Turning his head, Khalid saw the somber-faced hawker with two rectangular-shaped containers, each balanced on the end of a pole balanced on his shoulders. Several children were already surrounding him. The Ting Ting candy was a sweet, chewy and powdery indulgence. Khalid recalled the last time he had had it was a few months ago with Ibrahim and Samad on their street.

With a jerk of his head, Khalid gestured in the direction of the hawker. Ravinder followed behind him. The queue moved fairly quickly thanks to the efficiency of the hawker. Ravinder tilted his head from side to side, following the rhythm of the metallic 'ting ting' sound made as the hawker's hammer knocked candy off the pan.

'Ting Ting,' Ravinder said. 'I've actually never tried it.'

'What?' Khalid asked, raising an eyebrow in surprise. 'How is that possible?'

When it was his turn, Khalid bought a packet of candy but Ravinder looked hesitant to do so. The packet of candy was half the size of his palm and he knew he could easily finish it that afternoon. The hawker also sold sour plums. Khalid bought a bag full of plums for his mother while Ravinder bought two bags of sour plums for his family to share. As he held the bag in his hand, he thought of the next time he would see Mak Aisha again.

Khalid tore the packet of candy open and held it out to Ravinder who look hesitant.

'I don't know if I'll like it,' Ravinder said. 'It looks so hard.'

'You won't know what you like till you try it,' Khalid said.

Ravinder took a piece and popped it into his mouth. 'It's hard!' he said.

'It'll get chewy,' Khalid said before popping a piece into his mouth himself.

They continued sharing pieces of candy as they waited for the bus home. Khalid wondered again why it was Lily that he thought about when he had had only two prior encounters with her. As he munched on the candy, he decided he had no time to try to understand these confusing feelings, not when the fate of his academic future was yet to be determined.

Chapter X

4th December 1939

That Monday morning, the Raffles Institution students were making their way to the examination hall for their Additional Mathematics paper. Khalid could feel the tension in the air as he walked behind Ravinder and another one of his classmates. His body was rigid with fear. Additional Mathematics was not his favourite subject but he had prepared as adequately as he could for it. I can do this, Khalid thought. Just be calm and take it one question at a time, like Mr Menon advised.

As he walked towards the hall, Khalid thought about how all their futures depended on how well they did for their Senior Cambridge examinations. Since November, the speculation among Pak Ambi and a few anxious neighbours about the war coming to Singapore had waned considerably. Pak Ambi's concern had switched to Khalid's examinations. He had instructed all their neighbours, much to their consternation, to keep their volumes down, especially in the evening and night, so Khalid could focus on studying. 'Hello!' he had shouted whenever someone was making noise in the hallway. 'My son's studying, you know!'

'Ready?' Ravinder asked, turning back to look at Khalid. His backpack was slung on only one shoulder. Khalid thought Ravinder looked like he might be going to attend an ordinary class and not for his Additional Mathematics paper.

'No, I'm not ready at all,' Khalid said, managing a wry smile. Ravinder let loose a loud, tinkling laugh.

'Keep that sense of humour, K,' Ravinder said. 'I'm definitely keeping mine. It'll take us far in life.'

Khalid grinned. 'Yeah. Now let's go ace this paper, Rav.'

'Yeah! See you later, K.' The boys exchanged a firm handshake before leaving their school bags outside the hall. With their water bottle and pencil boxes in hand, they walked down the aisle to their assigned seats.

As he put his pencil box on the table, Khalid watched as the invigilator, Mr Balhetchet, took the microphone at the front of the stage. Mr Balhetchet was one of his favourite teachers. Khalid was sure he would miss him once he graduated. Mr Balhetchet always had something witty to say with a twinkle in his eye. However today, he was playing the part of the solemn invigilator.

'Take your seats, boys. We will start the exam at eight-thirty sharp.' Mr Balhetchet said. Khalid took a deep breath as he watched the seconds tick by on the clock at the front of the hall. A few students were running into the hall, looking anxious, as other students took their seats.

When Mr Balhetchet gave the cue, the examination began. Khalid wrote his name down quickly then perused the instructions carefully. Mr Menon had said the most important thing to do first after receiving the paper was to read the instructions line by line. He took a breath, flipped the paper over and started work on solving the first question. When there were more difficult questions, Khalid took his time to work out the equation step by step. Stay calm, he told himself. Step by step. You'll get the answer right if you're calm and focused. Apart from the tricky logarithm questions, he found the rest of the paper fairly doable. Khalid was so focused on the paper that he did not look up even once. Two hours later, time was up and Mr Balhetchet instructed them to put their pens down.

'Please leave your examination papers on the table and exit the hall in an orderly manner,' Mr Balhetchet said in an authoritative voice. 'No talking.'

Khalid reunited with Ravinder outside the hall where he was talking to Roy.

'I'm glad that's over,' Roy muttered, massaging his left temple.

Khalid nodded in full empathy. He was aware that Additional Mathematics was not Roy's favourite subject either.

'How was it?' Ravinder asked, turning to Khalid.

'Okay. I tried my best,' Khalid said.

'That's all we can do,' Ravinder replied. He put his arm around Khalid.

'Shall we have lunch together?' Roy suggested at that moment. 'I don't want to go home right now and face my Geography textbook.'

Khalid laughed. He could not imagine going home to study either. 'Sure, let's have lunch,' Khalid said.

Out of the corner of his eye, Khalid spotted Harry. Harry smiled and waved at the trio.

'I bet Harry breezed through the paper,' Roy said, scrunching up his nose.

Ravinder rubbed his temples and pretended to be thinking hard. 'Prediction: He'll be the top student,' he said with a slightly crooked smile on his face.

Khalid felt a pang of envy course through him though he knew Roy and Ravinder were probably right. 'It could be someone else. Maybe Barker,' he said.

'Yeah, Harry or Barker are always coming in first in the examinations,' Roy said, shaking his head. 'If it's not one, it'll be the other.'

'I still think it will be Harry,' Ravinder said.

Khalid knew how bright both Harry and Geok Choo were. Intelligence was a quality he greatly admired in a person. However, it was their work ethic that he admired more. 'Intelligence is nothing without hard work, character and ambition,' Mr Shepherd had said to the class last year.

'They're both smart and hardworking,' Khalid said, deciding to be more magnanimous with his praise, and putting aside the envy that lurked in his heart. 'Whoever comes in first will have fully earned it.'

Khalid started walking to the canteen just then, with Roy and Ravinder falling into step behind him.

'I'm so hungry!' Ravinder said as they reached the canteen which was thronged with fellow schoolmates about to have their lunch.

'One of our last meals in the canteen together,' Roy remarked, as his face fell slightly.

'Don't remind me,' Ravinder said.

Khalid grinned widely at Ravinder. 'You'll miss us, won't you?' he asked, a teasing glint in his dark eyes.

Ravinder groaned and shook his head vigorously. 'I refuse to think about all this right now.'

Khalid put his arm around Ravinder's shoulder while Roy patted him on the back.

'Okay, okay,' Ravinder protested, wriggling free from their grasp. Khalid chuckled, knowing Ravinder's discomfort with expressing his emotions.

The three boys reached the canteen and dropped their bags on to the nearest empty table.

'Go buy your food first,' Khalid offered as he sat down. 'I'll watch our bags.'

'Okay, thanks K,' Ravinder said as he retrieved his wallet from his bag.

As Roy and Ravinder walked away, Khalid found himself thinking through a question that had stumped him during the exam. He bet his solution and answer was wrong. He turned his head and spotted Harry again, this time walking into the canteen with another schoolmate. Khalid caught Harry's eye at that moment. Harry smiled in response. He still looks cheerful, Khalid thought as he offered a small wave back. Harry had probably figured out the right answer to that same question. Khalid frowned, wondering if his goal of obtaining a Grade I certificate would not be met. Roy came back to the table, carrying a bowl of bak chor mee in his hands.

'That smells very good,' Khalid said as he inhaled the medley of smells emanating from the bowl. He recalled how Roy had told him before about the stewed mushroom, minced pork and pieces of deep-fried lard that went into bak chor mee.

'You can't eat it though,' Roy remarked as he used his chopsticks to pick up the noodles.

'I know,' Khalid said with a wry smile.

'Free smells though,' Roy said, chuckling before he put the noodles on the chopsticks into his mouth.

'The best things in life can be free,' Khalid said, winking at Roy as he stood up, his wallet in hand, to buy his food. Roy shook his head a little as he turned his face to his bowl and lifted his chopsticks to his mouth. As he took steps away from the table, Khalid realised that Roy might be about to tear up as he thought of how it would be one of their last lunches together in the canteen.

* * *

Lily stood looking out at the rain gently falling through the air well. It was a rare, quiet moment that she had all to herself, after finishing lunch and before starting embroidery. She sometimes helped the majies who would have to rush to carry the bamboo pole in when there was a sudden downpour. When the skies darkened, Leng Jie, who sometimes stood at the air well and stared up melancholically at the clouds, would be the first to scurry into the house, pat Zhu Jie on the arm and say 'Bring clothes in'. Lily sometimes would help the majies to carry the heavy poles of clothes in.

Lily took comfort in rainy days. When it rained, everything seemed softer to Lily; the streets would empty as those on the streets rushed for shelter. Little looked more peaceful when he napped in his favourite corner under the living room table. Mak Kong seemed to speak in a gentler voice. Leng Jie always looked like she smiled more.

Rain showers brought good luck—that was the belief that Peranakans had. These are showers of luck, Lily thought so she closed her eyes and started to wish for the things she wanted. The only thing that came to mind was courage. She wanted the courage to write a letter to Khalid, the courage to stand up to Mak Kong and ask for what she wanted, and the courage to reach out and hold Mak Wee's hand.

'Woof!' Little barked as he came running up to Lily. Lily scooped him up and pressed her face into his soft fur just behind his ears. His ears had a light yeasty smell which she always found pleasant in its familiarity.

'Do you like it when it rains?' she asked Little. Little sighed, as he rested his head on Lily's chest.

'Is that a no?' Lily said. 'You're like a baby sometimes, my Little, my sayang.' She giggled as she continued looking at the falling raindrops. She felt an impulse to feel the raindrops falling on her.

She knew Mak Kong was taking her nap upstairs. Now would be a good time to play in the rain, Lily thought.

She put Little down on the ground, knowing he would whine the moment she did so.

When he let out a whine, Lily said, 'You don't like rain.' Little barked and watched Lily, with his ears up and head slightly cocked. He bounded off to Thunder's jar and barked at him.

Lily took off her slippers, feeling the cold floor beneath her feet. She lifted up her baju panjang and quickly dashed out into the rain. She laughed and lifted up her hands up to the sky. She felt the raindrops on her skin and head as they dripped down the face. How glorious it was to be in the rain! Each raindrop brings me luck and courage, Lily thought. Just what I need.

'Lily!' she heard Zhu Jie's voice at that moment. She turned and saw Zhu Jie's mouth slightly hung open so it looked like a small letter 'O'.

Lily laughed, luxuriating in the thrill of doing something new, and slowly, Zhu Jie started to laugh too. Zhu Jie watched Lily for a little while before shaking her head and moving away to tidy up the house. After a few more seconds, Lily darted in to take shelter. Now she would have to change her clothes before she started embroidery. I hope Mak Kong is not awake, Lily thought. She headed upstairs, trembling a little with a smile creeping across her face.

The door to Mak Kong and Pak Kong's room was slightly ajar. Lily walked past it and headed straight to her room. She wondered if Mak Kong would notice she was wearing a different baju panjang from the one in the morning. Opening her cupboard, Lily took out a fresh set of clothes and underwear. If Mak Kong notices, I will just say that I perspired a lot so I decided to change clothes, Lily thought. She felt certain that Mak Kong would admonish her for playing in the rain. 'You could get sick,' she imagined Mak Kong would say. She pulled her long tunic over her head and proceeded to change her bra.

When she emerged out of the room, she immediately saw Mak Kong outside her own room. Mak Kong turned her head slightly and spotted Lily out of the corner of her eye.

'Going to start embroidery?' she asked.

'Yes,' Lily said.

'Did you change your clothes?' Mak Kong asked.

Lily hesitated. 'Um,' she said. 'Mak . . . '

Mak Kong stood there, waiting for an answer, her right eyebrow raised slightly in annoyance. Charles appeared at the top of the stairs, his backpack slung over his shoulder. He had stayed back in school for a project discussion with his classmates.

'Hello Mak,' he said.

'Did you eat lunch?' Mak Kong asked.

'Yes,' Charles said. 'Going to rest.'

Mak Kong followed Charles to his room, seemingly forgetting about Lily's change of clothes.

Lily heaved a sigh of relief and hurried towards the stairs. It's kind of exciting, she thought. To have done something Mak Kong did not know about. She hoped Mak Kong would forget to ask about her change of clothes again.

Mak Kong did forget. She seemed preoccupied, lost in thought, for the rest of the day. By dinner, Lily found out why. Charles had lost his wallet on the bus. Pak Kong was furious, and reprimanded Charles for being careless in taking care of his belongings. Charles sat there, sullen, muttering apologies. Lily wondered how much money had been in Charles' wallet. Ivy, in an attempt to help, said they should call the police. But Pak Kong said there was no need to bother the police over a lost wallet. By the end of dinner, Lily felt relieved. She glanced over at Charles, who got up from the table and walked away, without saying a word.

On the third Sunday of every month, Lily and the Kongs visited Mak Wee. In Pak Kong's car, Lily pressed her nose close to the window. She liked looking at all the houses they passed and the people they saw on the way to Mak Wee's house. It was a short ride so sometimes they walked instead. Lily liked walking better; she felt the pulse of the area and part of the people living and moving on the street. She was the driver when she walked instead of a mere passenger.

'I'm hungry,' Ivy said.

Charles rolled his eyes. 'We had lunch.'

'That was hours ago,' Ivy said.

'You don't do any work and you're hungry,' Charles chuckled.

'I did my homework!' Ivy protested.

'I mean like chores, in the kitchen,' Charles said.

'Children,' Pak Kong said.

Soon, they reached Mak Wee's house, a shophouse painted sunshine yellow with white windows. There was a white frangipani tree in a brown pot on the five-foot way that Lily loved to admire. Pak Kong grabbed the handle of the door knocker to let the majies know of their arrival. Wen Jie, one of the family's two majies, came to the door. As they walked into the main hall, Lily saw Mak Wee sitting on her chair and her grandmother, Mama, in her rocking chair. Her elder brother, his wife and the younger two of their five children were there too.

Ivy bounded in and greeted everyone, a wide smile on her face. Lily remembered how in comparison, at ten, she had walked stately in.

'Apa khabair, Mama, Tua Ku, Tua Kim, Patrick, Alice,' Lily said.

As everyone returned her greetings, Lily took a seat. Wen Jie brought out a plate of kueh baulu and tea. It was like any other visit; it was the adults who did most of the talking. Alice and Patrick were close to Lily's age but they did not usually talk much to each other.

Then Tua Ku announced that they had found a match for Patrick and he would be getting married next year. Lily studied the inscrutable expression on Patrick's pale face. She could not tell how he felt about being matchmade. Glad it's not me, Lily thought as she leaned back on the sofa, her hands placed in her lap.

As if Tua Ku could read her mind, he asked, 'What about Lily?' Mak Kong exchanged a glance with Mak Wee but neither replied. I'm only sixteen, Lily wanted to reply.

But she knew that sixteen was considered old enough to get married. She looked down, hoping someone would change the subject.

'One day,' Mak Wee said finally. I hope one day is far away, Lily thought. Especially if I'm to be matchmade. Tua Ku seemed to accept this answer and resumed talking about Patrick's wedding. They had consulted an astrologer to determine a suitable engagement date and wedding date. Lily bit into a kueh baulu. Kueh baulu was one of her favourite snacks; it was slightly crusty on the outside with a soft and fluffy inside.

Pak Kong chuckled heartily. 'In a few years' time, it would be Charles' turn,' Pak Kong said. Charles raised his eyebrows in alarm. Lily almost laughed as she swallowed the piece of kueh in her mouth.

'I want to get married too!' Ivy piped up. Everyone started laughing much to Ivy's dismay.

'What's so funny?' she asked with her hands on her hips.

'You're too young,' Mak Kong said. 'Someday.'

Charles reached over and tugged on Ivy's ponytail. Ivy frowned at him. The rest of the visit seemed to pass by in a haze to Lily. She was not interested in the marriage discussion so she tuned out the adults' conversation and silently practiced spelling out English words in her mind. She turned to Alice a few times and they exchanged knowing glances and secret smiles. Alice shrugged and tilted her head. Then she whispered, 'I'm glad it's not my wedding.' Lily nodded, feeling a weight in her heart she could not explain.

Chapter XI

23rd December 1939

Preparation for Chinese New Year at the Kong house started on Tung Chek, the Winter Solstice Festival. Glutinous rice-flour balls, kueh ee, were prepared by the majies, Ah Huat, Lily and Mak Kong. Charles and Ivy joined in too. Ivy made five rice balls before she stopped, looking tired and bored, and asked if she could go out to play. Mak Kong said she could take a break for fifteen minutes but would then have to continue making kueh ee. Lily knew that Mak Kong was becoming firmer with Ivy because she wanted to prepare her as a young nyonya.

Charles shaped ten rice balls then stopped and said he needed to do his homework. Lily watched as Mak Kong nodded and patted Charles on his back. Charles receives a pat on the back for making ten rice balls because he is a boy, Lily thought. His place was not in the kitchen but in his room, in school and outside in the world. Without looking up from the rice ball she was shaping in her hands, Lily felt an uncomfortable warmth spread across her cheeks. She had had Mr Tan as an English tutor for seven months; now she was teaching herself. For the past two months, she had been sneaking into Ivy's room late at night when she was asleep to bring her English textbook back to her room to read it. Once she mustered up the courage to casually ask Ivy what the animal on the cover on one of her books was when she saw Ivy holding it. The animal's face looked a bit like a rat and it had pencil-thin feet.

'Ah, ini kancil,' Ivy answered.

'Kancil,' Lily repeated before asking for what the animal's name was in English.

Ivy said that it was a mouse deer. As she was about to turn away and head up the stairs, Lily stopped her and asked her to repeat herself. Wrinkling her brow, perhaps confused by why Lily wanted to know this animal's name so much, Ivy said the words slowly.

'Mouse deer,' Lily said. 'Terima Kasih, Ivy.'

'Sama sama,' Ivy had said.

Lily put down a red ball she had just rolled on a plate. Her balls were round and more or less the same size. She looked over at the kueh ee that Ivy had made. They were not equal in size; some were considerably larger than others. Lily stifled the urge to laugh as Ivy traipsed back into the kitchen just then and rejoined the group at the table.

'How many balls do I have to make?' Ivy asked Mak Kong.

'Eight more,' Mak Kong said, glancing over Ivy's kueh ee plate. 'Make sure you only take one piece of dough each time.'

'Like this?' Ivy asked, showing Mak Kong the piece of dough in her hand.

There's too much, Lily wanted to say. Mak Kong took the dough from Ivy's hand and put some back on the woven bamboo tray.

'This is enough,' Mak Kong said. 'Roll into a ball like this. Remember: one piece of dough each time.'

'Bigger balls would be better,' Ivy said, pouting.

'The kueh ee are supposed to be small,' Mak Kong said.

'But the balls made for worship are big,' Ivy said.

Mak Kong ignored her but Ivy persisted.

'Why?' Ivy asked.

'We are generous with our ancestors and Gods,' Mak Kong said.

Ivy seemed to accept this answer. Later, Lily, the majies and Ah Huat would cook the laok semayang, the offerings for worship.

Lily rolled the dough between the palms of both hands using a circular motion. How much better these balls would taste, Lily mused, if there was a paste inside. Like red bean or sesame. But the tradition was to make the glutinous rice balls without any filling. The round balls symbolised family unity. Once all the balls were ready, it would be time to prepare the syrup by boiling water, pandan leaves and sugar together. All the balls would be added to the pot and cooked till they floated. They would offer kueh ee to Tua Pek Kong and their ancestors. According to tradition, it was also important for a person to consume kueh ee otherwise they would not grow a year older. Lily remembered a few years ago, Ivy had consumed kueh ee after kueh ee, believing that she could grow older quickly the more balls she ate. Lily was not one to go against tradition but she did think it seemed like a silly superstition. A person would grow older whether they ate a kueh ee or not, Lily thought as she placed another ball on her plate.

Before lunch, Ivy recited a panton for Tung Chek that she had memorised. Everyone clapped for her when she was done. Ivy's face lit up as she took in the applause. She bowed and giggled before taking her seat at the dining table, looking pleased with herself. The majies brought out the bowls of kueh ee. Hungry after her efforts in the kitchen, Lily could hardly wait until Pak Kong invited everyone to eat. She bit into her first ball eagerly, feeling the festive spirit. Tung Chek was her favourite holiday after Chinese New Year. Everyone else seemed to be in a better mood on festive occasions. Lily felt more like a member of the family on festive occasions. She smiled at Ivy, who had her mouth full.

'Sedap!' Ivy said after she swallowed.

'Remember, don't speak with your mouth full,' Mak Kong said.

'I didn't,' Ivy protested, stirring the syrup in her bowl.

'Just a reminder,' Mak Kong said.

'By the way, you mispronounced a word just now,' Charles said to Ivy.

'Which one?' Ivy asked, her brow furrowed.

'You said men-ja-lang, it's men-je-lang,' Charles said.

'Oh,' Ivy said, frowning at her bowl. Lily knew she did not like to be corrected.

'Next time, you can take part in a panton competition,' Pak Kong said.

Charles laughed. Ivy considered the idea for a moment before declaring, 'I want to win!'

'I won a panton competition when I was in primary school,' Chek Chuan said, eliciting a smirk from Mak Kong.

'Ooh,' Ivy cooed. 'I want to win too!'

Everyone continued eating till their stomachs were full. Though nothing particularly good or interesting happened, Lily would always remember that Tung Chek because, though she did not know it at the time, it would turn out to be her last with the Kong family.

* * *

'I haven't decided,' Mrs Lee said. Khalid tried not to look impatient. Since his exams had ended about a week ago, Pak Ambi had tasked him to help out with collecting chap ji kee bets. Every morning, he would walk around the neighbourhood so people could place their bets with him. He had come to anticipate the numbers some of his neighbours would bet on. Mrs Lee would always say she had not decided but after a few minutes, she would invariably ask to place a bet on the numbers 2, 4, 6 or 10. Mrs Chong always bet on some combination of 3, 5 or 8. Khalid supposed the numbers were lucky numbers in Chinese culture or perhaps numbers that meant something to the bettors. Some of the neighbours like Mak Kong conveyed their bets through their majies.

'Do you want me to come back later so you have more time to decide?' Khalid asked. He had come to realise that with a bit of pressure, Mrs Lee would then have to tell him her bet.

'I've decided,' Mrs Lee said after a few seconds. '4 and 10. Two-way bet.' She handed Khalid a 50-cent coin. Khalid scribbled this down in his notebook. A one-way bet was for the combination of numbers in a particular order, and paid out hundred times the stake for a win. A two-way bet was for the two numbers to appear in either order, and paid fifty times the stake. Mrs Lee was one of the more conservative bettors, never betting more than 50 cents. But every day she would place a bet with Khalid. He supposed chap ji kee made the lives of housewives like Mrs Lee more exciting.

Khalid made his way to the next house where he could see Mrs Chong waiting for him. She waved him over, looking a bit stressed.

'Numbers 5 and 8. One-way bet,' Mrs Chong said in hushed tones, handing Khalid a five-dollar note. Her eyes darted from side to side, wary of being caught by a police officer.

'Okay, Mrs Chong,' Khalid replied, scribbling Mrs Chong's name, the numbers and her betting amount in his notebook.

'Thank you,' Mrs Chong said, rubbing the gold ring she wore like it would bring her luck.

'No problem, Mrs Chong,' Khalid said with a small wave. 'See you tomorrow.'

Zhu Jie was waiting at the five-foot way when Khalid appeared outside the Kong house. She presented him with a small colourful bowl of kueh ee. Khalid grinned; free food was a perk of collecting the bets.

'Eat,' Zhu Jie said.

'Thank you,' Khalid said. 'Happy Tung Chek! It was yesterday, right?'

'Yes,' Zhu Jie replied. 'We make kueh ee.'

Khalid wolfed down the four kueh ee and wondered if it was Lily who had made it. Then he drank the sweet, light syrup as Zhu Jie stood there, humming to herself. When he was done, Zhu Jie took the bowl from him.

'So good, Zhu Jie,' Khalid said.

'We make together,' Zhu Jie said, her face beaming. 'Me, Lily, Leng Jie . . .'

'Lily too?' Khalid whistled, impressed. 'You must be great cooks.'

Zhu Jie smiled broadly before clearing her throat and pointing at Khalid's notebook. 'Mak Kong want 2 and 4. One-way bet, $5,' she said.

Khalid put the five-dollar note in his pocket and wrote down the bet. Pak Ambi had taught him that a cross inside a circle represented a dollar. For five dollars, he just wrote the number '5' next to the cross-circle. Collectors had to use symbols to keep track of accounts to avoid being caught by the police with evidence of the lottery on them.

'Okay noted. See you tomorrow, Zhu Jie.' Zhu Jie gave Khalid a big wave, the way she always did. Khalid marched off to the next house, ready to take the next bet. Though he was initially hesitant to help Pak Ambi collect the bets, he admitted that it was now somewhat of a thrill for him, working in secret to avoid the police.

* * *

Inside the house, Lily had her face pressed to the peephole in the floor of her room, where she had been peering at the top of Khalid's head and eavesdropping on the conversation between Khalid and Zhu Jie. At that moment, she was wondering how she would ever have the opportunity to speak to Khalid. What can I do? she wondered.

'If only I could place the chap ji kee bet,' Lily mumbled to herself. 'Then I could see Khalid every day.' What can I do? Could I write a letter? Lily wondered. The purpose of language was to communicate. If I can't speak to him in person, maybe I should write a letter, Lily thought. That might be a good way to establish contact.

Slowly, with the spark of her new idea lighting a small flame in her mind, Lily slid the tile over the peephole and got up from her crouched position. She felt tired of living her life behind doors and peepholes. But I'm not a prisoner, Lily thought. I'm a nyonya. I should be thankful for everything I have. With a glance at the clock, she stepped out of her room to start her new set of embroidery work.

Part II

Chapter XII

8th February to 14th February 1940

Lily smiled to herself, admiring the white and red kueh ee that Mak Kong had stuck to the back of the main front door. The kueh ee was supposed to bring good fortune to the family and ward off evil. For the past month, all the women had been busy with spring cleaning and the preparation of food for Chinese New Year. They filled bottles with kueh like pineapple tarts and a container of kueh lapis, multi-layered cake. The day before, Lily, Zhu Jie, Leng Jie and Mak Kong had made kueh wajek, glutinous rice candy. Lily wished she could open the front door. She did not know who or what she would be looking for. The chances that Khalid would walk or cycle past were slim and she knew it was too early for Mak Wee to visit. Still, she stood there for a while longer, touching the door.

'Selamat Taon Baru!' Lily heard Chek Chuan call out. She stood up straight as the entire Kong family entered the reception hall, followed closely by Zhu Jie and Leng Jie. They would welcome the new year at 7 a.m. ever year. This year was no different. Pak Kong strode to the front doors and threw them open with a flourish. He boomed his new year greeting. Ivy clapped her hands, jumping up and down, and smiled brightly at Charles. Lily felt her spirits rise as she looked at everyone in the room with more fondness than usual. She loved the new year because it represented new beginnings and new clothes. Feeling grateful to be dressed in a new kebaya set and wearing the kasut manek she had painstakingly beaded, she exchanged a smile with Zhu Jie. Now that the front doors were open, it was time to pray to Ting Kong, the Jade Emperor, followed by the Monkey God and Kitchen God.

On the prayer table in the main hall, Zhu Jie and Leng Jie had arranged three combs of bananas so they looked like a blooming lotus. There were also fifteen sticks of skinned sugarcane stacked into a pyramid and twelve mandarin oranges. The offerings were banded with red paper that Lily had carefully cut. Pak Kong led the prayers. As Lily bowed three times with the glowing incense in hand, she silently prayed, 'Ting Kong, please grant us all health and happiness.' The prayers ended with everyone planting the joss sticks in urns and burning joss paper.

In the afternoon, Mak Wee arrived, carrying a container of kueh bakul on one arm and holding the hand of a young girl. Lily peered at the fair, diamond-faced girl dressed in a pink kebaya top and green batik skirt. Mak Wee patted Lily on the arm and then turned to the young girl.

'This is Irene, your cousin.' Mak Wee said. 'Irene, this is Lily.'

'Selamat Taon Baru, Mak Wee and Irene,' Lily said, wondering why Mak Wee brought Irene to visit. Irene looked up at Lily with wide eyes as if noticing her for the first time and then ducked behind Mak Wee. Mak Wee bent down so she was eye-level with Irene and whispered something in her ear. But Mak Wee always visits alone, Lily thought, feeling an unwelcome prick of jealousy as she watched how gently and warmly Mak Wee spoke to Irene.

'Come, come inside,' Mak Kong welcomed Mak Wee and Irene in. 'Terima Kasih for the kueh bakul. It is Charles' favourite.' No one except Lily seemed to think it was unusual that Irene had come along too. She watched as Irene settled next to Mak Wee on the wood sofa. Zhu Jie brought out a tray with a selection of kueh and tea. How much do I know about Mak Wee's life? Lily thought. Apart from the fact that Mak Wee lived with her mother, two brothers and their families, the rest was an empty space Lily could fill in with her imagination. Visiting Mak Wee once a month made them akin to relatives and not mother and daughter.

After Mak Kong and Mak Wee exchanged pleasantries enquiring about the other's health and family, Ivy came up to Irene and showed her a set of five stones.

'Want to play?' Ivy asked.

Pak Kong chuckled. 'Ivy loves to play five stones.'

Irene managed a small smile and clutched Mak Wee's arm with her right hand. Lily realised that Irene was sitting on her left hand. It looked uncomfortable to Lily.

'Yes, go on, Irene,' Mak Kong said. Mak Wee gave Irene an encouraging nod. Lily watched as Irene stared at Ivy as if wondering if this was someone she could trust.

Slowly, Irene got up and joined Ivy on the floor for a game of five stones. For a while, the group sat in silence. As Chek Chuan and Charles helped themselves to more kueh bakul, everyone watched Irene and Ivy play together. Ivy tossed a stone up in the air before catching it together with one on the ground, eliciting an admiring expression from Irene. Childhood should be the best time in a person's life, Lily mused. But it isn't that way for every child.

'How is Irene doing?' Mak Kong asked.

'Baik,' Mak Wee said. 'But sometimes, she cries . . . Nya Nya in her sleep.' Lily hung on to every word, as she tried to put the pieces of the puzzle of why Mak Kong brought Irene to visit. Mak Wee turned to Lily, her voice dropping to a whisper. 'Irene's parents passed away in a car accident last month.'

'Oh!' Lily said.

'Kesian,' Chek Chuan said. 'How old is Irene?'

'Turning seven,' Mak Wee said.

How were Irene's parents related to Mak Wee? Lily thought. She wanted to know more about Mak Wee's life. Was Mak Wee going to take care of Irene? Was Mak Wee lonely? Question after question sparked in her mind but then died out like flames with not enough air. Lily sat in pensive thought for the rest of the visit, speaking only when spoken to.

* * *

'What did you think of the movie?' Khalid asked as he turned to Dorothy. They had just watched the afternoon screening of *The Return of Dr X*, a mystery thriller starring the Hollywood actor Humphrey Bogart.

'I liked it, but there was not enough blood and gore for a horror movie,' Dorothy said, clutching onto her purse with both hands. 'What about you?'

It was boring, Khalid thought. 'Yes, I liked it too,' he said, wanting Dorothy to believe he liked the same things as her. He had finally summoned the courage to ask her out on a bus ride home a little over two weeks ago. When he had suggested watching a movie on Valentine's Day for their first eagerly anticipated date, he thought Dorothy would have suggested a romance movie but instead she wanted to watch the follow-up to *Dr X*, which neither of them had watched when it was released seven years ago. Khalid had baulked at this in his mind. Why would she want to watch a movie about bloodthirsty murders and corpses that are not really dead on Valentine's Day? After he found out it starred Humphrey Bogart, he had warmed up to the idea. But if he was being honest with himself, he just wanted to please Dorothy. He could not reconcile the horror movies Dorothy liked with the princess image of the girl before him. Maybe Dorothy likes comedies too, Khalid asked. He decided to ask her about the screwball comedy he enjoyed.

'Did you watch *Stand-In*?' Khalid asked.

'No,' Dorothy said. 'That was the comedy about Hollywood?'

'Yes,' Khalid said, finding himself holding his breath as he awaited her answer.

'I heard it was hilarious but I prefer thrillers and horror movies.'

Khalid nodded, wondering if he should tell her the truth about his movie preferences. He preferred romantic comedies like *It Happened One Night*. How ironic, Khalid thought. I'm the boy here but I prefer romance while Dorothy likes horror. Maybe not on the first date, he thought.

'Do you want to eat something?' he asked.

'Yes, it's tea time! Do you want to eat curry puffs?' Dorothy asked. Khalid agreed affably.

The pair wove their way through the crowd milling outside the cinema hall, where musicians were playing, the orchestra conductor swishing his baton with gusto. Dorothy stopped to watch for a few minutes before gesturing to Khalid that they could leave. They soon stepped out into the open air. The sun's rays shone down as they walked past the kacang puteh pushcart where two couples were queuing.

'One sugar-coated peanuts!' a young man said to the pot-bellied vendor. Khalid glanced at the vendor as he scooped out peanuts from a container and filled a newspaper cone to the brim. Dorothy had eaten the sugar-coated peanuts while he had murruku during the movie, crunching on the spiral-shaped fried snack and trying to refrain from yawning during the slower parts of the movie.

'Okay,' Khalid agreed. They made their way to a nearby coffee shop which was empty save for a couple of men and two women with young children. Khalid looked around the coffee shop and caught the eye of a middle-aged man who was puffing on a cigarette. A wispy cloud of smoke accompanied the man's exhale.

'Shall we eat the food outside?' Khalid said to Dorothy. He could not picture Dorothy sitting and eating in this coffee shop.

Dorothy was quick to agree. 'Let's go to the beach?' she suggested, frowning as she waved her hands in front of her face.

'Okay,' Khalid said. 'What's wrong?'

'It's a bit smelly here,' Dorothy said.

'Oh,' Khalid said, his brows creasing together. 'Yes, we'll go to the beach.'

A young girl in plaits stood next to her, holding her mother's hand. With her free hand, she reached out to touch Dorothy's skirt. Dorothy pursed her lips at the girl, who glared at her, a defiant look in her black eyes. Dorothy pulled her skirt away from the girl and frowned.

'Ibu,' the little girl said to her mother.

'I'm going to wait outside,' Dorothy said to Khalid. Khalid turned around, surprised. He had just placed his order with the waiter. Before he could reply, Dorothy glided out of the coffee shop. Khalid looked at the little girl who was pointing Dorothy out to her mother.

'Jangan sentuh baju orang,' the mother said, ignoring Khalid who stood looking from mother to daughter. Don't touch another person's clothes.

The little girl paused for a second before she nodded. Khalid smiled kindly at her but she grimaced at him and clutched onto her mother's hands tightly. Turning away from them, Khalid decided to wait for his order to be ready.

In a few minutes' time, the stall owner handed Khalid his order of four curry puffs and two cups of teh tarik. After Khalid collected his order, he met Dorothy outside, where she was fanning herself with a paper fan.

'Always so hot,' Dorothy said as she waved the fan in front of her face.

'Yes,' Khalid said, wishing he could come up with a better reply.

'Look at my new paper fan. Isn't it beautiful?' Dorothy said. 'It was a gift from a fan of a friend of my father's.'

Khalid looked at the fan for a second. It was pastel pink with white flowers on it. He supposed it was pretty. Dorothy looked even prettier holding the fan in front of her face.

'My father told me that the number of strips of wood on each fan reflects the rank and status of the owner back in the Heian period in Japan,' Dorothy said.

They walked to the beach, exchanging polite conversation about their family. When they reached the beach, lined with coconut trees, Khalid looked around for a shady spot under a rain tree.

'Let's just stand,' Dorothy said, wrinkling her nose, just as Khalid was about to suggest sitting under a nearby rain tree.

'Okay,' Khalid replied affably. 'There's shade there, under that rain tree.'

'Oh good,' Dorothy said. She hurried over to the tree.

Under the umbrella-like shade of the rain tree, Khalid passed Dorothy a curry puff. They watched the junk boats swaying and creaking in the water and the children frolicking in the white sand in front of them. Khalid realised this was the first time he was at the beach sitting down to admire the view instead of swimming in the sea or walking on the sand. He took sips of hot tea and munched on the curry puffs, the warm potatoes in the pastry satiating his hunger. As they ate, they exchanged stories of their families. Dorothy, Khalid learnt, enjoyed being the youngest of three girls in her family.

'I'm very much doted as the youngest daughter,' Dorothy said, as she ran her fingers down her skirt to smooth it out.

Khalid did not know what to say in response to that. He finally settled on, 'That must be nice.' He told her about Pak Ambi and how he felt pressure from him to do well in his Senior Cambridge examinations.

'That's expected, is it not?' Dorothy asked, turning to look over at him. Khalid nodded his head, feeling a bit uncomfortable. Yes it was expected, he thought. But he had hoped for a bit more empathy from Dorothy for the pressures he faced. Maybe he did not adequately explain how he felt. He decided to share a bit about his relationship with Ibrahim.

'Ibrahim, my elder brother, obtained a Grade II certificate. I hope I can do a bit better than him and get a Grade I certificate,' Khalid told Dorothy.

Dorothy's eyes gleamed in delight. 'Ooh, you should!' she exclaimed. Pleased that he had managed to impress Dorothy, Khalid leaned back and stretched his legs out. I will strive even harder now for a Grade I, he thought.

When they were done eating, Dorothy wiped her mouth with her handkerchief. Then she leaned over and kissed Khalid's cheek.

'Thank you for a lovely day,' she said.

Khalid felt his cheeks grow warm as he felt the imprint of Dorothy's lips still on his skin. He pretended to be interested in gathering their empty cups and the brown paper bag in his hands. Dorothy giggled, flipping her hair off her shoulder. Her laughter was high-pitched and it seemed to echo in the air. They walked to the bus stop slowly, without holding hands. Each time Khalid thought of reaching out to hold Dorothy's hand, he stopped himself. He guessed it was the nervousness of not knowing what the right thing to do was. He wanted to ensure it acted in a manner befitting a young gentleman. Although he and Dorothy had not discussed it, he was sure that Dorothy was being courted by other men. The thought made him feel a bit uncomfortable.

However, the day seemed to be a success so he thought he would soon figure out how to ask her out on another date. When they reached their bus stop, Khalid started walking in the direction of Dorothy's house but Dorothy was still standing at the bus stop, her hands clasped in front of her.

'You don't have to walk me home,' Dorothy said, as she flipped her hair over her shoulder.

'Oh,' Khalid said. 'Why?'

'I don't want my father to see us,' Dorothy said quickly. 'He's very strict. If I continue seeing you, he'll want to meet you for sure.'

'Oh,' Khalid said. This upset him. Did Dorothy not want her father to see him because he was Indian and came from a poorer background? Were these simply his insecurities about being a brown man, a member of the minority race in Singapore, or perhaps a truth that Dorothy could not bear to tell him yet?

'Yeah, so . . . ' Dorothy's voice trailed off. 'I'll see you.'

'Thank you for going out with me today,' Khalid said, though he felt his heart sinking a little.

'Thank you too,' Dorothy said. Her fingers fluttered in the air in a coquettish wave.

Khalid watched Dorothy walk away, her hair swishing behind her. Could he ask Dorothy out on a date again? After all, she had said, 'See you.' Did she mean in general or on a date? Khalid wondered. He guessed he would find out the next time he saw her. All in all, Khalid thought his first date with Dorothy had been a success. He allowed that thought to please him on the way home, as he thought of Dorothy, her sweet-smelling hair and shining smile.

Chapter XIII

10th March 1940

After her evening bath that day, Lily sat at her vanity table and tried to write a letter to Khalid. She pressed her pencil carefully into the paper to write out the letters. Next to her was her English textbook for reference; it was open to the page on greetings. Mr Tan's slow, monotonous and patient voice would come to her in these moments. She remembered how slowly he would sound out each word. At first she had thought that the pace of his lessons was slow because of his age but now that he had passed on, she felt grateful that he had tried to make sure she understood before moving on to the next word or sentence. Maybe after someone's death, we appreciate them more, Lily thought. She certainly felt that way about Mr Tan. In his absence on earth, all the things that seemed to annoy her about Mr Tan had faded into the deep crevices of her mind. Lily leaned forward in her chair and stared hard at the words she had just written.

Hello Khalid,
How are you?

Had she spelled every word correctly? She checked every single letter twice. When she felt confident her words were written accurately, she wrote her name at the end. Glancing at the clock next to her, she saw that it was past her bedtime. Lily wished she could share more of her thoughts with Khalid but she did not know how to translate them to words on the page. There was no one she could ask to write the letter on her behalf. For a brief moment, she considered asking Charles for help but soon came to the conclusion that would be too embarrassing. He would want to know why she was writing to Khalid and undoubtedly would share the matter with Mak Kong.

Lily reassured herself that her short note would just have to do. She folded the paper into four and then put it into her bedside drawer. Before she switched off the desk light and settled into bed, Lily knew her nervousness and excitement would keep her awake for a while. She would finally communicate with Khalid. If he writes back, Lily mused as she lay in bed, clutching on to her blanket. When she woke up, she would remember that she dreamt that she gave Khalid her note herself. But the rest of her dream was fuzzy. She could not remember if he had accepted the note and what he had said. In real life, he will reply, Lily thought.

A few days later, Lily woke up early, feeling waves of excitement course through her body. Today was the day she would give Khalid her note through Zhu Jie. When she had asked Zhu Jie about helping her pass the note to Khalid in the kitchen, she had agreed readily. As she fluffed up her pillow and tucked her sheets in, she imagined him reading her note outside of their house. Would he reply to her? Would he think that she was too forward? Was she allowing herself to be seen by writing a note? Young nyonyas were supposed to be cloistered away until after marriage. Lily tried to reassure herself that she was not doing anything wrong. After her bath, she got dressed and immediately hurried down the stairs, hoping to find Zhu Jie in the kitchen alone.

She spotted Zhu Jie in the hallway, walking purposefully to the kitchen.

'Zhu Jie,' she whispered as she ran up to her.

Zhu Jie did not hear her. When she reached her, Lily tapped her on the back. Zhu Jie turned around. With her eyebrows raised, she asked what was happening.

Lily passed the note to Zhu Jie. As she looked at the empty lined note, she wished she had written Khalid's name on it.

'It's a note for Khalid,' Lily said. 'Could you try to pass it to him later?'

Zhu Jie wiggled her eyebrows. 'Yes, when I bring out tea.'

Lily smiled. It was a small, nervous smile tinged with her hope that her note would, at the very least, gain her a friend.

She felt nervous the whole time while cooking and during lunch. Once, she almost wanted to ask Zhu Jie for the note back but she could not get Zhu Jie alone. Mak Kong's presence that day made Lily feel nervous. Lily thought that this might be her most terrible idea or the best one depending on the outcome. Her nervousness did not abate when it was time to do embroidery. She sat still in the sewing room and waited till she heard Khalid's voice.

Khalid tried to stifle a yawn. As much as he liked tutoring Charles, watching him read a comprehension passage was not on top on his list of things to do on a Wednesday afternoon. But until his Senior Cambridge results were released and he could find another job, tutoring Charles was a good way to earn some income. Khalid checked his watch. Soon Zhu Jie would serve them some snacks.

'What does this word mean?' Charles asked, as he pushed his textbook closer to Khalid.

'Interminable means endless,' Khalid said. 'Have you finished reading the passage?'

'Yes.'

'Then let's try answering the first question.'

'Okay,' Charles agreed.

At that moment, Zhu Jie entered the room, carrying a tray. Khalid turned his head and saw a tray of sugee cookies, a kamcheng and two glasses. Zhu Jie grinned her usual broad smile that made her eyes disappear. As Charles' head was bent over his textbook, Zhu Jie slipped Lily's note under Khalid's plate. Khalid looked up at Zhu Jie, wondering what was under his plate. He had been tutoring Charles for one and a half years. Every week, Zhu Jie would bring out a tray of snacks for tea time but she had never slipped a piece of paper under his plate before.

This was probably the most unusual thing that had happened in his tutoring session at Everitt Road. Without a word, Zhu Jie walked away. Somehow Khalid knew that he should not look at what was under his plate. He supposed satisfying his curiosity would have to wait till the end of the session.

After Charles completed his comprehension and they had gone through the answers, Charles thanked him and stood up to walk Khalid to the door. When Charles' back was turned, Khalid slipped the note from under the plate and into the pocket of his pants. Then he followed Charles to the door.

'Bye,' Charles said. 'See you next week.'

'Bye Charles,' Khalid said as he stepped out of the door. He looked from left to right as he always did to make sure Little was not around. Though Mak Kong made sure that Little stayed upstairs whenever Khalid was around out of respect for his Muslim practice of avoiding dogs, Khalid still had some fear that Little would somehow escape. Once he felt sure Little was not in the vicinity, Khalid hurried to his bicycle. He took the note out of his pocket and looked at it. Then he unfolded it. Lily wrote me this note, he thought as he read. But why? He read it again and turned the paper over but there was no reason he could infer from what she had written. Shrugging his shoulders, he put the note back into his pocket. He pushed his bicycle to the main road as a thought came to him. Maybe she's lonely. Maybe she needs a friend. By the time he reached home, he had decided he would reply to her note once he figured out what to say.

After dinner, Khalid was alone in his room. Pak Ambi had gone out for a drink with his friends and he did not know where Ibrahim was. He wondered how Lily had learnt to write in English. As far as he knew, Lily did not go to school or have a tutor. He took out his pen and letter pad from his drawer.

Dear Lily,
Thank you for your letter.
It was a nice surprise.

I am well. How are you?

He did not know what else he should say. Lily's letter had just asked how he was. Maybe she didn't know what to write, Khalid thought. He heard footsteps in the hallway that sounded like the sound Ibrahim's new shoes made. Instantly, Khalid shoved the letter pad into the drawer, knocking his pen onto the floor in the process. Khalid ran after his pen, picking it up just as Ibrahim entered the room.

'What's up?' Ibrahim drawled.

'Nothing much,' Khalid said. 'Where were you?'

'On a date,' Ibrahim said.

'With whom?' Khalid asked.

'A girl,' Ibrahim said as he tossed his towel over his shoulder. 'Going to bathe.'

Khalid sighed in relief as he watched Ibrahim walk out of the room to the toilets.

That was close, he thought. He could imagine the round of teasing he would face if Ibrahim had caught him writing a letter to a girl. Even if it was an innocent letter, like the one he was writing to Lily, Ibrahim would find a way to twist it into something he could make fun of.

Deciding that he would continue the letter tomorrow, Khalid put the pen in the drawer. He stretched his arms behind him, feeling a bit restless. I'll see if Samad wants to take a walk or play soccer, Khalid thought as he left the room, closing the door behind him.

'I want to be a soccer player,' Samad declared later that night.

'Why not?' Khalid said. 'You can be one!' He and Samad were kicking the ball back and forth at the courtyard.

'Don't know if good enough,' Samad replied, kicking the ball towards him. 'You ever thought of it?'

Khalid shook his head. 'No . . . soccer is a game.'

'Doesn't mean you can't make money from a game!' Samad said.

'That's true,' Khalid said.

'I hope I don't fail my exams,' Samad said. He sighed and stopped the ball that was coming towards him with his feet.

Khalid racked his brain for something encouraging to say. He did not know what examinations in Alsagoff Arab School were like but he knew, from what Samad shared about his results, that Samad was not a good student. 'It'll be okay,' Khalid said finally. 'Hope for the best.'

'Are you going to study more?' Samad asked as he shifted his weight from one foot to another. Then he kicked the ball to Khalid who received it easily.

'Probably not,' Khalid said. 'Need to earn money.'

'Ya,' Samad said with a heavy sigh. 'If only we are rich man's son eh.'

Khalid chuckled as he looked at Samad. 'That would be nice.'

'Ya!' Samad said. 'Can do anything, go anywhere.'

Khalid thought of Barker whose family was well-off. Barker studied harder than anyone he knew.

'Well,' Khalid said after a brief pause. 'Rich men's sons have to go to school and study too.'

Samad paused. 'Guess so,' he said. 'I want to go to England. Learn soccer there.'

Khalid tried to imagine himself flying on an airplane just then. He could not quite picture it; flying was a lavish affair reserved only for the richest. One day, he promised himself that he would take an airplane, though the thought scared him a little. He would see the world and visit England, Germany and other parts of Asia.

Khalid ran to stop the ball from getting away from him. He ended up punting it past Samad. The ball hit the base of a nearby tree.

'Hey!' Samad shouted.

Khalid laughed. 'Sorry!'

Samad glanced at his watch. 'I better go. Or Mak will be shouting my name soon.'

'Okay,' Khalid said.

'Coming?' Samad asked, looking at Khalid.

'Not yet,' Khalid said. He felt secretly a bit glad that Samad was leaving because he wanted to spend some time alone.

Samad waved and strode off, leaving Khalid alone with the ball, listening to the sounds of a stray cat meowing. Ball in arm, Khalid decided to look for the cat, following its sounds. It was a black cat, darker than the night, standing on the drain. The moment the cat saw Khalid approaching, it darted away. If I see it again, I will give it some food, Khalid thought. He knew Samad's mother would try to feed the stray cats in the neighbourhood whenever she could. 'Be merciful to Allah's creation,' she would say when Khalid spotted her putting out food for the strays. Khalid sat at the base of a tree, watching to see if the cat would return. As he listened to the silent sounds of the night, his thoughts meandered to Lily, elusive Lily, whose letter was like a question he wanted very much to answer. He leaned back, feeling his head touch the bark of the tree. There were so many questions about life that he wanted an answer to, Khalid thought as he dozed off, not sure what that meant.

Chapter XIV

1st April 1940

The Senior Cambridge results had been sent to Singapore from England by Imperial Air Mail. For months, Khalid and his fellow schoolmates had waited for the results on which their futures depended. There were three possible outcomes: attend college, seek employment, or for the unfortunate ones, repeat the academic year. Now that results day was finally here, Khalid found himself back at his alma mater. The clerical staff of Raffles Institution had prepared the pass lists and posted them on a bulletin board in the school hall. There was a growing swell of students crowded in front of the board. Khalid turned his body sideways and tried to squeeze through the tiny space between two students in front of him. His eyes scanned the list of passes in front of him till he found his name. He exhaled in relief and turned around to see more anxious faces. They would have to wait a while before they received their individual certificates.

He saw Roy, Barker and Rahman standing together, each one wearing serious expressions on their faces. He hurried over to join them.

'Pass?' Rahman said once he saw Khalid.

'Yes,' Khalid said.

'Congrats!' Roy said. 'Us too.'

'I hope I get a Grade I certificate,' Barker said in a low voice.

Rahman laughed and clapped his hand on Barker's back. 'You will.'

'Yeah, you definitely will,' Roy said readily.

'Barker, if anyone will get Grade I, it'll be you,' Khalid said, biting his lip a little. 'I don't think I will.'

'You will, K. But if you don't, it'll be alright,' Roy said, putting his arm around Khalid's shoulder. 'We're going out to work anyway.'

Rahman nodded his head vigorously. 'I have four younger sisters to support. Can't study further even if I wanted to.'

Barker looked at Rahman, his brown eyes filled with empathy.

'Raffles College isn't for everyone,' Rahman said as he scratched his chin.

'The important thing is that we all passed,' Khalid said. He watched as one student, standing some distance away, buried his face in his hands. The student was sandwiched between two friends who both put their arm around him. He could not imagine having to retake the Senior Cambridge examinations as a private candidate, the grim fate that awaited those who had failed. The student's shoulders were shaking now. Khalid tore his gaze away from the sad sight and met Roy's eye.

'Shall we play a game of soccer while we wait for our certificates?' Roy asked, looking around eagerly at his friends.

'Good idea,' Khalid said. 'I see Noor and Zaid over there too. Let's ask them.'

'I don't think I'll be able to think of anything else but getting my hands on my certificate,' Barker said, his brows creased together.

'Take a breath,' Rahman said. 'Soccer will take your mind off results.'

Barker nodded as Roy took out his ball from his backpack.

'Let's go,' Roy said, leading the way out of the hall and towards the soccer pitch. Khalid gestured to Noor and Zaid, who understood his signal and joined the group. The boys played 3v3 soccer, running up and down the length of the field. Khalid noticed that his head was not in the game at all. He felt like he was just going through the motions of playing like it was a practice session he had to attend though he was ill. Khalid felt his hands and legs tremble as he ran after the ball, tension radiating throughout his body that made it hard to fully enjoy the game. No one it seemed wanted to keep score though Khalid noted privately to himself that Noor, Zaid and Barker's team scored two goals while his team with Roy and Rahman scored three goals. Soon enough, they heard the announcement over the loudspeaker that their certificates were ready for collection.

'Moment of reckoning,' Barker muttered. Khalid put his arm around Barker's shoulder as they walked off the soccer pitch together.

Later that evening, Khalid sat at his desk, perusing his certificate again. He had obtained two distinctions, for English and Elementary Mathematics, and five credits for Additional Mathematics, History of the British Empire, Malay, Geography, and Hygiene and Physiology. He could hardly believe it. Ibrahim had obtained a Grade II certificate two years ago and had bemoaned how impossible it was to obtain a Grade I certificate. Even when Khalid was studying for his examinations, Ibrahim would, from time to time, mention how lucky he would be if he too obtained a Grade II certificate. But Khalid had exceeded Ibrahim's expectations. He stared at his watch. He expected Pak Ambi and Ibrahim would both reach home in about twenty to thirty minutes.

Maybe I should go for further studies, Khalid thought. He imagined himself walking through the halls at Raffles College, looking dapper and confident, and sitting in class, answering the teacher's questions with ease. What was the alternative? He could be a clerk perhaps like Ibrahim. He certainly did not want to work as a tutor forever or be a chap ji kee collector and driver like his father. Khalid thought, at that moment, of Harry. Mr McLeod had announced Harry as the top student. Harry would attend Raffles College. Khalid thought of how sure Barker had seemed when he said he was going to attend Raffles College as well. Barker dreamt of reading law at Cambridge University in the United Kingdom. Khalid envied their certainty of purpose. He had spent the past few months scanning the job advertisements and wondering which job would suit him best.

He opened his drawer and took out his half-complete letter to Lily. They had been steadily exchanging letters for almost a month. He had written three letters to her and received two letters in return. Khalid felt glad that he could openly be himself with Lily and share his innermost thoughts. It was different from dating Dorothy. With Dorothy, Khalid felt like he could not really be himself for fear of judgement.

He took out the last letter he had received from her. He had wanted to know more about what her life was like. The letter was written mostly in Baba Malay and the rest was in English.

Dear Khalid,

Today was a long day. I woke up before dawn as usual to the sound of the rooster crowing. After my bath, I rushed down to the kitchen to have breakfast. Zhu Jie and Leng Jie were there. They were speaking in Hokkien. That's their dialect. Apart from that, they also speak Baba Malay, and they can also speak a bit of English. When they saw me, Zhu Jie stopped and smiled widely. Zhu Jie is a good friend. I cannot imagine life without her.

Then we started preparing the ingredients for lunch with Ah Huat, our cook. Ah Huat is a really good cook. Mak Kong came into the kitchen to supervise us. We made rendang daging and sayur lemak. Do you like to eat rendang daging?

Khalid put the letter down at that moment. Yes, he thought. I love beef rendang.

Grabbing a pencil, Khalid quickly wrote:

Dear Lily,

How are you? I would like to taste your rendang daging one day and sayur lemak as well. I'm sure that you are a talented cook.

I have good news to share with you. I obtained a Grade I for Senior Cambridge!

Khalid paused as he took his hand off the paper slightly. What would Lily think of that? Khalid wondered. Did it sound like he was boasting? Lily had never even had a chance to attend school; he did not want to remind her of that. Shaking his head at himself, Khalid considered using his eraser to rub off the words he had just written. Then he realised that he really wanted to share his results with her. He wanted to understand her and have her understand him in return though he did not, at that moment, fully know why. A while ago, he had seen Dorothy and she had professed her admiration and pride for his results with a gasp and a hug. In spite of himself, Khalid had felt his body stiffen. Dorothy had said she hoped that she would do as well as him when she took the Senior Cambridge this year. Khalid had bit his lip, feeling awkward, and told her she would do well. But at that moment, he found himself thinking once again of Lily as he was speaking to Dorothy.

Just as Khalid was rereading what he had written to Lily, he heard Pak Ambi's voice down the hall. In an instant, Khalid shoved his letter into the drawer. I don't want Pak Ambi to see this, he thought.

'How?' Pak Ambi said once he strode into the room eagerly.

Khalid grinned and showed Pak Ambi his certificate. 'I did well!' he said.

'Wow!' Pak Ambi exclaimed, his handsome face lighting up with pride. 'Well done!'

'What are your results?' Ibrahim asked. Khalid turned around to see Ibrahim standing there, looking curious yet guarded. It was an expression like a half-opened door.

Pak Ambi flourished the certificate in front of Ibrahim's face.

Ibrahim was quiet for a minute then he said, 'Well done.'

Pak Ambi grabbed the certificate from Ibrahim and strode out of the room. 'Must tell the neighbours,' he said, a broad smile upon his face. Khalid felt overwhelmed with such pride that he could make Pak Ambi feel happier than he had ever remembered seeing him.

Khalid stood there for a while, eavesdropping on Pak Ambi sharing his results with Mr Rashid. Turning around, he watched as Ibrahim unbuttoned his shirt and sat down on a chair. In Ibrahim's eyes, he thought he saw a tiny glint of envy. Khalid knew he would have felt the same way if his results had been worse than Ibrahim's.

'Hungry, Ib?' Khalid asked.

'Yes, very,' Ibrahim replied. After a pause, he continued, 'You know, the working world is very different from being a student, Khalid.'

'I know,' Khalid said.

'Just because a person is a good student doesn't mean they will be a good worker,' Ibrahim said as his fingers grasped his shirt.

Khalid frowned as he met Ibrahim's glance. Ibrahim looked away quickly and continued undressing in front of his cabinet. Khalid fixed a hard stare at the back of Ibrahim's head.

'I don't mean you, of course,' Ibrahim said. 'I meant in general.'

'Okay Ibrahim,' Khalid said. Why don't you just be quiet? He wanted to say but did not.

'Well, going to wash up before dinner,' Ibrahim said. He walked out of the room with a smirk playing on the edges on his mouth. Khalid exhaled and sat down on his chair. He would not let the envy which he expected from Ibrahim ruin his buoyant mood. Ibrahim had been in a bad mood ever since his wedding date was set on 15th December. Probably he is also envious that I am not being matchmade like him, Khalid thought as he stretched his feet out. So far anyway.

Pak Ambi's voice was growing fainter and fainter now. Knowing his father would not be satisfied until he had informed all the neighbours in the entire shophouse, Khalid leaned back on his chair. He guessed it would be a while till his certificate was safely back in his possession.

He took out the most recent letter Lily had written to him in Baba Malay. There were spelling errors but he understood all of it. She said that she had never had the opportunity to attend school though she desperately wanted to. Her English tutor had taught her for less than a year before dying. She thought writing a letter in English to Khalid would help her improve her command of the language. She complimented Khalid for being a good tutor to Charles. Khalid smiled as he reread the compliment. He wondered what Lily would say about his Grade I certificate. Unsure if she would understand the significance of it, Khalid added to the letter he was writing to explain that a Grade I was the best certificate a Senior Cambridge student could get.

* * *

Lily was embroidering a tablecloth when she heard Khalid's voice. He's here, she thought, as her heart leaped like a cat jumping up a tree.

What would his letter today say? She had heard Charles mentioning that the Senior Cambridge results would be out on Monday. Maybe Khalid would share with her how he had fared in the examinations. Though Lily had no idea what the examination process was like, she felt reasonably confident that Khalid would do well. She had been listening to him tutor Charles in English for almost a year now. She pierced the needle she was holding through the tablecloth. Lily thought that each piece of embroidery meant something special because of the emblems on them.

The tablecloth would feature two majestic phoenixes surrounded by a flurry of pink peonies and sweet green leaves when she was done. A phoenix was associated with imperial power while the peonies symbolised wealth and status. At that moment, she could hear Khalid and Charles exchanging greetings. Lily felt tired at that moment; she was not in the mood to do embroidery. She pulled the needle out of the cloth and paused. All she wanted to do at that moment was lie down and take a nap. She closed her eyes for a minute as she felt a wave of pain overcome her. Lily leaned back in her chair and took deep breaths. Once in a while, she would get these painful menstrual cramps. Slowly, she got up and walked to the kitchen. Zhu Jie and Leng Jie were both in the kitchen. Lily stood before them, pale-faced as she felt her body breaking out into cold sweat.

'Cramps,' Zhu Jie said at once. She got up and headed straight to the kettle, where she started boiling water. A few minutes later, Lily was sipping ginger tea, cradling the cup with both her hands as Zhu Jie massaged her back. She supposed that she could not do her embroidery work that afternoon. She fervently hoped Mak Kong would not be angry at her. The tea provided her a bit of relief but Lily still felt the cramps in waves of pain rolling through her stomach.

'Go rest,' Zhu Jie said when Lily was done with the tea.

'Okay,' Lily said. 'Thank you, Zhu Jie.' Leng Jie gave her a look that Lily supposed was sympathy though it was hard to tell. The sides of Leng Jie's mouth were drooped downwards as usual. Lily left the kitchen and went up to her room. She fell into her bed and slept till it was almost dinner time. It felt good, Lily thought as she closed her eyes. To take a nap for once. Lily combed her hair back into a bun, smoothed out her baju panjang and left her room to help prepare dinner. A thought came to her as she walked to the kitchen. Every week, she sat in the next room and tried hard not to eavesdrop on Khalid for it was not polite to do so. But inevitably she would hear his voice speaking to Charles. She imagined Khalid's steady, measured voice speaking to her instead. But today she could not listen to Khalid's words which had inspired her to learn more English.

With a pang, Lily thought that Khalid would not have missed her; there was no way he could have known she was not in the next room. To be so close and not have her absence felt made Lily feel sad. With that sadness sinking like a hook in her heart, Lily slowly fell asleep.

What if Khalid stopped writing to her one day? Lily thought as she took out the dinner plates from the cabinet later that evening. She was sure she would feel forlorn. The future felt like a big white void that she could not see. It amazed Lily how no one could predict the future but lived like tomorrow was certain. But nothing in life ever was. Humans are brave, Lily decided as she placed the plates down on the kitchen table. Living life is a courageous act.

Seated at the dinner table that night, Chek Chuan announced in a merry voice that he had found a job.

'Yay!' Ivy cheered, as she swung her legs back and forth. Chek Chuan winked at her before taking a gulp of water from his glass.

Pak Kong spoke in his firm voice. 'Kerja betul-betul.'

Lily was sure that she saw a slight smirk on Mak Kong's face.

'Then you can get married. Now you have a job,' Ivy said.

Chek Chuan laughed. 'I don't want to get married,' he said.

'Why?' Ivy asked.

'If I wanted to get married, I'd be married by now,' Chek Chuan said, as his eyes twinkled, glancing over at Ivy.

'Why didn't you want to get married?' Ivy persisted.

'Just not for me,' Chek Chuan said with a shake of his head. 'Marriage isn't for everyone.'

'Why not?' Ivy asked.

'Being single means more freedom,' Chek Chuan said.

Mak Kong frowned at Chek Chuan, but he did not seem to notice.

'Freedom,' Ivy repeated. 'Like a plane has freedom?'

'Planes don't have freedom, silly,' Charles said. 'They have to fly from one country to another.'

'Okay, like a bird then,' Ivy said. 'Free like a bird.' She stretched her arms out and tilted them left and right.

Charles shrugged nonchalantly as he scooped steaming curry from the serving bowl onto his plate.

'So, what is this job?' Mak Kong asked.

'Assistant at the medicinal hall,' Chek Chuan answered.

Mak Kong nodded slowly then she aimed at Charles a piercing gaze that Lily interpreted to mean was a warning not to be like Chek Chuan. This is what happens when you don't study hard, Lily imagined Mak Kong saying. Charles swallowed the food in his mouth and pursed his lips.

'Will it be fun?' Ivy asked.

'Work is not about fun,' Charles said, laughing as he shook his head. Ivy stuck her tongue out at him.

'Work can be fun,' Chek Chuan said, winking at Ivy.

'Oh?' Mak Kong asked, sniffing before putting the rice cupped in her hands in her mouth. Her eyes were ablaze with red-hot judgement. Lily looked at Mak Kong and then averted her eyes.

'Why not?' Chek Chuan asked.

'Fun is for after work,' Pak Kong said as he lifted his glass of water. 'Or on weekends.'

Chek Chuan winked at Ivy again, who giggled as she leaned her hand on her face and sighed dreamily.

Being single means more freedom, Lily thought, pondering over Chek Chuan's words. For men, she supposed, that was true. But she knew an unmarried nyonya of a certain age would be regarded as most undesirable in society.

Chapter XV

6th May 1940

Khalid wiped a bead of perspiration away from his temple. There were many things he liked about staying in Singapore, but the humid climate was not one of them. The ceiling fan spun slowly above him like it was giving up in its daily battle of fighting the heat.

'I know about your girlfriend,' Ibrahim said, wiggling his eyebrows. He was stretched out on his bed, on his stomach, filling out a crossword puzzle. He turned to look at Khalid as he slid his pencil between his ear and head.

'What?' Khalid asked, looking up from the copy of the *Straits Times*. He did not welcome the interruption, especially since he was reading an article about the Saigon soccer team visiting Singapore. It was a welcome break from studying the job advertisements, especially on a Sunday.

'I saw you holding hands with a girl yesterday,' Ibrahim said. He put his pencil behind his ear and tossed his book on the bed. Khalid thought he looked rather triumphant, as if he had uncovered a big secret.

'Oh,' Khalid said. 'I didn't see you.'

'How come you didn't tell me you have a girlfriend?' Ibrahim asked. 'What's her name?'

'You don't tell me everything about your life either,' Khalid said, feeling defensive.

'Not answering the question,' Ibrahim retorted.

Before Khalid could reply, Pak Ambi strolled into the room. 'Let's go,' Pak Ambi said, snapping his fingers. Ibrahim smirked at Khalid as he ran his fingers through his thick, wavy hair. Khalid felt glad that Ibrahim had not found out he had been exchanging notes with Lily. Although he and Lily were just friends, he felt sure Ibrahim would tease him endlessly if he found Lily's notes in his desk drawer. He made a mental note to be more organised with her letters. He would place the notes in a box than in the drawer. This would serve as another layer of protection from Ibrahim's inquisitiveness. He got up from his chair and grabbed his wallet which was on the table. Khalid watched as Ibrahim stood up and adjusted the strap of his watch on his wrist. It was time to go to visit Mak Jah and their half-sisters for Sunday lunch.

'Hai pasu bunga!' Ibrahim called out as he stepped into Mak Jah's house at Ceylon Road. 'Satu hitam, satu putih.'

Khalid watched as his half-sister Leha rolled her eyes at Ibrahim's greeting of choice.

'I'm not a vase!' she protested and stopped short of complaining about the remark on skin colour. But Khalid knew she was writhing on the inside. She did not like her skin colour, especially since people tended to compare it to her younger sister Fatimah's much fairer one. Khalid felt glad that no one commented on his dark chocolate skin or compared it to Ibrahim's caramel-coloured skin. On the other hand, women had their skin colour commented on far more often. They have it tougher than men, Khalid surmised. Skin colour is seen as an indication of beauty for women here. The fairer, the better, Khalid thought. He took a deep breath. If he ever had a daughter that was darker skinned like Leha, would she face the same teasing?

'The appropriate greeting is Assalamualaikum,' Leha said, her thick eyebrows knitting together as she frowned at Ibrahim.

Ibrahim did not respond. He wrinkled his nose slightly as he strode into the house towards Mak Jah and her parents.

Khalid glanced from Ibrahim to Pak Ambi who had an impassive look on his face. He had never taught his sons to greet others with 'Peace be upon you' but he knew Mak Jah taught her daughters that they should always greet everyone they met by wishing them peace. The very word 'Islam', Khalid knew, meant submission in Arabic. After they greeted Mak Jah and her parents, Ibrahim flopped on the walnut sofa in the living room. Khalid took a seat in the matching chair opposite him and waited for the conversation to begin.

Pak Ambi started by making polite enquiries about Mak Jah's parents' health. Every week, the answer from Mak Jah's father would invariably be 'not good' then he would resume staring into the distance. Mak Jah's mother would say 'Sihat, Alhamdulillah'. She was well, praise be to Allah. Leha and Fatimah usually engaged in quick chatter with each other but today they were rather silent. Leha stifled a yawn as she examined her fingernails. Fatimah was sitting on the floor with her legs tucked under her. She swayed her body from side to side as she looked around at everyone.

'Did you all know Khalid is courting a girl?' Ibrahim announced at that moment as if he wanted to end the short silence that was uncomfortable for him. Khalid grimaced, sinking lower in his seat. He had had a sinking feeling Ibrahim would not be able to keep the news to himself and now he was proven right.

Everyone began talking at once. Leha and Fatimah looked at each other, their eyes widening with this piece of news.

'He's courting someone?' Leha asked. 'Who?'

'Ooh,' Fatimah cooed.

'Of course, he is! Handsome like the father so he can get any girl he wants!' Pak Ambi boomed.

'Ah,' Mak Jah said.

In his rocking chair, Mak Jah's father yawned and closed his eyes, as he rocked back and forth.

Khalid stayed silent as he tried to think of another topic that he could bring up to change the subject. Leha tried to elbow him from her chair but could not reach him.

'Well? Who is she?' she asked.

'Leave him be,' Ibrahim said in a teasing voice. 'He's shy.'

Khalid shot Ibrahim a dark look. It was one thing to tell Pak Ambi about Dorothy but to share it with almost everyone else in the family was another. Besides it was not like he and Dorothy were going steady. Khalid wished there was something juicy he knew about Ibrahim that he could disclose as revenge. But his older brother kept his personal life a mystery. He never referred to any girl by name; it was always 'some girl' or 'a girl'. Khalid had never caught him walking alone with a girl. When he did spot Ibrahim outside their home, he was either alone or with a few friends.

'I shall ask around to find out,' Leha said, twirling her hair around her finger.

Fatimah giggled, her black curls bouncing as she looked from Leha to Khalid. She placed her hand on her mouth as if to contain her laughter. Khalid exhaled, letting his irritation out with his breath. He moved slightly on his chair, hoping that lunch would be served soon. He looked hopefully at Mak Jah who did not look at him. At that moment, however, Mak Jah got up and walked into the kitchen, a signal that she would heat up the lunch she had cooked. Leaning back in his chair, Khalid smiled to himself. It was as if Mak Jah could read his mind. Once the food was brought out, he was sure everyone would forget about the topic of Dorothy. He watched as Leha sauntered into the kitchen to help Mak Jah, with Fatimah following closely behind. Khalid could already taste the spicy curry in his mouth. He decided to follow them into the kitchen and ask if he could help out. That would be preferable to sitting opposite Ibrahim and trying to avoid his smirk. Getting up from the chair, Khalid made sure to avoid Ibrahim's gaze as he walked away. He thought that he should announce that Ibrahim too had a girlfriend at lunch. While he had not seen Ibrahim with a girl, Ibrahim talked about going on dates often enough. Maybe he has more than one girlfriend, Khalid thought as he watched Mak Jah heat up the curry in a big pot. But wouldn't the parents of these girls want to meet Ibrahim before they allowed him to take their daughters out on dates? Khalid wondered. It was proper dating etiquette. But Khalid knew he could not say anything. Pak Ambi would be angry that Ibrahim had a girlfriend when he was engaged to their cousin. He took out the plates from the cabinet, stacking one on top of the other, as he thought of the other ways that he could make Ibrahim pay.

* * *

Lily was sitting in the sewing room, trying very hard to focus on embroidering the tablecloth in front of her. Just an hour ago, Mak Wee had visited with Irene for lunch. Lily still felt painful pricks of jealousy every time she watched Mak Wee interact with Irene. Since Chinese New Year, she had been pondering why Mak Wee had given her away to the Kongs. She was told that Mak Wee felt like she could not take care of a newborn on her own. But now Mak Wee was much older, which surely would make caregiving more challenging, yet she had chosen to assume an adoptive mother role. Lily could not understand it. Questions tumbled around in her mind at night when she was in bed, trying to sleep. She knew that the only way to get an answer was to ask Mak Wee. The answer feared her as much as it intrigued her. Had it been an unwanted pregnancy? What if she was considered bad luck? Was it her mole? Absent-mindedly, Lily poked her mole with her left finger.

She looked at the pink silk thread she was stitching into the fabric. Lily sighed softly, threading the needle through and then pulling it out. No point brooding anymore, she told herself. Next time she saw Mak Wee, she would try her best to ask why she was given away. Even if the answer was hard to accept, at least she would know. Knowing the truth was better than endless speculation.

She felt like she was yearning to belong to someone most of the time. Sometimes, she wished she could be free like the phoenix she was stitching. But the phoenix was not real. If it was, was it truly free just because it could fly? If Lily did not belong within the walls of the Kongs' home and she was not free to leave the home, to fly away like a bird, then neither belonging or freedom were possible. Maybe it is just human nature to yearn for things we can't have, Lily thought. Her time would be better spent focusing on completing the tablecloth. Lily completed one stitch after another and watched the body of the phoenix slowly come together. She let her thoughts float away like passing rainclouds.

'How is it?' Mak Kong asked as she walked into the room. She examined the cloth, studying the intricate stitching. Lily was quiet, waiting for Mak Kong's judgement. It felt to Lily like minutes passed in uncomfortable silence.

'Okay,' Mak Kong said after a while. She gave Lily a nod and marched off. Lily took a deep breath and continued sewing till her eyes and hands were tired. She packed up the sewing kit and folded the tablecloth neatly. When she left the room, she saw Ivy with Leng Jie in the main hall. Ivy was reading a book, looking engrossed. Lily caught Leng Jie's eye as she passed. She ascended the stairs to her room and walking past, she saw that Mak Kong's door was closed. Mak Kong was taking her afternoon nap. Lily entered her room and closed the door. She wondered at that moment if Mak Kong had always been the way she was now. What had she been like at Lily's age? Had she wanted to marry Pak Kong? The marriage had been arranged; Lily knew that much. Mak Kong was around the same age as Zhu Jie and Leng Jie but to Lily, she seemed older. Sometimes she wished she could find out what Mak Kong really thought of her. Mak Kong was not her mother, so Lily supposed it did not matter. Still, she would be lying to herself if she said she did not want Mak Kong's approval. But to live her life waiting for recognition that might never come was proving to be tiring. She would have to be content without knowing.

Lily sat down on her bed. She glanced around the room and then got up and went to her drawer. She opened it and took out a square pouch. The pouch contained her green jade bracelet. Her father had given it to her mother when she was pregnant with Lily. It was one of the five possessions Lily had been gifted by Mak Wee. She held onto it, feeling its cool surface with her fingertips. This was her gift from her parents. I was wanted, Lily said to herself. I was loved. Mak Kong had shared with her children and Lily about the story of an orphan child in Singapore whose mother had died at birth and whose father had died soon after. Pak Kong had also told them once about children in other countries who had lost their father in World War I. She could not remember the exact number he mentioned but there were tens of thousands of them. She was far more fortunate; her father had not died in a war and her mother was still alive. She would choose to be grateful for all she had. She slid the jade bracelet on her wrist. It fit snugly. I am wanted, Lily thought as her fingers ran down the bracelet. I am loved. Just as I am.

Chapter XVI

16th June 1940

Lily stood at her bedroom window, looking outside and waiting expectantly. Her neighbour across the road was getting married today. At any minute, the bridegroom's procession would arrive at the shophouse opposite theirs. She took to examining the shapes the clouds made in the sky and counting the number of men, women and children that passed by as she waited. Maybe Khalid would cycle past, Lily thought. She found herself dreaming of the next time she would see him. Then she heard the strains of melodious music from a distance. First, Lily saw an older man, perhaps in his fifties. She figured he had to be the pak chin dek, the ceremonial father. She spotted the groom, who was hard to miss. He was the tallest person in the group. He was all decked out in his wedding robes and flanked by two best men carrying umbrellas. Lily looked on in awe, admiring the intricately embroidered robe, which glistened in the sunlight. He looks like a king, Lily thought. How grand.

She spotted the musicians playing the serunai to herald the arrival of the groom, a page boy and four men in the procession carrying magenta lanterns adorned with deer and qilin. As she noticed the serious expressions on the groom's face, a contrast to the fanfare of the procession, Lily assumed that her neighbour was probably in a glum mood herself. Soon she would meet her husband, an almost-stranger, for the first time. Lily imagined being dressed in wedding wear herself, a long-sleeved tunic over a pleated skirt, with a fancy headdress and a black veil over her face. On her wedding day, she would finally know what it was like to be a queen for the day. Who would she marry, if she married at all? Would it be a stranger? Was there any chance at all it could be Khalid? Till the next time she saw him, she could write a letter to him about the wedding she had witnessed.

Lily walked away from the window and opened her drawer. She took out the biscuit tin where she kept Khalid's letters. At the very top of the tin lay the most recent letter Khalid had written to her.

Dear Lily,

How are you? I am looking forward to playing soccer tomorrow with my brother and neighbours. I love playing soccer. I miss playing at school with my team. A few of my teammates have enrolled in Raffles College and they are busy with schoolwork. I don't see them anymore.

I am still looking for a job. Hope to find one soon although I am trying to make the most of the leisure time I have now. What do you do like to do in your leisure time?

Yours Sincerely,
Khalid

Lily did not understand what 'Raffles College' or 'leisure time' meant. She was hoping that Charles or Ivy would help her translate. Maybe she could ask May Geok the next time she saw her. It suddenly dawned on her that the next time might be the last time she saw May Geok as an unmarried woman. May Geok's wedding was a week and a half away. Lily clutched the letter to her chest as if she was afraid to lose it. She feared that there would soon come a day she would no longer be able to hear from Khalid. Maybe their destinies did not lie with each other. She knew he was Muslim. She assumed that he would probably want to marry a Muslim girl. She had to marry a young Baba. This is just the way life is, Lily told herself as she pinched her arm and looked out of the window. Wu wei. Go with the flow. Lily folded the letter and put it safely back in its biscuit tin.

The next day, an elderly woman delivered a red and brown basket to the Kong house. Leng Jie collected it and brought it promptly to Mak Kong who was supervising the cooking of lunch in the kitchen.

Mak Kong nodded almost imperceptibly at Leng Jie. She opened the basket immediately and revealed something shaped like a triangle. Lily stopped slicing lady's fingers to watch. She wondered what that object was.

'Sa kapor siray,' Mak Kong said. Betel leaf and areca nut.

'Is it for May Geok's wedding?' Lily asked, overcome with curiosity.

Mak Kong looked up with raised eyebrows, narrowing her eyes at Lily. 'Yes, this is a token of invitation. I will attend The Opening of Marriage Day lunch and Pak Kong will attend the dinner.'

Lily slid the cut okra off the chopping board and into a bowl. Despite herself, her face fell into a grimace. Why can't I attend the lunch too? She thought. Was it only for married nyonyas? She glared at the okra. Turning her head, she caught Zhu Jie's eye. Zhu Jie gestured to the stove; her face soft with sympathy. Lily tried to muster a smile as she brought the bowl of okra to the stove. She braced herself as she lit up the stove. She thought cooking on the stove was quite unpleasant because the heat made her sweat. Lily fried the okra in the wok until they darkened in colour.

'Teck Soon is still unmarried,' Mak Kong mused as if the thought had just occurred to her. Lily could feel Mak Kong's eyes trained on her. Mak Kong stood at arm's length, so no oil splattered on her.

'Parents still looking for a match,' Mak Kong continued. Lily felt a lump of words she could not voice out settle uncomfortably in her throat. A feeling of deep trepidation flooded her body. She knew what was to come and the thought of being matchmade, of stepping into a future married to Teck Soon made her feel giddy with worry.

She simply did not want to be matchmade to Teck Soon. He reminded her of a pencil drawing that had been partially erased so it looked faint; Teck Soon had barely any eyebrows and no spark in his eyes. She vowed she would rather run away than marry someone she did not love. But how could she take control of her own destiny? Lily pondered. As overwhelming as her thoughts were, she had to focus on her task with Mak Kong's commanding presence behind her. Lily took the okra out of the wok and then added oil to it, turning the heat up.

'Wait till the oil starts giving out smoke,' Mak Kong said.

I know, Lily thought. Stir-fried okra was a new recipe they were trying out after their Indian neighbour in the next street had given them some to try the week before. Whenever they tried a new recipe, Lily could feel pressure from Mak Kong for the dish to turn out well. Lily added mustard seeds, lentils and curry stalks and moved the spatula briskly till the seeds popped. She put tomatoes in the wok and cooked them till they were soft. When she was done, she placed the dish on a plate and brought it to Mak Kong at the kitchen table. She stood there; her hands clasped in front of her as Mak Kong pierced a piece of okra with a fork.

'Okay,' Mak Kong said without looking at Lily. 'Boleh makan.' Lily pursed her lips together. She supposed 'edible' was the best compliment she could elicit from Mak Kong who seemed to reserve her words of praise for food that guests, or friends brought over. Lily sighed internally. She could not wait till it was time to feed Little because she hoped that she would see May Geok. May Geok would know what 'leisure time' meant. Lily wanted to know how May Geok was feeling with her wedding day coming up. Did she ever think of running away? An image of the two nyonyas running away from home came unbidden to Lily's mind. Where could they go? Lily wondered.

During lunch, Lily sat at the table, bringing one mouthful of food to another. She did usually say much at lunch to begin with but during this lunch, she did not utter a single word.

'I don't want to eat this,' Ivy said as Lily passed the plate of okra to her.

'Just try a bit,' Mak Kong said. 'One.'

Ivy made a face and took one piece of okra. She put it by the side of her plate and continued eating.

'You only eat the same things,' Charles said. 'No wonder you're so skinny like chichak kering.'

'You are skinny too,' Ivy retorted.

'Not as skinny as you.'

'Enough, children,' Mak Kong said, frowning.

Lily did not look up from her plate, lost in thought. Absent-mindedly, she put a piece of fish into her mouth. She bit into something sharp and spat it out immediately.

Everyone at the table turned to look at her.

'Fish bone,' Lily said, feeling an ache in her cheek that had nothing to do with the bone.

'Excuse me,' she said and rushed to the toilet. She splashed water on her face a few times and leaned against the sink. If she did not return to the table soon, she supposed Mak Kong might come to the toilet and ask if she was alright. Or maybe she would not. Lily stayed in the toilet and let herself cry till she felt a sense of relief. She felt a deep sense of foreboding; she would be matchmade with Teck Soon. Her life as she knew it would be over.

In the afternoon, Lily crouched on the five-foot way next to Little, who was barking at any stranger who walked past. She watched as a middle-aged man, who was walking hurriedly past, threw Little a glare. Little continued barking, unperturbed by the man's disdain.

'Ssshhh,' Lily whispered to Little, though she knew any attempt to silence him would be futile.

'Hi Lily. Hi Little,' May Geok said. Lily turned and saw May Geok standing in front of her, her brows knitted together like a cloud of gloom was hovering over her head. Little woofed at May Geok, who managed a small smile.

'What's wrong?' Lily asked, holding onto tightly to Little's leash as he barked at a passer-by.

'What else? Invitations were sent out today,' May Geok said. 'I'm in mourning.'

'Maybe it won't be so bad,' Lily said, wondering what she could say to make May Geok feel a bit better.

May Geok let out a snigger and shook her head. She stared at the five-foot way. 'What could be worse than marrying a man I don't know? I have to serve him every day.

I have to sleep next to him. I have to sleep with him.' She shuddered and put her arms around herself. Lily put her hand on May Geok's shoulder to give her a small pat. She had never thought of May Geok as a good friend; she was merely the beautiful neighbour she would encounter every so often. But at that moment, she realised it did not matter whether May Geok was a neighbour or a friend. She cared for May Geok as a fellow woman, a fellow nyonya, and she did not want her to be unhappy. Little seemed to realise May Geok was feeling down. He woofed at her as if to say 'Cheer up'. Lily loosened her grip on his leash as Little licked May Geok's big toe.

'That's ticklish, doggy,' May Geok said, moving her foot away.

'It is very difficult,' Lily said.

'Yes,' May Geok said. 'It is. I hope you don't suffer the same fate as me.'

'Do—do you think they would try to matchmake me with Teck Soon?' Lily asked.

May Geok paused and then looked at Lily in the eye. 'If your horoscope is a match. I know my parents are considering you,' May Geok said.

Lily bit her lip and stared at the mosaic tiles on the ground.

'Don't worry,' May Geok said. She fluffed up her permed bob. 'My parents are so busy with my wedding. They won't think of Teck Soon's until I'm married off. Then my second brother will be next.'

This thought did not comfort Lily at all. It seemed like only a matter of time before she was matchmade as well. Lily felt certain she would never feel as attracted to Teck Soon as she felt to Khalid. She remembered then what she wanted to ask May Geok.

'May Geok?' Lily began.

'Yes?' May Geok replied.

'What does leisure time mean?' Lily asked.

May Geok laughed darkly. Lily turned her head to look at her.

'It is something that we will not have much of once we are married,' May Geok said, her lip curling up. Lily stared at her, feeling confused. Little whimpered, demanding some attention. Lily bent down and stroked him slowly, letting his fur run through her fingers.

'It means the time you have for relaxation,' May Geok continued, looking at Lily's face. 'Why?'

Lily tilted her head. 'I saw it in Charles' book. Terima Kasih.'

'Sama-sama,' May Geok said. 'You know a nyonya's life ends when she turns twelve.'

'Not much leisure time,' Lily said.

'Exactly,' May Geok said.

The two nyonyas stood outside for a little while longer, with Little by their side, watching as people and vehicles passed them by. Lily thought about how it had been a short window of time where she played freely in the street with May Geok and other neighbours before each of them turned twelve. Then the door had slammed shut on Lily's freedom. She and May Geok had grown apart. Fleeting were their occasional meetings on the five-foot-way.

After a while, Lily asked May Geok if she could attend The Opening of Marriage Day lunch.

'I don't know,' May Geok said. 'My parents didn't even ask me who I wanted to invite.'

'Oh,' Lily whispered. Her face fell slightly as she stared at the geometric patterns on the five-foot way.

'If I have children, I won't matchmake them,' May Geok declared, her eyes blazing. 'Let them find love on their own, if they do.'

'Okay,' Lily said. She bit her lip, feeling hopeful. 'Good idea. If I get married, I think perhaps that's what I'd do too.'

May Geok nodded. 'But having no children with this man would be ideal,' May Geok said.

Lily noted how May Geok never called her fiancé by his name. She wondered what May Geok would call him after the wedding.

'I hope you'll have a happy married life, May Geok,' she said.

May Geok did not reply. She just stared out onto the street. Lily let the silence stretch out between them. May Geok seemed far away though she was standing right next to her.

Later, when she was in her room before dinner, Lily turned the heart-shaped cockle shell that she had brought home from the beach in her palm. Love, Lily thought. The shell reminded her of love. She closed her eyes and prayed that May Geok would be happy and would grow to love her husband. Then she prayed that she would marry Khalid and no one else. Part of her believed her prayers would be answered somehow although they seemed impossible, like a flight of fancy, and the other part of her felt resigned to accept her fate.

Teck Soon, Lily thought. I don't even like his name.

She put the shell back on her dresser before heading to the toilet to wash up for dinner.

Chapter XVII

12th July 1940

Khalid glanced at his watch as he watched a bus halt to a stop in front of him. A few commuters streamed out. Khalid did not seem to notice any of them. For a few weeks, he had been thinking about how he had been courting Dorothy. He had wanted to take her out on dates. Khalid wondered. But now here he was on the verge of breaking up with her. Except for Ibrahim, he did not know anyone who had broken up with a girl before, so he did not have anyone to turn to for advice. I guess I should have asked Ibrahim, Khalid thought, scratching his nose as a fly appeared in front of it. Desperate times, desperate measures. He swatted the fly away with his hand.

Maybe I'll say, 'We can't see each other anymore,' Khalid thought. He did not know what he should say in response if Dorothy asked for a reason why he wanted to stop dating her. He could not very well say, 'You ask too many questions' or 'I don't think we really understand each other.' Maybe he could offer a vague but true excuse like he wanted to focus on looking for a job. His thoughts wandered to his job search, which had proved to be fruitless thus far. He had been for two interviews, one as a clerk for the Singapore Improvement Trust and another as a clerk at the Oversea-Chinese Banking Corporation but had received no job offers.

'What do these people want?' Pak Ambi had asked a few days ago. 'Grade I certificate not good enough, is it?'

'Some job experience,' Ibrahim had answered.

Khalid was worried but Pak Ambi had assured him he would find a job soon. 'Job will come,' Pak Ambi said as if a job was a person who would visit Khalid soon. Khalid chuckled internally, thinking of Pak Ambi's complacency about employment. Pak Ambi had claimed to have quit another driving job just last week.

He glanced over at the white-uniformed traffic marshal at the road junction, his rattan wings directing the flow of traffic.

'Hey!' Dorothy said just then.

Khalid turned to his right and was surprised to see Dorothy standing there in her school uniform of navy pinafore and white blouse. She waved at him cheerfully. Khalid tried to gulp down his nervousness.

'Where did you come from?' Khalid asked as he sat up straight.

'I stopped at the bus stop before this one. Wanted to talk to my classmate a bit more,' Dorothy said. She took off her backpack and sat down next to Khalid at the bus stop, smoothing down the pleats of her uniform as she did so.

'Oh,' Khalid said. 'That's nice.

'So, what did you do today?' Dorothy asked, shielding her face from the sun with her hand.

'Looked for jobs,' Khalid said.

'Found anything?' Dorothy asked, an eager look on her face.

'No, not really,' Khalid shook his head and ran his fingers through his hair, expecting to find more hair. He had gone for a haircut a few days ago and was not used to his trim cut yet.

'You should apply to Raffles College,' Dorothy said, moving her fingers down the pleats of her pinafore as if to iron them out.

'Trying to find a job first,' Khalid breathed out. He and Dorothy seemed to have the same conversation every few days. He tried to summon the courage to tell Dorothy what he wanted to say at the bus stop. But as another bus dragged past, Khalid thought it might be better if they took a walk.

'Can we take a walk?' Khalid asked. He seemed to notice the humidity in the air more than usual.

'Okay,' Dorothy said. 'Are you okay?'

'Yes,' Khalid said. He tugged his collar away from his neck, where it had been stuck with sweat.

'You look strange,' Dorothy said, peering at Khalid. 'Are you sick?'

'I—I'm fine,' Khalid said without looking at Dorothy. 'How was school?'

Dorothy proceeded to regale Khalid with what she learnt that day and the gossip she had exchanged with her friends. Khalid tried to listen as best he could though his mind was preoccupied with how to break up with Dorothy. As he was about to speak, he espied Ibrahim walking towards them. Ibrahim darted behind a rickshaw and jogged towards them, clutching his briefcase. Khalid sighed, cursing his bad luck.

'What?' Dorothy asked.

'My brother,' Khalid said as Ibrahim saluted him. Frowning, Khalid did not salute back; he wished Ibrahim would leave them alone.

'Hello!' Ibrahim said, his eyes dancing with mischief. 'You must be Dorothy.'

How did he find out Dorothy's name? Khalid wondered. Did one of my friends tell him? Was it Samad?

'You must be Ibrahim,' Dorothy said, grinning as she flipped her braid behind her.

'Yes,' Ibrahim said. 'Khalid's older, taller, more handsome brother.'

Dorothy giggled, looking delighted, as Khalid turned his head to the side to roll his eyes. He watched Dorothy and Ibrahim chatting and laughing together as if they were old friends. There goes my plan to break up today, he thought. He folded his arms across his chest and waited for a pause in the conversation. He turned his head slightly and saw a rickshaw being tugged by with a British couple in it, its rickshaw puller shirtless and bare-footed. Hard work for 60 cents a day, Khalid frowned. He thought about how the British and locals who worked in comfortable offices were paid well while labourers toiled under the blistering sun for a pittance.

When he turned back to face Dorothy and Ibrahim, they were still talking. He tried to stop himself from rolling his eyes as Ibrahim grinned at Dorothy with a twinkle in his eye.

'Sorry,' Khalid interrupted. 'I have to walk Dorothy home.'

Dorothy looked up at him, surprised but Ibrahim shrugged nonchalantly.

'See you around, Dorothy,' he said.

'Oh, you too, Ibrahim,' Dorothy replied. She hurried after Khalid who had already started walking off.

'What's wrong?' Dorothy asked. 'You seem to be in a bad mood.'

Khalid shook his head vigorously. 'I'm fine.'

'People are never fine when they say they are,' Dorothy observed.

'That's not always true,' Khalid said. As Dorothy flipped her ponytail over her shoulder, he thought that she seemed a tad annoyed with him. Was it because he had interrupted her conversation with Ibrahim that she was enjoying? He sighed and decided that he would have to postpone letting Dorothy know that he could not see her anymore. Lily came to his mind just then. What was Lily doing at that very moment? Khalid wondered.

* * *

Lily had just about given up on asking Mak Wee why she had been given away to the Kongs. She could never seem to get Mak Wee alone for this question that she did not wish to have other family members gathered around for. So, she assured herself that there was no truth lurking behind the reason she had been told. Mak Kong simply could not care for her at that time.

Irene had warmed up considerably since her first visit to the Kongs. Now she did not have to be prompted to play with Ivy. They played five stones, hopscotch and congkak. Today, they were just sitting on the floor and talking. Ivy was sharing a story Chek Chuan had told her about a young girl who lived in a rainforest in Malacca. This elicited 'oohs' and 'aahs' from Irene. Lily watched them play as she popped pineapple tarts into her mouth. The pineapple tarts had been made by Mak Wee. Lily thought they tasted better than the ones she had made previously with the majies. Lily wondered what the difference in the recipe was.

'It is time for Lily to get married, Tachi,' Mak Kong was saying. Lily snapped to attention. She had assumed that she would not be privy to the conversation she had been dreading but here it was about to happen right in front of her.

Mak Wee glanced at Lily but did not say anything. Lily tried to read the expression on Mak Wee's face. Was it reluctance, disinterest or preoccupation with another matter?

'She is seventeen,' Mak Kong continued. Mak Wee jerked her head slightly.

Mak Kong pressed on. She sniffed and said, 'The horoscope of Teck Soon and Lily is a match. If you agree, I can tell them to proceed.'

Still Mak Wee was silent. Lily wanted to scream 'No!' but she too kept silent. What had been the point of her letters to Khalid? She would have to marry Teck Soon. She stared at Mak Wee, her eyes wide and pleading. But Mak Wee's attention seemed to be focused on her hands.

'Teck Soon comes from a good family. He hopes to become a dentist in future,' Mak Kong said. This was news to Lily. If he is studying, he should just focus on that, she wanted to say. Teck Soon was only a year older than her. She did not think he was ready for marriage; what did he know about being a husband? How were Babas prepared for their marriage? Nyonyas had to learn so much just to be regarded as a prospective wife and daughter-in-law. Lily pictured herself making a kasut manek in preparation for her wedding to Teck Soon. The thought made her feel sick to her stomach.

'I can arrange a meeting with Teck Soon's parents,' Mak Kong continued. 'If you're agreeable to it, Tachi.'

'Okay, Adek,' Mak Wee finally agreed after a long pause. She sat still, her face like a dark cloud, as she stared at her palms.

Lily dug her fingernails into her palm, growing angrier and more frustrated that neither Mak Wee nor Mak Kong seemed to care about what she wanted when it was her marriage and future they were discussing. Look at me! She wanted to scream at Mak Wee. I'm your daughter. Please look at me, Mak. Please.

Lily wanted to reach out and kneel before Mak Wee to beseech her to say something to stop the marriage from proceeding. But Mak Wee did not look up at Lily. She was now staring at a spot on the floor in front of her.

I'll just have to run away then, Lily decided. There was no other choice. But where could she go?

That night, Lily's mind drifted from thoughts of her childhood to thoughts of her father and mother to thoughts of her future. When she was little, Lily used to wish her Mak Wee would come for her. She would sit by the window of her room and imagine the ways it would happen. Maybe one day, Mak Wee would show up after lunch, her grim, steely resolve broken and dissolve into tears. She would tell the Kongs that she wanted Lily back. After all, Lily was her only child. Or she would appear early in the morning when the rest of the house was asleep, wake Lily up and embrace Lily. Hold her like she had never been been held. All the desire, all the hope and then inevitably, all the disappointment Lily felt when she woke up and realised, she was still in the same bed in the Kong household. Nothing had changed. She was no one's child, it seemed. She belonged to herself. But how Lily had longed and still longed to belong to someone else who loved her just as much she loved them.

Lily sighed and took her pillow from underneath her head. She hugged it as if it was a real person she could lean on. After a while, she let go of the pillow and rolled onto her back. Lily told herself to stop with the self-pity because it was fruitless. Wu wei, she reminded herself. Follow the simple course of nature and accept her fate.

Chapter XVIII

10th August 1940

Khalid padded back to his room, treading carefully so as not to wake up the neighbours. All appeared still in their shared quarters. All doors were closed; Khalid guessed the families in them were either out, winding down for the day or already asleep. His shoulders slumped, as he suddenly felt the exhaustion from the events of the day. He had gone for another job interview, a temporary administrative position with Braddell Brothers, an independent law practice. The job advertisement had listed out the requirements: 1) A knowledge of King's English essential, 2) Below 30 years of age, 3) Education Senior Cambridge, and 4) Hardworking and organised.

Khalid believed he had all those qualities, especially organised. He was naturally neat, ordered and efficient, not to mention, detailed. He always kept his belongings in the same place every day at 90-degree right angles to the table and kept meticulous accounts of chap ji kee bets for Pak Ambi. Khalid was confident of getting the job. After the interview, however, while running after the bus, he fell down and dropped his wallet on the ground. He rushed home to change then headed to the Kongs for his tutoring session with Charles. He had hoped that Lily would come out to serve the tea, but he did not see her that day. When he met Dorothy afterwards, he finally confessed to her that he wanted to stop seeing her. Dorothy was initially confused but then she seemed to grow bigger in front of Khalid as she seethed with anger, baring her teeth.

'Why?' Dorothy asked, demanding a reason for the breakup.

'I don't think we're compatible,' Khalid said.

'Is there someone else?' she asked. Khalid shook his head as vigorously as he could, determined not to reveal a thing about Lily. He knew that telling Dorothy about Lily would only make her angrier.

'No,' Khalid had insisted several times after she pressed him for an answer. He did not want Dorothy to become even more angry with him.

Finally, Dorothy had stormed off in a fury, calling Khalid names like 'coward' and 'child'.

But now as he was nearing his room, Khalid wondered if there was someone else. Did he like Lily? he wondered. He certainly looked forward to receiving her letters each week and enjoyed writing letters to her. His History teacher Mr Bayliss had taught their class at the start of the year when they were studying the Regency era of British history that to correspond was to build a commitment towards matrimony. Was that the direction he and Lily were headed towards? Last week, he had felt concerned when she said she did not feel well. He felt immediate relief when this week, her letter said she had had a slight cold but was now better. Since they had started corresponding, his curiosity was piqued about what her life was like beyond the cooking, embroidery, beadwork and other chores. She had never attended school. Did she feel stifled or suffocated? Was she unhappy?

When he was with Dorothy on a movie date, he found himself thinking sometimes of Lily. Lily who had never been to a movie theatre, let alone the Alhambra. Lily who had never seen a movie before. He pictured himself at the Alhambra with Lily; how everything there would seem new to her, things he took for granted like the live orchestra. Still, Khalid tried to convince himself that none of this meant he had romantic feelings for Lily. He did not want to be one of those men, if he could consider himself a man now, who strung a woman along with no intention of committing to her. Had he done that with Dorothy by taking her out on dates? Khalid felt steeped in a guilt that weighed him down.

Lost in his thoughts, Khalid leaned against the wall outside of Samad's room. He stood there for a while, reflecting on his feelings and actions. Samad's door swung open just then and Samad strolled out.

'Hey anak jerung,' Samad said when he spotted Khalid.

'Hi Samad,' Khalid said as he stood up straight.

'You okay?' Samad said, raising an eyebrow. 'Penat?'

Khalid took in the bemused expression on Samad's face.

'I finally broke up with Dorothy,' Khalid said softly.

'Ohhh,' Samad said. 'She cried?'

'No, she didn't cry,' Khalid said.

'Then okay, right?' Samad said. 'If she cried, then it's bad.'

Khalid almost chuckled at Samad's take on the situation. 'I guess so.'

'Going to the toilet,' Samad said. 'Don't think so much.'

Khalid watched as Samad rushed to the toilet. Yes, he thought. It would be good not to think too much. He tried to open the door to his room. To his surprise, it was locked. After fishing out the key from the pocket of his backpack, Khalid opened the door. He glanced around the empty room, feeling glad that neither Pak Ambi nor Ibrahim were there. He was not in the mood to converse with either of them. Khalid decided he would wash up and head to bed earlier than usual.

* * *

'On On Saturday, Mrs Chong will come to look at you,' Mak Kong informed Lily that morning before breakfast.

Lily frowned, her face falling into a sulk she was sure was reminiscent of Mak Wee's. She couldn't help herself as she felt her hands tremble.

'Why?' Mak Kong asked, peering closely at Lily. 'What's the matter?'

Surprised that Mak Kong had noticed her discomfort, Lily paused then heard herself saying the words, 'I—I don't want to marry Teck Soon.'

'Teck Soon is a nice boy. From a good family,' Mak Kong said. She sniffed and examined her fingernails. There was an air of finality to the discussion that Lily felt she could not say anything in response to.

Lily fixed her gaze on a spot on the floor. I want to marry Khalid, she wanted to say. But she knew that there was no way she could ever tell Mak Kong that. Without even asking, she knew that Mak Kong would not approve of Khalid because he was Indian Muslim. He was good enough to be her son's tutor but not Lily's husband. Lily could hear Mak Kong's criticisms of Khalid's family now, delivered in a sharp tone that Lily imagined piercing into her heart. His parents were poor and divorced and he had a father who works as a collector for chap ji kee, never mind that Mak Kong herself was an avid chap ji kee gambler.

Lily stood in front of Mak Kong and waited, not daring to move or say anything. Unexpectedly, Mak Kong's face softened at that moment. 'Don't worry,' she said. She stood up and glided away, leaving Lily to contemplate how quickly the matchmaking was proceeding.

Should I not be free to choose who I want to marry? Lily thought, as anger bubbled up inside her. It is my life and happiness. But nyonyas were supposed to matchmade.

Lily shuffled her feet into the kitchen and stared at the scene around her. Zhu Jie was peeling potatoes. Lily watched the potato skin come off with the knife. At the sink, Leng Jie was washing vegetables. Ah Huat was grasping a fish firmly by its tail and scraping away the scales. Lily watched the knife moving quickly from the tail to the head of the fish. She did not know how she was going to help with the cooking today when she was in a daze, willing time to stand still. But the world around her moved along anyway, going about its usual activity, seemingly unaware of her inner turmoil. Lily felt like she was about to cry.

'Stop!' Lily wanted to scream. 'Stop and help me get out of this match!'

As if in a daze, she approached Zhu Jie, feeling like she could not take another breath.

'Zhu Jie,' she began. Zhu Jie looked up at Lily and handed her a freshly peeled potato as if to say not to worry.

'Help me peel potato,' Zhu Jie whispered. 'Anything can happen. Future take care of itself.'

With both hands, Zhu Jie held the potato out to Lily and looked deep into her eyes. Lily found her breath again. After a moment of hesitation, Lily took the potato. She used the knife to peel the potato skin off, her mind lost in thoughts of how to escape her predicament. Zhu Jie interrupted her with a warning, 'Careful. Finger can slice!' Lily took a deep breath to compose herself then she resumed slicing the potato slowly. If the world would not stop, she had no choice but to take part in it.

* * *

Khalid started work at Braddell Brothers on a Monday morning. He arrived at their office before nine in the morning to find the office manager, Mr Ong, already there waiting for him. Mr Ong was a trim, middle-aged man with a receding hairline. He's even shorter than me, Khalid thought as his eyes settled on Mr Ong's hairline.

'Good morning, Mr Ong,' Khalid said when he reached Mr Ong's desk.

Mr Ong looked up from the thick file in front of him. 'Oh yes, good morning, Khalid,' Mr Ong said. 'Today is your first day.'

'Yes,' Khalid said, clutching onto the new briefcase Pak Ambi had bought for him.

'I will give you a tour,' Mr Ong said. 'Just give me a few minutes.'

'Okay,' Khalid agreed. He stood there, feeling awkward as he wondered what he should do for the next couple of minutes. He glanced around the office. It looked the same as the day of his interview, except that this morning it was still empty. There were about eleven other oak desks and chairs in open cubicles and a kitchen at the other end of the office with a water dispenser, a fridge and a sink. There were four doors on the perimeter, with shiny name plates on them. Khalid supposed they belonged to the bosses. He read the name on one of them: John Braddell. At that moment, a tall British man entered the office.

Mr Ong stood up immediately, almost spilling the water in his glass. 'Good morning, Mr Braddell,' he said.

'Good morning, Ong,' Mr Braddell said.

'Is this our new hire?' Mr Braddell asked, as he gave Khalid a small nod.

'Oh yes, yes it is,' Mr Ong said, turning his head slightly to face Khalid. 'His name is Khalid.'

Khalid tried to smile but his nerves overcame him and his lips twisted into a grim line instead. Mr Braddell seemed not to notice as he strode into his office.

'Next time you see Mr Braddell, greet him,' Mr Ong said, closing his file.

'Okay, I will. I'm sorry,' Khalid said, as he made a mental note to greet Mr Braddell.

'Okay, I'll give you a tour now,' Mr Ong said.

Mr Ong brought him around the office, pointing out where the filing cabinets were.

'Do not leave files lying around,' Mr Ong said, his hands gesturing to the cabinet. 'After you are done filing, return the files to the cabinet. Understand?'

'Yes, Mr Ong,' Khalid said, wondering how come Mr Ong could leave the file on his desk if that was the case.

'This is your desk,' Mr Ong said as he reached a desk at the corner of the office. 'You can sit now. I'll give you documents to file in a moment.'

Khalid sat down and put his briefcase on his table. He had told Pak Ambi that he did not need a briefcase, but Pak Ambi had insisted on buying one for him anyway.

'Good to look professional you know,' Pak Ambi had said.

For the rest of the day, Khalid filed law documents into file after file, making sure he returned them to the cabinet when he was done. It was dull work, but he was thankful he had a job. He would be steadfast in carrying out his duties at this job. Besides, Khalid thought, it kept his mind busy from other matters that only muddled his mind and more specifically, his heart.

In the evening at home, Khalid was resting after his first uneventful day at work. He decided to write a letter to Lily. He took his pen and paper from the drawer. He thought for a long time before he started to write.

Dear Lily,
Would you like to go on a date with me?

Khalid read what he had just written down on the paper. This felt very different from asking Dorothy to a movie. Dorothy had freedom of movement, but Lily did not. If I want to ask Lily out, it would be proper to ask Mak Kong or Mak Wee for permission first, Khalid thought. Young nyonyas are not permitted to date. But as far as he knew, young nyonyas did not write letters to boys they were not acquainted with either. He thought that somehow Lily would not appreciate him asking Mak Kong if he could take her on a date. As for asking Mak Kong, that was even more of a foolish notion. Maybe he would be fired from his job as Charles' tutor. So, Khalid continued writing the letter. He acknowledged that Lily might not be able to go out with her, but he thought he would try asking anyway. He ended the letter with three words he considered over and over again before he wrote them down—'I like you, Lily.' I like you a lot, he thought.

He did not know what he was doing apart from following his heart. Maybe he was being foolish. If it was unlikely that dating Dorothy could last, perhaps it was even more unlikely that he and Lily could go out on a date. He sighed. But as Coach Choo had said before, 'You miss all the chances you don't take, team' so he had to try. Khalid folded up the note into the shape of a heart. He felt as if his own heart was leaping over a high wall. Recognising this emotion as hope and excitement, he told himself to calm down and not to have any expectations. He would have to wait till Saturday to give Lily the note. Ever since he started work at Braddell Brothers, he had to change the day he gave tuition to Charles.

Khalid heard Pak Ambi's voice down the hallway. Swiftly, he put the note in his pocket. He could hear Pak Ambi talking about the Battle of Britain, which had started in July. He did not know the audience for Pak Ambi's monologue because they seemed silent. Khalid continued to listen in. A few minutes later, Ibrahim entered the room, shirtless with his shorts on and drying his hair with a towel. Khalid flipped open the newspaper and continued reading an article proclaiming the readiness of the British to receive German invaders.

'Britain is ready!' Ibrahim said, reading over Khalid's shoulder. 'I hope so.'

Pak Ambi appeared at the doorway just then. 'So many people starving in Europe!' he said, shaking his head. 'Eighteen million. We are very lucky.'

Khalid wondered what the rest of the article said. He had seen Pak Ambi read just headlines of articles and then expound on the matter as if he had swallowed a textbook.

'But Germany won't surrender,' Pak Ambi continued. 'Hitler won't be happy till he wins the war. He will destroy Britain. Wait and see.'

Pak Ambi paused, waiting for a reaction from his sons. Ibrahim nodded solemnly. Khalid grimaced at the thought of Britain being destroyed. Pak Ambi resumed talking.

If only you had studied harder in school, Khalid thought to himself. He was sure that Pak Ambi had missed his calling to be a teacher or politician. Even with the inevitability of war coming to Singapore and changing life as they knew it, Khalid was determined to work hard at his job. He wanted to have a career as much as Pak Ambi did not want him to follow in his footsteps. What the parent cannot achieve, the child must, Khalid thought, wondering where he had heard that saying from. Probably one of my teachers, he decided. Already he was starting to forget not what his teachers had taught him but which saying could be attributed to which teacher unless the teacher was very memorable and unique. He did not want the memories of Raffles Institution to fade in his mind with time. Maybe I should visit soon, Khalid mused. Ask some of the boys along too.

Part III

Chapter XIX

5th September 1940

Lily could not believe it. Khalid had asked her out on a date with a heart-shaped note. To be sure, she did not know what the word 'date' meant. But he had asked her out for a meal, so she gathered that that had the same meaning as 'date'. Whatever the word meant, Lily thought it was most exciting but also very scary. How could she manage to sneak out to meet him? It would be better to meet at night when they were less likely to be seen. But was it dangerous to do so? Lily wondered. Could she trust Khalid? She wanted to trust him very much. She had to take a leap of faith.

Perhaps she would have to wait till the Kongs were out of the house. What if that never happened? Lily thought. She felt afraid that she might not ever be able to see Khalid out of the house. If she wanted to run away though, which required a great deal of gumption, then she could be brave enough to sneak out. She read the note again, relishing in every single word written by Khalid.

She was sure this was the best day of her life. She twirled around her room, feeling younger and at the same, older, than she had ever felt. Lily wished she could sing a dondang sayang like Chek Chuan. As she hummed the only tune she knew, she got ready to take her bath before dinner. She could not wait to show Zhu Jie her note. It was

Zhu Jie who had brought it to her, with glee in her eyes, after Khalid had gone home that day. Zhu Jie was convinced that this note, shaped differently from the ones before it, which had been squares, surely held something promising inside. But Lily had not dared to hope lest she be disappointed. She wanted to tell Zhu Jie that she was right. This note was different; it held a question that could be the start of a very different future than the one that had been planned for her.

After dinner, when she was sure Mak Kong and Pak Kong were in their room, Lily quickly showed Zhu Jie the note. Zhu Jie's eyes widened and she clapped her hands together.

'But how?' Lily asked.

'We make plan,' Zhu Jie said.

'A plan?' Lily asked.

'Yes, we think,' Zhu Jie went on. 'Tomorrow, I tell you.'

Lily took a deep breath. 'Okay.' She hoped that Zhu Jie could think of a fool proof plan. Leng Jie tiptoed into the kitchen then, looking morose as usual. Lily cast a furtive glance at her.

Had she been eavesdropping? Lily worried. Without a word, Leng Jie took a seat at the kitchen table. She sighed softly as she stretched out her feet in front of her. Lily frowned as she looked at Leng Jie. There was more she wanted to say that could not be said in front of Leng Jie. As quiet as Leng Jie was, Lily did not trust that Leng Jie would not carry stories back to Mak Kong.

'Bye Leng Jie,' Zhu Jie said. 'Take rest.'

Lily left the kitchen together with Zhu Jie and bid her goodbye as Zhu Jie was leaving the home to return to her rented room. If only I could go with her again, Lily found herself thinking. Then we could plan together.

Lily resigned herself to returning to her own room for the night. Adventures rarely happened in her life so she would seize every opportunity that presented itself, starting with the date with Khalid. Certain she would find it hard to sleep that night, she lingered in the hall a little while longer. She figured that soon Chek Chuan would be home. It seemed as if he had stopped drinking last month but he still traipsed home late, often after dinner. Mak Kong had complained that she bet he had just exchanged one vice for another one.

'Gambling or smoking,' Mak Kong scoffed. 'Ya, when boys are pampered, they grow up to be irresponsible men.' Lily thought that it was strange that Mak Kong would have said that when she certainly thought that Charles himself was spoiled. He did not have to lift a finger around the house. But Lily thought that Mak Kong was confident in her child-raising abilities, the way she spoke about Charles to her friends when they were visiting to play Cherki last week.

'Charles will grow up to be a responsible man,' Mak Kong had said.

Lily certainly hoped that that would be the case. She wanted Charles to succeed in life and become a good man in the future.

* * *

Khalid woke up around six in the morning to use the toilet. He bumped into the night soil carrier changing the oval bucket in the toilet. He felt sorry for the man, having to touch the dirty soiled bucket. When he was in primary school, he remembered that Pak Ambi would use the night soil carrier as an example of an occupation he would have to do should he fail at school.

'You see ah, if you don't study hard, you will have to become a night soil man,' Pak Ambi said. 'Or a Chinese coolie.'

Recollecting the memory now, he realised how funny it was. He could never be a Chinese coolie because he was not Chinese in the first place. But they were the backbone of Singapore's labour force according to Mr Braddell, who seemed to have great respect for them.

The night soil carrier trudged past Khalid, balancing two iron buckets with a pole on his shoulder. Khalid refrained from covering his nose, not wanting to offend the man. Instead, he held his breath but he got a whiff of the faeces left behind by one of his neighbours. He made a beeline to the toilet to relieve himself. When he was done, he came out to find Ibrahim standing outside.

'Why you take so long?' Ibrahim grumbled.

'Sorry,' Khalid replied. He knew Ibrahim was in a bad mood with the date of his impending marriage looming over him. Pak Ambi and Mak Aisha had met with Ibrahim's future parents-in-law to discuss the wedding. Ibrahim met his future wife that day.

'Can't stay married but can get along well enough to arrange my wedding,' Ibrahim complained to Khalid.

After the meeting, Ibrahim returned home, sulking. 'Pretty, fair, short, quiet' had been his report to Khalid. He finally confided in Khalid that afternoon that he had been dating a Chinese girl whom he really liked. Although the wedding was now only two months away, he was still dating the Chinese girl. When Khalid had suggested that he end things with the girl, Ibrahim had practically shouted, asking him to mind his own business.

Khalid shuffled back to his room to sleep. By the time he awoke, it was past eight in the morning. Without making his bed, he rushed to get ready for work. Pak Ambi was still sound asleep and snoring but Ibrahim had left for work. Could have woken me up, Khalid thought. He could not be late for work. Later that night, he would be meeting Lily for dinner so he would have to leave the office on time. He had been surprised when Lily had suggested dinner and not lunch. Part of Khalid wondered whether Lily would show up to the date. He knew how difficult it would be for her to leave the house. I guess I'll find out later, he thought as he dashed downstairs.

Lily put on a floral dress, one of two dresses she owned, and coiled her hair up into a bun. She stared at her reflection in the mirror. She looked different in a dress, younger and more modern. Afraid she would lose her nerve, she took a deep breath and peeked out of her room. She could see that the other doors were closed except Chek Chuan's; she knew Mak Kong, Pak Kong, Charles and Ivy were usually in their rooms at this time of night. Lily stepped outside her room and closed the door behind her.

Lily tiptoed down the stairs. It seemed as if there were more steps than on other days. She had counted them before. Twenty-three steps from her room to the first floor. Each step made her heart thud furiously. When her feet touched the cool tiles of the floor on the first level, Lily fled, walking as fast as she could and hoping that she did not bump into Chek Chuan on the way out. There would be no good reason she could come up with for being dressed differently.

It was five minutes to seven-thirty at night when she snuck out of the house, convinced that if she was back by eight-thirty, no one would miss her. Zhu Jie said she would stay later than usual at the Kongs and keep a look-out. She wished that she could have had a conversation with Zhu Jie but there was simply no time. She stood there on the five-foot way, waiting for Khalid. Then she saw him walking towards her, dressed in a shirt tucked into his pants. Lily felt so nervous that she thought she might faint.

'Hello Lily,' Khalid said when he reached her.

Lily stood there, gaping at him a little. She gulped. Khalid was actually right in front of her. She took in his warm brown skin, his tightly curled hair and his eyes. These were eyes she could trust. Lily felt that with every fibre of her being.

'Shall we go?' Khalid asked, gazing into Lily's eyes though he did not take a step forward towards her.

'Yes,' Lily whispered.

They walked off silently till they reached the end of the road. Lily tried to find something to say while Khalid wondered he could do to make her feel more comfortable. He tried to keep at least two hands' spacing between them.

'Have you had dinner?' Khalid asked. He had wondered about that, if Lily could avoid eating dinner at home.

'No,' Lily said. In fact, she had had dinner at home to evade suspicion but she did not want to let Khalid know that.

'What do you want to have for dinner?' Khalid asked.

'Mm,' Lily said. 'I don't know.'

'Indian food?' Khalid suggested.

Lily had never eaten Indian food in her life. What did it taste like? she wondered as she bit her tongue.

'Okay,' Lily said.

They walked to another street till they reached a small restaurant.

'This place is good,' Khalid said.

Lily looked at the green signboard that spelled out 'Mumtaz Mahal Restaurant'. She read each letter one by one.

Khalid stood there and waited. Lily looked over at him. 'Mumtaz Mahal,' she said.

Khalid nodded. 'Yes,' he said. 'Do you know the last word?'

Lily stopped and read it out. 'Rest . . . '

'Restaurant,' Khalid said. 'Ini tempat makan.'

Lily nodded, her breath catching in her throat.

A restaurant, she thought. She followed Khalid in. There were two other couples and a family in the modestly decorated interior of the restaurant. The walls were a burnt orange and tinged with a red that made Lily feel even more hungry than she already was.

They sat down at a table and a waiter promptly brought two menus over. Lily kept her head bent. She felt like everyone should be staring at her but no one was. She wondered if any of these people knew the Kongs. Would someone see her and report that she was out on a date with Khalid? Lily worried as she wrung her hands. Then she realised she was being silly. Even if they knew the Kongs, they would not recognise her unless they had been to the house.

'Do you like Indian food?' Khalid asked.

'I don't know,' Lily said.

'Can you handle spicy food?' Khalid asked after a few seconds.

'Yes,' Lily replied. 'I can.'

'Oh good. Me too,' Khalid said. 'Butter chicken?'

Lily imagined a creamy chicken dish cooked in a lot of butter. She loved eating butter with her bread in the morning. It tasted divine.

'It's like a curry,' Khalid explained.

'Oh, I see,' Lily said.

'Naan is like a bread that is flat but fluffy,' Khalid said.

'Okay,' Lily said. She did not know what to say next. Her hands trembled a little on her lap. She assumed Khalid wanted to order naan. She started looking through the menu. Pra-ta, she read. She had eaten that before when Pak Kong brought home plain prata for everyone in the family.

'So, we'll order naan and butter chicken. What about vegetables?' Khalid asked.

'Um,' Lily said. She thought Khalid must find her utterly boring.

'Aloo gobi is potatoes and cauliflower and some spices,' Khalid said. 'I'm not sure what they are exactly.'

Lily smiled slightly, tilting her head to the side. 'You don't cook,' she said.

'No,' Khalid said. 'But I like to eat.'

At that moment, Lily thought about what Mak Kong had said once in the kitchen as she fanned herself. 'Makanan itu jalanan ke hati lelaki,' she smirked. 'Pak Kong suka makan.' Food is the way to a man's heart, Lily thought. One day, she would cook every day for Khalid. He was the only man she wanted to be with and marry, Lily mused. What should I say next? she wondered. She had no idea what to say. Khalid is going to think I'm not good company, Lily thought. She wondered what other girls said when they were out on dates with boys. What did Mak Kong and Pak Kong talk about when they were alone?

The waiter came to their table. Lily looked at the waiter's belly protruding under his singlet. With his heavily lidded eyes, he had a sleepy look about him. Lily half-expected the waiter to yawn in front of them. The next second, he did, as he brushed the back of his hand over his mouth. Lily stifled a giggle.

'One butter chicken, two naan and one aloo gobi,' Khalid said.

'Drinks?' the waiter asked.

'Oh yes,' Khalid said. He glanced at Lily.

'What do you feel like drinking?' he asked.

'Tea?' Lily said.

'You like tea too?' Khalid asked.

'Yes,' Lily said. She really liked drinking tea.

Khalid placed the order and the waiter lumbered away from the table.

'So,' Khalid began. 'How did you manage to come out tonight?'

'Mak Kong doesn't know,' Lily confessed, as she worried if Khalid would think she was too forward and bold for a young nyonya. I should not have snuck out of the house, Lily thought as guilt pricked her.

'It is a secret,' Khalid replied.

'Yes,' Lily said. 'A secret.' She remembered at that moment that she would have to be back by eight-thirty.

'I have to be back soon,' she blurted out.

'What time?' Khalid asked.

'Eight-thirty,' Lily admitted.

'That's forty-five more minutes more,' Khalid said, glancing at his watch. Lily almost sighed in relief. There's still time, she thought. Calm down.

Soon, the waiter brought the food to the table. Lily peered at the bowl of butter chicken. She used the common spoon to take a spoonful and put it into her plate. Then she looked over at Khalid. He was eating the naan with some of the orange butter chicken gravy with a spoon and fork. He looked up at Lily and swallowed the food in his mouth. Lily looked at some gravy dripped down his mouth. Khalid wiped it away with the back of his hand.

'It's better if we eat with our hands,' Khalid said.

'At home, we eat with hands,' Lily said.

'Me too,' Khalid said. Their eyes met for a moment, and Khalid thought he had never felt so comfortable with someone. It's like I've known her in a past life, he thought. Or is it my future one?

'There is a sink here,' Khalid said, gesturing with his thumb to the back of the restaurant. 'We can wash our hands.'

'Okay,' Lily said. They got up from the table and walked to the sink, Lily feeling self-conscious as she walked past the tables of other patrons. She was curious what the dishes on their tables were but she tried her best to refrain from looking.

Back at their table, Khalid and Lily tore the naan with their hands and dipped it into the butter chicken gravy. It is delicious, Lily thought, admiring the rich and smooth texture of the butter chicken gravy and wondering if she could recreate it in the Kongs' kitchen. She was sure she tasted tomatoes and turmeric in the gravy. The naan itself was light and fluffy.

'Do you want to try the aloo gobi?' Khalid asked, passing the plate to Lily.

'Oh yes,' Lily said. She scooped a spoonful of the aloo gobi and let the sliced potatoes and cauliflower florets fall off the spoon onto her plate. Khalid looked on as Lily tried the dish.

'How is it?' Khalid asked. He wanted Lily to like every dish on the table. He hoped, as his heart twinged, that she liked him as much as he was beginning to like her.

'Good!' Lily beamed. She had been so busy eating that she forgot to check the time.

'What time is it?' she asked.

'Going to be eight,' Khalid said. 'Don't worry.'

'Okay,' Lily said. She continued eating, sure that this would not be the last time she would try Indian food. It made her happy to try new things and make her world a bit bigger.

'Are you a good cook?' Khalid asked.

Lily blushed. She wanted to say that she was but she did not think it was becoming to praise herself.

'I like all the kueh I've eaten at the Kongs,' Khalid continued. 'Did you make any of it?'

'Yes,' Lily said. 'I help Zhu Jie and Leng Jie.'

'Then you're a good cook,' Khalid said. Maybe it was kueh that was the way to Khalid's heart, Lily thought. She would find out all his favourite kueh and his favourite food slowly. Lily blushed more, avoiding looking Khalid in the eye. They ate until all the food on the plates disappeared. Lily thought that no matter what happened in the future, that night would always stay in the brightest corner of her memory. The first time she went out with Khalid, Lily thought. All the food they ate. The questions he asked her. Her answers. How he had waited patiently for her to read the word 'restaurant' on her own. Lily blushed as she thought of it all.

When dinner was over, Khalid walked Lily home, wishing that he could summon from the depths of his deepest being, some courage to reach out and hold her hand.

'Good night, Lily,' Khalid said finally when they reached the Kongs' home.

'Good night,' Lily whispered, her voice soft with sadness. She did not want to part ways. 'Khalid.'

Khalid stood on the street outside the Kongs' home while Lily dashed into the five-foot way. Before Lily could use her key to open the door, it swung open. Lily held her breath and braced herself for an anticipated reprimand from Mak Kong. To her immense relief, before her stood Zhu Jie, her round face creased with lines of worry and fear.

'Quick,' Zhu Jie said. 'Come.' Lily slipped in and Zhu Jie rushed out of the home.

'Thank you, Zhu Jie,' Lily whispered. Zhu Jie did not seem to hear her. She waved her thanks away and then motioned her to go upstairs. Lily waved as Zhu Jie closed the door and locked it. As Zhu Jie bustled to the bus stop, Lily tiptoed upstairs. She knew no one would be asleep yet; it was a terrifying thought. She hurried into her room and swung the door behind her, her heart pounding the entire time. Leaning against her closed door, Lily wondered if all the stress of sneaking out was worth it. She stared at her shadow on the floor as she prayed fervently to all the Gods that she knew, hoping against hope that she would never get caught.

Chapter XX

15th October 1940

Khalid rubbed his temples with some Axe Oil. Around mid-afternoon, he would start to get a headache, low on sugar from fasting. The fasting month of Ramadan had started two weeks ago. From dawn to dusk, Khalid was abstaining from food and drink. Muslims also had to refrain from sexual activity and bad habits such as gossiping or fighting. He had asked Mr Rashid if he ever felt hungry or tired during Ramadan but all Mr Rashid would let on was that it was for the sake of Allah. Khalid wished he had Mr Rashid's level of piety because fasting sometimes made him feel grumpy. If only I can nap now, Khalid thought as he pressed down on the hole puncher. He placed a stack of documents into the file in front of him. Glancing at his watch, he tried not to sigh. Four more hours till he could break his fast over dinner with Lily, Khalid thought. He hoped that Lily would be able to meet him tonight. The last time they were supposed to meet, Lily could not sneak out because Mak Kong and Pak Kong decided to sit in the main hall to listen to the radio after dinner. That had only met two times since their first date. The second date had been a short walk in the Everitt Road Park that only lasted about twenty minutes. The third date was when Lily met Khalid once again at Mumtaz Mahal Restaurant. It's becoming our special spot,

Khalid thought. But he wanted to take Lily somewhere different on their next date so that she could see a different restaurant.

'Done?' Mr Ong asked, appearing at Khalid's desk.

'Yes,' Khalid said.

Mr Ong handed him some handwritten papers. 'You can type this out,' he said. 'Notes of meeting. After that, do organise these case materials in chronological order.'

'Okay,' Khalid said. He took the papers and glanced at them. At the very top were meeting minutes from Mr Braddell's meeting with a client that morning. Khalid knew that the typist had gone home sick that day. She was three months' pregnant with her first child so he had to cover her typing duties. He did not mind. Khalid thought that time would pass faster if he had a task to do. He made sure to be careful because he did not want to make any mistakes. He turned to the typewriter on the desk and placed a piece of paper behind the cylinder.

When Khalid was done typing the notes of meeting, he stapled the sheets of paper together. Mr Ong came to his desk and Khalid handed him the document.

'Thank you,' Mr Ong said, without looking up at Khalid. He perused the document.

As Mr Ong walked away, Khalid turned to the thick stack of case materials and started skimming through them. There were legal terms, some typewritten in shorthand, that he did not understand. Luckily, all I have to do is file them, Khalid thought. He wondered what Lily was doing at that moment. Was she perhaps doing embroidery work? he thought. He pictured her behind in the next room, behind the screen, where she would sit and decorate fabric with a needle. Maybe she was embroidering blossoming pink peonies with big green leaves, he thought.

Mr Braddell came out of his office just then. His brows were furrowed and his forehead was creased with lines of worry. Khalid knew he was working on a difficult case. Mr Braddell strode past the desks and out of the office. Khalid figured he was going to the toilet. He stole a glance at his watch. It was five minutes past four in the afternoon. If I stop looking at it, time will pass faster, he told himself. By the time he was done organising and filling the documents, he decided it was time for a toilet break. He stretched his arms and legs out a bit before getting up. Khalid decided he would have to eat and drink more during sahur to have more energy. He had been fasting the whole day since he was fourteen but he was still figuring out what was best to eat for the pre-dawn meal. He rarely ate eat rice though that was what Pak Ambi and Ibrahim ate, rice and leftovers from dinner the night before. Khalid usually had two slices of bread with hard-boiled eggs and sardines but maybe that was not filling enough. Tomorrow morning, I'll try eating rice again, Khalid thought.

Khalid gulped as he waited across the road from the Kongs' home. Seconds ticked by on his watch and still Lily did not come out. She was seven minutes late. Khalid looked at the closed windows on the second floor. He wondered if Zhu Jie would come out again to tell him Lily could not leave home. Then he saw the door open and a shadowy figure emerged. His heart leapt like a soaring bird; it was Lily. Looking worried, Lily crossed the road and quickly walked up to him. She was wearing the same dress she had worn on their first date.

'Hi,' Lily said, almost breathlessly.

'Hello,' Khalid said.

'Sorry about the other time,' Lily said. 'When I couldn't come out to meet you.'

'No problem,' Khalid replied. 'Have you had your dinner?'

'Yes,' Lily said with a sheepish look. 'I'm sorry.'

Khalid shook his head. 'No, don't apologise!' he said.

'Have—have you eaten?' Lily asked.

'No,' Khalid said. 'I have not.'

Lily's brows furrowed in concern. 'You must be hungry. I mean, you were fasting today, right?'

'Oh, I mean I broke my fast with two dates and water,' Khalid said. 'But I haven't eaten dinner.'

'Okay,' Lily said. 'Where do you want to go?'

'Satay? There's a stall but it's by the roadside . . . '

'I've always wanted to eat by the roadside,' Lily grinned.

A bright smile spread across Khalid's face. 'Let's go then, Lily.'

Lily thought that Khalid had the most genuine smile. It was because of his teeth that were just the right shade of pristine white, Lily decided. The thought pricked her with guilt and sadness. Once she married Teck Soon, she would only see Khalid's smile in her memory. He would age and she would never see how the years would change the look of his smile. How would he face life's challenges? she mused. She wanted to be by his side and face everything together with him. Marriage, children, birthdays, accidents, loss, death. She hoped so much to share in Khalid's every joy and every sorrow for she was sure that she had found the one whom her soul loves. Khalid's my soulmate, Lily thought. She had known him in a past life, she found him in this present one and she would find him in the next life.

It seemed to Khalid like Lily had a lot on her mind and he was concerned that she would tell him she could not see him anymore. He knew that they could both get into trouble with Mak Kong and Pak Kong. Deciding that he would be silent and leave Lily to her thoughts, he walked alongside her, looking at her every once in a while. Soon, they reached the satay stall. The inviting smells of barbequed meat and the noisy chatter of people jolted Lily out of her brooding. She saw some occupied tables, a few empty ones and a row of four stalls next to each other.

'Chicken and beef, okay?' Khalid asked as they sat down at an empty table.

'Okay,' Lily said. Khalid left the table to order from the satay seller. Lily saw the satay seller seated on a stool with a towel around his neck, fanning the skewered meat. In front of him, smoke billowed in curly wisps. Lily had eaten satay a few times before when Pak Kong brought it home. Maybe it was from this stall, Lily thought.

At the next table, a young girl and her brother were poking their satay sticks against each other like toy swords. Lily smiled a little at them. She thought that she would slip in and out of this freedom until she got married. But until her marriage to Teck Soon was confirmed, she would choose not to think of it. Just focus on the present, Lily told herself. The present is here with Khalid.

Khalid returned to the table after he placed the order. Lily smiled what she hoped was an easy, confident smile but she felt sure it came out as more of an uncertain, awkward look.

'Are you okay?' Khalid asked.

'Oh yes,' Lily said, her head bobbing up and down.

'Have you eaten satay before?' Khalid asked. He was curious about what Lily had tried and what she had not. The ordinary things he took for granted like eating at a roadside stall were things Lily yearned to do. In a way, it was refreshing. He was glad that he could bring her to try new experiences. She struck him as the kind of person who liked to try something at least once. In that way, he thought Lily and him were similar.

Lily nodded shyly in response to Khalid's question just as the satay man brought the sticks of chicken and beef satay with rice cakes and peanut sauce to the table. Lily picked up a stick of chicken satay and blew on it. Khalid bit into a stick of beef satay.

'Hot,' Khalid said but continued eating anyway.

'It's nice,' Lily said after she had taken a bite from her stick.

'Yes, this place has my favourite satay,' Khalid said. 'The Beach Road one is nice too.'

'This tastes like the satay I had at home,' Lily said.

'Should be the same one.'

Lily smiled as she dipped her stick in the peanut sauce. The young girl at the next table stared at her but Lily did not notice. She counted the sticks on the plate. There were ten sticks left. She was surprised that she could eat more after dinner. Before going out with Khalid, she had never considered eating more after dinner.

'What's your favourite food?' Khalid asked.

'Hmm,' Lily said. She had never thought of it.

'Yoghurt rice or briyani is mine,' Khalid said.

'I like a lot of food,' Lily said. 'Maybe chicken rendang. Durians are my favourite fruit.'

'Oh,' Khalid said. 'I don't really like durians.'

'That's okay,' Lily said. We can't always like the same things, she thought. What's more important is that we have the same values. I hope we do. I think we do.

When they were done with dinner, Lily wiped her mouth with her handkerchief. She smiled to herself behind it. For the rest of the dinner, they had talked about Khalid's family. Lily had told him about the Kongs but more about Zhu Jie and Little, both of whom she loved with all her heart. Lily thought that Khalid's family life seemed so interesting. He had a father, an elder brother, a mother, a stepmother, and two half-sisters. She had always wondered what it was like to have siblings, she told him. Khalid said that the grass is always greener on the other side. After he explained the phrase to Lily, she agreed. Humans always seemed to want something different from what they had.

Chapter XXI

1st November 1940

Lily had felt an impending sense of doom ever since Mak Kong informed her that she would be matchmade with Teck Soon. Before Mrs Chong visited them with the matchmaker on the day of Ghost Festival, Lily fantasised about the different ways she could sabotage the day. She could spill hot tea on Mrs Chong or speak rudely or rub something smelly on her clothes. But anything she did would get her into trouble and bring disrepute to the Kong family. So, Lily did nothing; she was demure, dutiful and graceful. After consulting with a Feng Shui master, the Kongs and Mrs Chong found an auspicious wedding date. Lap Chai, the ceremony of exchanging wedding gifts, was held soon after. The Chongs had sent four trays of gifts in a multi-tiered basket: jewellery and red packet containing dowry money, a raw pig trotter, twelve oranges, a pair of candles and two bottles of brandy and pieces of cloth for Lily to sew into a full set of garments for the groom. The Kongs had returned the bakul siah with gifts of their own: a ring tied to a silk handkerchief, a belt and a buckle, a portion of the pig trotter received, a pair of candles, two bottles of syrup, two packets of longans, oranges, and the completed set of clothes for the groom.

Lily stared at the chicken wing next to the rice on her plate. She looked up and saw Charles observing her. Charles is only sixteen, Lily thought.

It'll be a few years before he gets married. She frowned at Charles and looked away, not waiting to see how he would respond. She had met Khalid thrice since their first meeting. It's only a matter of time before I'm caught, Lily thought. Maybe I shouldn't even try to hide it. This idea was at once so liberating but scary and unlikely that Lily wanted to laugh at her naïveté.

'Did you know Thunder can survive on land for up to ten hours?' Charles said.

'No,' Ivy said. 'How do you know?'

'My classmate told me,' Charlies replied. 'His father works at a fish farm.'

'Maybe I'll work on a fish farm when I'm big,' Ivy said.

You'll get married, matchmade like me, and not have to work, Lily thought bitterly.

Charles laughed. 'They won't hire you!'

Ivy pouted. 'Says who?'

'Me,' Charles said.

Mak Kong threw both Charles and Ivy a look and they fell silent.

After lunch, Charles approached Lily in the kitchen as she was about to wash her hands at the sink.

'Are you okay?' he asked. Lily was taken aback; it was rare that Charles would initiate a conversation with her.

'I'm sorry that you will be matchmade,' Charles continued. 'I don't want to be matchmade either.'

Lily smiled sadly at Charles. She did not know what to say, but perhaps no words were needed. Charles tilted his head slightly and cleared his throat. Then he turned and walked away. Lily felt peculiar as she saw him leaving the kitchen; she knew Charles meant well but she realised she did not like being pitied. She picked up the bar of soap and scrubbed her hands clean. I'll have to tell Khalid I can't see him anymore, Lily thought. She wondered if he would be upset upon learning that she was engaged to another man. The window of freedom had been short-lived. Or maybe it was not a window but fragments. She had stayed over at Zhu Jie's dormitory, danced in the rain and gone on four dates with Khalid. It should be enough, Lily tried to convince herself. But it wasn't. She wanted more; she wanted a life of her own choosing.

Zhu Jie nudged Lily out of her reverie. Lily turned and saw the stack of dirty kitchenware. She moved away, silencing a sigh before it could escape her lips, as the majies started washing the dishes. She went up to her room to take a rest before it was time for embroidery work.

In her room, Lily decided to complete the letter she had started writing in reply to Khalid. They had continued writing to each other after their first date. She read what she had already written in Baba Malay.

Dear Khalid,
Yes, we should meet again soon.
I have something to tell you.

What else should I say? Lily wondered. She imagined how Khalid would respond to finding out she was engaged. Would he be shocked? Would he feel hurt? Would he try to help her find a way out of the marriage? Was there even a way out? Lily sighed and put the letter back in her biscuit tin. She might have to fight for the life she wanted; that was the only thing she could do.

* * *

Khalid turned and watched as Ibrahim stalked into the room, slamming the door shut behind him. Ibrahim dropped his backpack on the floor by his bed and sat on the edge of his bed.

Khalid stayed silent and waited for Ibrahim to say something but he did not. Khalid continued checking the money he had collected for the chap ji kee bets against his notebook.

Without saying a word, Ibrahim slumped out of the room. Khalid frowned, wondering how long Ibrahim's bad mood was going to last. He could not imagine starting a marriage in this way. He wished Ibrahim would just tell Pak Ambi he did not want to get married but he knew Ibrahim did not think that was possible. Ibrahim cared a lot about what Pak Ambi thought about him and did not want to disappoint him.

Khalid finished counting the money and kept it in Pak Ambi's money box. He leaned back into his chair and peered out of the room but he could not see Ibrahim anywhere. Khalid took out the latest letter Lily had written to him. It was in Baba Malay. He wished he could somehow help Lily with her English, as she seemed keen to learn, but meeting her was difficult enough so finding a way to teach her English would be next to impossible.

He had not yet received a reply to his letter from Lily on Wednesday and Zhu Jie did not bring him one either. It made him feel a bit anxious but he was hopeful he would get a reply. Feeling his stomach churn, he glanced at his watch. It was about an hour till they could break their fast on the last day of Ramadan. Tomorrow it would be Hari Raya. Khalid could not wait. Every year, he would visit Pak Ambi's parents, then gather at Mak Jah's home. The thought of all the good food and being surrounded by family made him smile. He put Lily's letter back in his drawer as he heard footsteps behind him. Ibrahim reappeared in the room and slunk into his bed.

'Hi,' Khalid said. 'Are you okay?'

'Ya,' Ibrahim replied.

'Cheer up,' Khalid said.

'I'm just hungry,' Ibrahim said. 'That's all.'

'Okay,' Khalid said, deciding to let Ibrahim be. He watched Ibrahim close his eyes. At that moment, he heard Pak Ambi's voice down the hallway.

'Tomorrow Hari Raya already,' Pak Ambi was saying. 'They spotted the moon in Johor.'

'Alhamdullilah,' Mr Rashid replied. 'You fasted the whole month?'

'Mm,' Pak Ambi said.

'May Allah reward you for your efforts,' Mr Rashid said.

'Thank you,' Pak Ambi said. Khalid heard some murmurs and then his father's footsteps nearing the room.

Pak Ambi emerged at the doorway and closed the door.

'Every year!' Pak Ambi said. 'Every year, Mr Rashid has to ask me if I fasted the whole month.'

Khalid wondered what would be safe to say. Perhaps he could say that Mr Rashid was religious and only meant well. Khalid knew that Pak Ambi tried to fast but his weakness for cigarettes and beer posed a challenge. He himself had never asked his father if he fasted the whole month but he was sure that there were days when Pak Ambi had broken his fast in secret.

'Tomorrow it's Hari Raya,' Pak Ambi continued. 'He cannot focus on that? No, because he's sad Ramadan is over.'

Pak Ambi shook his head as he unbuttoned his shirt. Khalid reclined in his chair, deciding just to listen to Pak Ambi's rant.

'Next year, I should ask him if he fasted the whole month,' Pak Ambi said. But the answer would be yes, Khalid thought. And that would make you feel more guilty.

'Good thing he doesn't ask me about solat,' Pak Ambi said. Probably because he knows you don't pray, Khalid mused. So, there was no point asking.

'You see, people should mind their own business,' Pak Ambi ranted. 'Am I right?'

'Yes,' Khalid answered.

Pak Ambi stopped and looked at his son just then. 'Did you count the money and check?'

'Yes,' Khalid said. 'All correct.'

'Good,' Pak Ambi said. He yawned and stretched his arms out. Khalid knew that this meant that Pak Ambi was ready to fall asleep soon. At that moment, Ibrahim woke up from his nap and looked around the room.

'Are we leaving to Mak Jah's soon?' Ibrahim asked.

'Ya, go wash your face and change your shirt,' Pak Ambi said. He put on a fresh shirt and then sat in his chair. Suddenly, there was a knock on the door. Khalid opened the door and to his surprise, he was greeted by Charles.

'Hello!' Charles said. 'Selamat Hari Raya. I know it's tomorrow. My mother asked me to come by and give you this. It's love letters.'

Khalid looked at the big tin of love letters, the delicate Chinese pastry, Charles was holding.

'Thank you, Charles!' Khalid said. 'That's so sweet of you.'

'You're welcome,' Charles said, nodding politely in greeting at Pak Ambi and Ibrahim.

'Hello,' Pak Ambi said, his face breaking into a smile. 'Charles, is it? All the best for your exams!'

'Thank you,' Charles said. 'Selamat Hari Raya to you all.' He grinned and then walked off.

'We can eat this later,' Ibrahim said as he headed to the toilet. Khalid considered this for a moment.

'We should bring this to Mak Jah,' Khalid said.

'Good idea,' Pak Ambi said.

Khalid started getting ready for iftar at Mak Jah's house. After washing his face, he combed his hair and put on a new shirt. Thoughts of fragrant tomato rice and crispy papadom filled his mind.

At midnight, Khalid, Ibrahim, Samad and other boys from the neighbourhood gathered in the streets below to set off fire crackers.

'Selamat Hari Raya!' Samad cried out as he lit his matchstick to light the firecracker on the ground. It crackled and exploded loudly, with bright sparks and clouds of smoke.

Khalid watched as his young boy clapped his hands in delight.

'No more fasting till next year!' Ibrahim yelled.

'May we meet next Ramadan!' Samad shouted.

Khalid took the set of matches from Samad and lit a match then he passed the box to Ibrahim. Together, the brothers lit their firecrackers before they dashed away to watch the explosion.

Khalid realised that Ibrahim would probably not be able to do this next year at Everitt Road. Once he got married, he would move in with his wife's family into their kampung house. The thought made Khalid feel like he was missing Ibrahim though he was standing right next to him. He did not feel ready for Ibrahim to get married and move out. Everything would change. Can we be boys for a little while longer? Khalid found himself wishing. He glanced at Ibrahim, who was taking in the scene of firecrackers going off to the delight of the gathered crowd.

'Hungry,' Samad said. 'Wish Mak's chicken rendang is ready now.'

'I hope we'll get some too,' Ibrahim said.

'Of course,' Samad said. 'Come visit as usual and Mak will serve some.'

'Great,' Ibrahim said. He turned to look at Khalid. 'What's wrong?' Ibrahim asked.

'Oh nothing,' Khalid said, shaking his head.

'Dreaming,' Samad said. He chuckled, gesturing to their rooms. 'Want to go up?'

'Yes, let's go up,' Ibrahim said. Khalid took one final look at the festive atmosphere; the squealing children, smiling adults and excited teenagers letting go of the exploding firecrackers. All that was left behind was scattered red shells and plumes of smoke.

Khalid glanced over, amused, as his father adjusted his songkok on his head. The one day a year that Pak Ambi looks like a proper Muslim man, Khalid thought. Ibrahim was a little in front of him. He took off his sandals and strode into the house.

'Selamat Hari Raya!' Pak Ambi said, as he stepped into the living room of Mak Jah's house. Fatimah rushed to salam Pak Ambi, with Leha close behind. Fatimah was dressed in a purple baju kurung while Leha was dressed in a pink kebaya and blue batik sarong.

'I didn't recognise either of you,' Leha said, guffawing as she put her hand over her mouth and looked from Khalid to Ibrahim. 'Wearing baju kurung and looking so respectable.'

'Not funny,' Ibrahim said, wrinkling his nose.

'Who says I was joking?' Leha retorted.

Khalid was proud of the brand-new blue baju kurung set he was wearing this year because he had bought it with part of his salary. As Ibrahim and Leha continued to tease each other, he went over to give salam to Mak Jah and her parents. There were four plates filled with snacks on the table and empty glasses next to a pitcher of bandung. Khalid sat down and waited for everyone to gather around. He was wondering which kuih he should eat first: sugee cookies or tapak kuda. As everyone took their seat and the attention shifted to the snacks, Khalid helped himself to the hooved-shaped cake. The vanilla sponge cake had a chocolate filling in it.

'We helped Mak make the tapak kuda!' Fatimah said.

'Won't eat those then,' Ibrahim joked. Fatimah rolled her eyes and flipped her long hair over her shoulder.

'Some people don't know how to appreciate good food,' Leha said, pursing her lips.

'Some people can't take a joke,' Ibrahim countered.

'It's good,' Khalid said. Fatimah beamed at him.

'Have more,' Fatimah said. She picked up the plate and handed it to Khalid.

'Later,' Khalid said. He turned to Pak Ambi who was talking to Mak Jah.

'Khalid and Ibrahim will go visit their mother after this,' Pak Ambi was saying. 'Yes, I'll stay here.'

'Are you looking forward to your wedding?' Fatimah asked as she tipped a piece of keropok into her mouth.

Ibrahim shot her a look which Khalid interpreted as 'Be quiet!' but Fatimah did not seem to notice.

'I feel bad for your wife,' Leha said, smirking.

Ibrahim pretended to laugh as he stared at her. 'I feel bad for your future husband!' he said.

Pak Ambi joined in the conversation. 'Yes, yes. After that, it will be Khalid's turn.'

'So, who is K going to be matchmade to?' Ibrahim asked.

Khalid held his breath. Pak Ambi leaned back in his chair. Wrinkles appeared in his forehead as if this was the first time he had been asked this question. 'We don't have a match yet for Khalid,' he said.

Khalid exhaled in relief. I'm going to marry Lily, he thought.

'That's not fair!' Ibrahim said. He put down his glass. It landed with a loud thud on the table.

'Ibrahim,' Pak Ambi said. 'Sara is a very nice girl.'

Ibrahim shook his head and turned away. Silence descended upon the room, punctuated by the sounds of chewing and munching. Khalid took sips of his bandung and decided it was best not to say anything. Fatimah and Leha started chatting between themselves about their clothes and make-up. Finally, Mak Jah said it was time for lunch.

As Khalid looked at Ibrahim's grumpy expression, he wondered what would happen next. Would the wedding be called off? He dared not imagine the impact that that would cause. Would Ibrahim's name be ruined in the community? He sat next to Ibrahim at the dining table and tried to keep fretful thoughts at bay. He inhaled the smell of the main dishes on the table, a plate full of longtong and a big bowl of chicken rendang. He could already taste the warm rice cakes and buttery, creamy, nutty, sweetness and spice of the chicken stew. Knowing rendang was one of Ibrahim's dishes, he passed the plate to Ibrahim and hoped that the food would put Ibrahim in a better mood. At least for today, Khalid thought. Today maybe Ibrahim will just enjoy Raya.

Chapter XXII

24th November 1940

Lily swallowed the lump in her throat and walked into the main hall. She had felt that something was wrong since the morning when Zhu Jie announced that Ibrahim was at the front door. Mak Kong had a quizzical look on her face before she instructed them to continue preparing lunch. Then she bustled out of the kitchen. Lily tried hard to strain her ears though she knew it was wrong to eavesdrop. She was overcome with a mixture of curiosity and worry. Why would Ibrahim come to the house? Mak Kong looked surprised which meant that Ibrahim's visit was unexpected. Had something happened to Khalid? Did he need help? But by the look Mak Kong gave her in the kitchen after that, Lily knew that Mak Kong knew that she had been sneaking out of the house to meet Khalid. She was in trouble with no discernible way out. During lunch, Mak Kong did not even look at her once. She went through the motions of scooping food up to her mouth, putting it in and chewing but she could not eat properly at all. In Lily's mind, she had fervently prayed to Ting Kong.

Mak Kong was sitting on her chair. She did not look up at Lily when she walked in, seeming lost in thought. Lily hurried off to the kitchen where she found Zhu Jie and Leng Jie washing the dishes. She was sure she would faint from worrying what would happen.

'Can I help?' she asked the majies. Anything to stop thinking, she thought.

Zhu Jie stopped scrubbing a plate and turned around to look at her.

'Going to finish soon,' Zhu Jie said.

'I—I don't know what to do,' Lily sputtered. The water from the tap ran down the plate in Leng Jie's hands. Leng Jie wiped it with a cloth and then stacked it on top of another clean plate.

'Don't know what they talk about,' Zhu Jie whispered. 'Don't worry.'

Lily caught Leng Jie's eye just then. Leng Jie frowned as she took a kamcheng from Zhu Jie.

So softly that she might have been talking to herself, Leng Jie said, 'She know.'

'She know?' Lily repeated, feeling like the ground beneath her feet was moving and her body with it.

'Yes,' Leng Jie said. 'The boy tell her.'

'Tell her what?' Zhu Jie pressed.

'The boy tell her Lily see his brother,' Leng Jie said.

Lily felt like air was leaving her lungs. Her throat closed up as she realized she would never see Khalid again. There was no question about that. Would she be asked to leave the Kongs' home? She stared into space and wrung her fingers. Zhu Jie dried her hands with a washcloth and patted Lily on the back. Lily could not bear to look at Zhu Jie. If she was in trouble, Zhu Jie would be in trouble too. She felt relieved that Khalid was going to end his lessons with Charles soon; Mak Kong was unlikely to fire him. But would she let Zhu Jie go?

At that moment, Mak Kong strode into the kitchen.

'Zhu Jie,' Mak Kong said. 'I want to speak to you.'

Lily wanted to stop Mak Kong and plead, 'Please don't blame Zhu Jie. It's my fault.' But she said nothing and watched helplessly as Zhu Jie followed Mak Kong out of the kitchen. She wished she could follow them and try to eavesdrop. Leng Jie sat down at the table and stared at Lily.

'What should I do?' Lily said. She did not know if she was asking Leng Jie or just thinking out loud. Leng Jie shrugged and looked down at her hands. She's just glad she's not involved, Lily thought. Leng Jie shuffled out of the kitchen. Lily sat down at the kitchen table and waited. It seemed unbearable as time stretched on. She expected that Zhu Jie would reappear in the kitchen soon but she did not.

Finally, she heard movement in the main hall. It sounded like Mak Kong was climbing up the stairs. Still Zhu Jie did not come into the kitchen. Lily kept still and listened. Then she realised that Zhu Jie must have gone out of the house. Where did she go? Lily wondered. What if Mak Kong had asked her to leave the home? Surely, she would not have been so heartless.

* * *

'Eh!' Samad called out. The ball went past him into the makeshift goal demarcated by two tin cans. Khalid pumped his fist into the air in celebration.

'Two-nil!' Khalid said.

'Not fair,' Samad said. He sighed as he took the ball from Khalid. Samad put the ball down on the ground and ran with it at his feet.

'Next goal is mine!' he cheered. Khalid ran after him and tried to tackle him but Samad slipped away, quick-footed. Khalid ran to stand in the goal to block Samad. Suddenly, he heard a woman's voice. He stopped and turned around. It was Zhu Jie. She was standing in front of him, looking frantic. She waved him over.

Samad kicked the ball into the goal with a flourish.

'Yay!' he shouted.

'What happened?' Khalid asked.

'Mak Kong know,' Zhu Jie said. 'Mak Kong know you and Lily go out.'

Khalid gasped. 'H—how?' he sputtered. 'Who?'

Zhu Jie hesitated. 'Mak Kong want to talk to you.'

'Now?' Khalid asked.

'Yes, now.' Zhu Jie said.

'Oh no,' Khalid said, groaning.

'Ya, come now,' Zhu Jie said, gesturing urgently with her hands waving about in front of her.

'I'm sweaty,' Khalid said. 'I go change first.'

'Never mind,' Zhu Jie insisted. 'Just come.'

Khalid took a deep breath and nodded. 'I have to go!' he told Samad.

'What's going on?' Samad asked, holding the soccer ball in his hands.

Khalid shrugged, trying to maintain a facade of calmness in front of Samad. 'Tell you later.'

He turned back to Zhu Jie who waved him over. Feeling as if he might choke, Khalid followed Zhu Jie who had already started walking away in a hurry.

They reached the Kongs' home in a few minutes. Zhu Jie walked in without leaving the door open for Khalid. Khalid swallowed his saliva as his heart pounded wildly. What would happen to Lily? Khalid thought. Had Mrs Kong already spoken to her?

Mak Kong looked up from her chair when Zhu Jie and Khalid entered the main hall. Khalid approached Mak Kong hesitantly, wishing that he could disappear. When Mak Kong realised Khalid's presence, she turned around and frowned at him.

'You are not to see Lily anymore,' Mak Kong said. 'Do you understand?'

Khalid gulped as the uncomfortable sensation of guilt pricked him. 'I'm sorry, Mrs Kong,' he said.

'She is going to be married,' Mak Kong said.

Khalid's eyes widened. 'Wh—When?' he sputtered. He felt like he had just been punched in the stomach. That had happened once before after a brawl on the soccer pitch with a rival school team. This time, if it was possible, Khalid thought he felt even worse. Lily would be getting married to someone else.

'Soon,' Mak Kong said. She sighed and shook her head.

Khalid stared at the floor, feeling like he was unable to move.

'You can go now,' Mak Kong said. 'Remember what I said.'

She started drumming her fingers on her chair.

'Okay,' Khalid said. 'I'm sorry, Mrs Kong.' Mak Kong did not respond. After a beat, Khalid turned to leave. He felt his heart sinking with each step that he took out of the Kongs' home.

Khalid stood on the five-foot way, feeling like he might be ill. He would have to stop seeing Lily. He did not know if he could do that. But Lily was going to be married. What choice did he have? Was he ready to marry Lily? He could not imagine never seeing her again. Lily, whose name and being reminded him of a precious flower. As he stumbled home in a daze, his thoughts turned to who it was that informed Mak Kong that he had been seeing Lily. Did it ever matter? Khalid thought he was foolish to ever believe that they could sneak around and not be caught. Living in a small neighbourhood, there were eyes everywhere that they could not see. Now it was too late for regrets. Khalid trudged home, staring at the pavement. Deep in thought, he only looked up when he had to cross the road.

As he reached home, he heard Samad's voice. Khalid looked up to see Samad smiling at him.

'What's wrong?' Samad asked as he peered at Khalid's face.

Khalid shook his head. 'The Kongs know,' he said after a minute. 'They know I've been dating Lily.'

Samad gasped. 'How?'

'I don't know, Samad,' Khalid muttered. He felt like getting as far away from home as he possibly could. He could take a long walk and see where he ended up. But he knew he had to be at home to tell Pak Ambi before he heard the gossip from someone else.

'Sorry, K,' Samad said. 'What you going to do?'

Khalid shrugged and bit his lip. He did not know what he could do.

'Talk to you later,' Khalid said, his shoulders slumped. Without waiting for a reply from Samad, he turned to his right and headed to their home.

* * *

Lily was sitting on her bed when she heard a knock on her door. She gulped and hesitated for a moment. What if it was Mak Kong at the door? Lily thought. She knew that she could not keep Mak Kong waiting and walked hastily to the door. She opened it to see Mak Kong's frowning face in front of her.

'I'm disappointed in you,' Mak Kong said, holding Lily's gaze firmly with a hard stare.

Lily looked down at the tiles on the floor. 'I'm so sorry, Mak Kong,' she mumbled. 'I truly am.'

'You know that as a young nyonya, you cannot go out with boys,' Mak Kong continued. 'You are going to marry Teck Soon. What if Mr and Mrs Chong find out what you did? The wedding will be called off.'

Lily did not look up nor respond.

'Do you understand?' Mak Kong asked.

'Yes,' Lily said weakly.

'I will tell Pak Kong about this matter,' Mak Kong said, sniffing. 'Tomorrow I will talk to you again.'

Determinedly, Lily avoided Mak Kong's gaze as she nodded. As Mak Kong turned to leave, Lily felt herself let out a huge breath. She slipped back into her room and sank into her bed. As she breathed in and out slowly, tears started to form in her eyes. Lily leaned back on her bed and tried to compose herself. She knew that she would have to stop crying soon. If she did not start her embroidery on time, Mak Kong would be even angrier. Lily took out her handkerchief and dried her tears. She peered at herself in the mirror. Her face was flushed and the irises of her eyes were tinged with red. No one is going to look at me anyway, Lily thought. She folded her handkerchief and brought it with her downstairs.

When she reached the main hall, she saw Leng Jie and Ivy there playing congkak. Ivy was dropping marbles from her hands into the congkak set. Lily was used to hearing the clinking sound of the marbles but at that moment, she wanted the sound to stop. She wished she could go to the kitchen to talk to Zhu Jie. Was she okay? What had Mak Kong said to her? Her thoughts turned to Khalid as she took out the embroidery stand and set from the cabinet. She hoped that he had not been too upset. Had Mak Kong been mean to him? She felt like crying again when she thought she would never see him again. She had not allowed herself to think of such thoughts till now. Lily sat down, feeling waves of regret overwhelm her. She knew she had been selfish. She would have to figure out a way to atone for her mistake. But first she wanted to apologise to Zhu Jie and Khalid. Khalid, Lily thought. Khalid. Would she really never see him again? His easy smile. His handsome face. His head full of dark, tight curls. His reassuring hands. Would she never hear him speak again? Already she missed his eloquent voice. She wanted so much to hear him speak again. Lily swallowed a scream and let it lie uncomfortably in her throat.

* * *

Khalid was trying to distract himself by reading an old book. But he was finding it hard to concentrate. Every time he heard a sound outside his room, he looked up from his book, hoping to see Pak Ambi or Ibrahim. He figured the chances of them hearing the news before he told them were high. Eager to explain his side of the story, it was hard for him to sit still and try to calmly read. Nonetheless, Khalid read on and on until he yawned. He closed the book, placed it back on his bookshelf and waited. Pak Ambi had gone to visit Mak Jah. He did not know where Ibrahim was. Khalid closed his eyes and tried to quiet his mind but he was unsuccessful. An image of Lily eating satay came to him. He opened his eyes quickly and looked out of the window. Khalid focused his attention on the second storey windows of the shophouse across the road. He could see his elderly neighbour's grey head. His neighbour looked like he was dozing off in his chair.

He could hear footsteps outside. Turning his head, Khalid was greeted by the sight of Ibrahim strolling into their room, whistling loudly.

'Hi,' Khalid said. 'Where were you?'

'Out,' Ibrahim said. He continued whistling loudly.

'Are you going to be in a bad mood forever?' Khalid said.

Ibrahim did not look at Khalid as he unbuttoned his shirt. 'No,' he replied.

'Okay,' Khalid said. 'Are you going to take a bath?'

'Yes,' Ibrahim said. 'I'll do that now.'

'Can we talk after?' Khalid asked.

Ibrahim paused and looked carefully at Khalid, his eyebrows knitting together. 'About what?'

'I don't know how to tell you,' Khalid said.

'Okay,' Ibrahim said. 'Talk later.' He swung his towel across his shoulder and left the room.

As Khalid waited for Ibrahim, he lay down on his bed. The next thing he knew, Ibrahim was shaking him awake. Khalid sat up in his bed and rubbed his eyes. He did not usually take afternoon naps but he felt so tired after his conversation with Mak Kong.

'You said you wanted to talk,' Ibrahim said.

'Yes,' Khalid said. He thought for a minute before he said, 'I did something and now I'm in trouble.'

Ibrahim did not say anything. He seemed to be thinking hard. Khalid stood up from his bed and started to pace up and down the length of his bed.

'I don't know how to tell you what it is, because I know you'll say I was stupid,' Khalid continued. 'And I don't really feel like hearing that. But I was—I was stupid.'

'I think I know what it's about,' Ibrahim replied.

Khalid stopped his pacing and stared at Ibrahim. He felt his heart drop. It couldn't be... His elder brother, his only brother, had been the one to betray him? Khalid's hands curled into tight fists. What do I do now? he asked himself.

'How did you find out?' Khalid hissed as his head pounded.

Ibrahim looked him straight in the eye. 'I saw you in the park,' Ibrahim said. 'One of my friends saw you at Mumtaz Mahal Restaurant. Did you really think you could hide it for long, K?'

Khalid felt anger, red-hot and burning, rise up in him as his muscles tensed. 'But you're my brother, Ibrahim,' he said. 'You're my brother! You're supposed to be the keeper of my secrets, not the person who betrays me!'

'I did it for your own good,' Ibrahim said, turning away from Khalid.

The sinking feeling in Khalid's chest deepened as his lower lip trembled.

'For my own good?' he said in a whisper of rage.

'You know single nyonyas are not allowed to date,' Ibrahim said. 'If I hadn't said anything, you would be in more trouble.'

'That's not why you did it!' he shouted.

'Lower your voice,' Ibrahim said as he ran over to close the door to their room. 'Do you want the neighbours to hear?'

'You got me into trouble! Lily too!' Khalid said. 'Don't say you did it for my own good!'

'Why else would I do it?' Ibrahim said, folding his arms across his chest.

'You're unhappy!' Khalid spat out as he released his fists and then curled them again into tight balls. 'Unhappy and jealous!'

Ibrahim snorted loudly. 'Jealous of who?'

'It's jealous of whom, Ibrahim,' Khalid sneered.

'Just be quiet!' Ibrahim shouted.

As his anger exploded, Khalid pulled his fist back and punched Ibrahim's face. Ibrahim howled and struck Khalid hard with a sweaty slap. Khalid's head whipped sideways before he charged at Ibrahim, burying his head in Ibrahim's chest. They crashed into the table and rolled onto the floor, both brothers' fists pummelling each other repeatedly. Khalid felt Ibrahim's fist slam into his jaw and he groaned in pain. He was smaller than Ibrahim but surely, he could fight just as hard, Khalid thought. The blood pounding in his ears, Khalid tried to stop the next punch from Ibrahim. Just then, the door swung open and Pak Ambi shouted at them.

'Ibrahim!' Pak Ambi said. 'Khalid! Stop!'

Ibrahim stopped, his fist raised in mid-air, as he was about to reach out to pummel Khalid further. Khalid stared blankly at his father. Why did you come home? he thought bitterly.

Ibrahim pulled himself upright, rubbing his jaw and he glared at Khalid.

'Nothing better to do, is it?' Pak Ambi asked, putting one firm hand on Khalid's shoulder and the other on Ibrahim's.

'He started it,' Ibrahim said as he continued to massage his jaw. Khalid sank into his chair and put his face in his hands.

'What's going on?' Pak Ambi said, looking from Ibrahim to Khalid. Neither of his sons replied. Khalid did not look up, as a tear rolled down his cheek. His face and fists hurt. He felt like there was nothing he could say that would make things better. Worse than that, he felt like there was nothing he could do.

'No one stopped him,' Ibrahim mumbled.

Khalid held his breath as he stared at Ibrahim. 'You told Pak?' he asked.

'Is this about the nyonya girl?' Pak Ambi said, looking from Ibrahim to Khalid.

'Her name is Lily,' Khalid said. 'I can't believe he told you.'

'I told you—I did it for your own good,' Ibrahim said. 'But Pak, why didn't you stop him from seeing Lily?'

Pak Ambi paused. 'I was going to talk to you,' he said finally.

'Instead of telling the Kongs, you could have talked to me first,' Khalid said. 'So, like I said, you did it because you're jealous of me.'

Ibrahim did not reply. He propped his elbows up on the table behind me and spread his legs out wide. Frustrated and exhausted, Khalid made a movement to walk out of the room. He did not want to be around his brother any longer.

'Come back and talk properly!' Pak Ambi shouted after him.

Khalid stopped, turned back to look at Pak Ambi and shook his head. He thought that his family would always protect him but it was Ibrahim, his elder brother, who had betrayed him. He did not know why Pak Ambi had not stopped him from seeing Lily. There were other questions he wanted answers to. But at that moment, he just wanted to be alone.

Chapter XXIII

15th December 1940

'Shame to the family,' Pak Kong's words echoed in Lily's ears. Pak Kong and Mak Kong were infuriated when they reprimanded Lily together that morning. Mak Kong had said that Lily would be very fortunate if the Chongs would still allow Teck Soon to marry her. But I don't want to marry him, Lily had thought as she stood in front of the Kongs, trembling in fear. I want to marry Khalid. The Kongs were very concerned that the Chongs would find out what had happened. They had done their part to make sure that the news did not travel by asking Leng Jie to inform Khalid and his family to keep quiet. Even in the Kong household, Lily did not know if Chek Chuan, Charles and Ivy knew about her seeing Khalid.

Lily moved through the house, her thoughts clouded by misery, for the rest of the day. After lunch, Pak Kong and Mak Kong had left to visit a friend and Lily wondered frantically if 'friend' actually meant Mak Wee. She was sure that sooner or later, Mak Kong would inform Mak Wee about Lily's deplorable behaviour. As she did her embroidery later that afternoon, Lily found herself worrying about how Mak Kong would use her as a cautionary tale with Ivy; to teach Ivy that if you do the wrong thing, you would be ashamed and live with regret.

'And no one will marry you,' Lily imagined Mak Kong saying to an Ivy whose jaw would drop. As if, Lily thought wryly, not getting married was the worst fate that awaited a person. If I can't marry Khalid, I'd rather not get married at all. As that thought spread across her mind unfurling itself like a flag raised up a pole, Lily knew with certainty what she had to do.

* * *

It was the morning of Ibrahim's wedding day. Khalid watched, bleary-eyed, as Ibrahim lay still in bed, seemingly sound asleep. After today, everything would change, Khalid thought. Khalid was not ready for Ibrahim to be married though he had scarcely thought of this day in the prior months. He and Ibrahim had barely spoken since last night when Pak Ambi had asked them to apologise to each other. But Khalid knew neither of them had been truly sorry, the way they avoided looking each other in the eye when the apologies were almost forced out of them by Pak Ambi's heavy hands on their shoulders. Khalid decided when Ibrahim woke up, he would apologise sincerely. He did not want to be on bad terms with his brother on his wedding day. But more than that, he was sorry that he had punched Ibrahim. Khalid loved his brother very much and would rather avoid having a physical fight with him again.

Pak Ambi strode into the room just then, with an eyebrow raised at Khalid. He gestured to him with his thumb to step outside the room.

'I want to talk to you about the nyonya girl,' Pak Ambi said.

'Her name is Lily,' Khalid said. 'Lily!' He could not keep the passion out of his voice.

'Yes,' Pak Ambi said, frowning a little. 'Okay then, I want to talk to you about Lily.'

'I get it. Difficult sometimes but no choice,' Pak Ambi continued. 'You understand?'

Khalid did not understand what Pak Ambi meant. He thought of the moment when he had heard Pak Ambi mumble a girl's name. Mary, Khalid mused if he remembered correctly. But he did not feel like talking about it. He just wanted to forget everything about that day, if that was even possible. Except Lily. Khalid did not ever want to forget Lily. He nodded his head and hoped Pak Ambi would stop talking.

'You see, you'll marry a Muslim girl, like Ibrahim. It is . . . easier,' Pak Ambi said, staring at Khalid carefully.

Easier? Khalid thought, as he gazed at his feet. What did easier mean? With dread, he imagined himself being matchmade just like Ibrahim. His solemn face would face an equally solemn bride whose face was blurred. Then he saw Lily's beautiful face, kind, smiling and open. Lily, his first love. The love of his life. Someone he wanted to protect and take care of. The only woman he wanted to marry and have children with.

'I don't know what to say, Pak Ambi,' Khalid said after a moment.

'But you understand right, Khalid?' Pak Ambi pressed on.

'I guess so,' Khalid said finally. What he had gleaned from the conversation was that he would make sure he did not follow in Ibrahim's footsteps. Maybe it's too late for Ibrahim, Khalid thought determinedly. But it's not too late for me. At once, he felt a mixture of relief and guilt that he could still decide his own marriage but the same choice was not given to Ibrahim.

Ibrahim stumbled out of the room just then, his towel hung across his neck. He did not look at them as he walked off in the direction of the toilet. To Khalid's surprise, Pak Ambi said nothing. He wore an expression on his face that looked heavy, like a long sigh.

'I had a girlfriend once,' Pak Ambi said in a low voice without looking at Khalid in the eye. Khalid's eyes flickered in interest as he looked at Pak Ambi's bent head. He knew next to nothing about who Pak Ambi had dated before he was matchmade to his mother. Was Pak Ambi about to tell him about the mysterious Mary? he wondered.

'Who was she, Pak?' Khalid asked, his curiosity piqued.

'Chinese girl, you know, like Lily,' Pak Ambi said. 'But her father and her mother said she cannot marry an Indian.'

Khalid's lips fell into a disappointed lump. 'That's sad,' he said, realising that Pak Ambi did not even want to mention her name. 'I'm sorry, Pak.' Khalid decided to not probe further.

'The lesson from this is it is better to stick with people like us,' Pak Ambi said with a nonchalant shrug. 'Anyway, get ready to bathe. Busy day today.'

Pak Ambi clapped a firm hand on Khalid's shoulder before he got up and strode back into their room.

Better to stick with people like us, Khalid thought, shaking his head. But you and Mak divorced even though you come from the same religion. How is that better? He stared hard into the room as Pak Ambi walked to his cabinet to take a fresh change of clothes. Then after a minute, Khalid too re-entered their room, feeling a renewed sense of determination to marry Lily. If I cannot marry her, Khalid thought. I will not marry anyone else. I will be a bachelor. It was Lily as his wife or no wife at all.

* * *

Khalid listened closely to the middle-aged kadi recite his mellifluous sermon in the mosque. Looking over at Ibrahim, Khalid thought his expression was most inscrutable but Khalid had a feeling that he knew how Ibrahim was feeling. He was married now to a woman he did not choose for himself. Everything will be okay, Khalid thought to himself over and over as the kadi's volume seemed to grow louder with each word. Maybe they will learn to love each other after marriage. He wanted Ibrahim to be at peace and to be happy.

Ibrahim had accepted his apology earlier that day and for the first time ever, the brothers had embraced tightly. Khalid thought later that perhaps it was because Ibrahim was motivated, not by remorse, but by needing some comfort on his wedding day. But it did not matter; he knew he would remember the way his brother hugged him, like he would never let go.

As the kadi finished his sermon, the nikah ceremony ended. Khalid hung back as people surged forward to congratulate the couple. Then he saw his mother crying on Ibrahim's shoulder and Ibrahim patting her back with a slow, awkward hand. Just then, Khalid felt a hand on his back and he heard his uncle's voice.

'Your turn next, Khalid,' his uncle said.

Khalid chuckled as his uncle wiggled his eyebrows and again, he saw Lily in his mind. But Lily is not Muslim, he thought. Somehow, he could not imagine her at a Muslim wedding ceremony. All things are possible, he thought as he bit his lip. The future is unknowable.

That meant if a person knew nothing about the future, then all things are possible. I have to believe that one day, Lily will be a true Muslim. With that thought moving through his mind, Khalid walked over to join the group filtering out of the house to the tables outside. It was lunch time. With the medley of inviting smells of mutton briyani, curry, naan and other food that was greeting his nostrils, Khalid felt a hunger that needed immediate satiation.

* * *

Later that night, Khalid stood in his room alone, letting the emptiness surround him like a cloak. Pak Ambi was not home yet. He had claimed that he would be meeting friends for supper. Ibrahim's side of the room was almost empty. Only his bed and some of his possessions were left. Khalid thought of the time when he was barely ten and his brother had told him ghost stories in the dark till he screamed loudly. Ibrahim had laughed maniacally before Khalid pelted a pillow at him. In the dark, everything had seemed scarier, but Khalid had never felt closer to his elder brother. Then Ibrahim turned thirteen, and he stopped spending time with Khalid and even in the dark, the distance between them grew bigger and bigger.

Khalid bit his lip as he switched off the light. There would never again be a ghost story told in this room, he thought and had he known it at the time, all those years ago, he would have tried to make the story last longer. Memory was a strange thing and he thought that the longer ago the memory was, the more he would forget till he would not know what had actually happened and what his mind had made up to fill in the gaps. With a sigh, he made his way to his bed and sat there, letting the ache of missing Ibrahim settle into his chest.

He lay in bed awake, as his thoughts turned to Lily. Lily who did not have a sibling, Lily who was brave enough to send him a note, Lily who was so determined to learn English, Lily who savoured food with such delight, Lily whose cooking he had not yet tried but felt sure would taste very good. Lily who would become his wife, Khalid decided at that moment as the certainty of knowing whom he wanted in his future dawned on him. He would find a suitable time to tell Pak Ambi that he did not want to be matchmade. He had already found his wife, Lily.

* * *

Two streets away, Lily was awake in her bed too. Tomorrow she would tell Mak Kong that she was truly sorry but she could not marry Teck Soon. Mak Kong would resist at first but Lily would refuse. They cannot force me, she thought. Marriage can't be forced. She would thank Mak Kong profusely for all that she had done for her. She would say she was grateful.

Eventually, Lily decided, Mak Kong would say that she would have to inform Pak Kong.

Everything would fall into place, Lily reassured herself. But still she lay awake. Finally, she decided she would just step outside the house for a short while. She changed into her baju panjang and crept downstairs. All was still. In her nervousness, she thought she saw Chek Chuan's form on the floor but it was only her imagination. Chek Chuan had quit drinking as far as she knew. Or at least he no longer came home drunk.

As she put on her slippers and stood on the five-footway, Lily started walking. She did not know where she was going. She walked down the street and stood there for a while. Then she put her arms around her and seized by the sudden urge to see Khalid, she knew, all of a sudden, where to go.

When she reached Khalid's shophouse, she took a deep breath. She looked up at the windows; they were open but she did not know which room was his. What had she hoped for in coming here? Lily found herself wondering. She would get into more trouble if she was found out. She saw a shadowy figure just then and her breath caught in her throat.

* * *

Khalid could not believe his eyes. He was sure he was dreaming so he blinked his eyes. He pinched himself and still the person who looked like Lily did not disappear on the street below. Without thinking, he dashed out of the room and ran down the stairs.

'You're real,' he said to Lily the moment he saw her. 'I thought I was dreaming.'

'I'm real,' Lily whispered. Her breath caught in her throat. At that moment, she stopped thinking. With a deep breath, she leaned in and let herself fall into Khalid's welcoming, reassuring arms. He held her tightly, in a way that Lily had never been held before. So, this is what safe feels like, Lily thought. I'm safe with Khalid. Before she knew it, they were kissing, their lips meeting in moments that felt so blissful Lily thought she might cry. Lily felt something she had never felt before, a love that felt like it would burst out of her heart. She did not even know she knew how to kiss a boy. When they pulled apart, Lily spoke first.

'I'm sorry,' Lily said, feeling like she might cry. 'I'm sorry.'

'What for, Lily?' Khalid asked, a note of concern in his voice.

'I'm sorry I didn't tell you that I was getting married,' Lily said, looking down at the floor. 'Maaf, Khalid.'

'It's okay,' Khalid said as he exhaled in relief. For a moment, he had thought that Lily would say something like she could not be with him or see him again.

It's not okay, Lily wanted to scream. She shook her head and put her arms around her.

'But you can't marry him,' Khalid said after a minute as if he could sense what Lily was thinking. 'You don't belong with Teck Soon.'

Lily stared at him, her eyebrows raised in surprise and hope. She had not expected him to say that. She had hoped he would but to actually hear him say it was another thing altogether.

'Do you want to come upstairs?' Khalid asked, looking at Lily. It was a question that he did not know if he should ask but the question came out of his mouth before he could stop himself. He paused then he extended his hand out.

Without hesitation, Lily took his hand and followed him into the house and up the stairs, past two rooms. Outside the third room, Khalid stopped and turned to face Lily. All of a sudden, he was afraid that Pak Ambi might come home. Noticing him pausing and sensing his fear, Lily wondered whether she should say something.

Then Khalid gently touched her hand and guided her inside the room. Lily did not have a chance to look around before Khalid spoke.

'Would you marry me, Lily?' Khalid said after a minute, looking deep into Lily's eyes. He wanted to ask her this alone, in his childhood room. He wanted to hear her answer to his question when it was just the two of them, alone, away from the street and people who might walk past.

Lily did not know what to say. She shook her head a little. Am I dreaming? she wondered. She believed that she might, at any moment, start to cry tears of glorious joy and deep gratitude. The man she had liked for so long had actually asked her to marry him.

After a beat, she spoke the word she had longed to say to him for so long. 'Yes,' she said breathlessly. 'Yes, I will marry you.'

Their lips met again and again. Lily dissolved into Khalid, feeling with all her heart that this was the right thing to do. She stopped thinking and let herself fall. Soon, she was in his bed. She felt his hands, his arms and his body move above hers in a rhythm she felt that she would get used to soon enough. Nothing else matters, she told herself as a bit of guilt clouded her mind. We're going to get married after all.

Everything is going to be okay, Khalid told himself. Lily will be my wife. Lily's name bloomed in his mind as he held her hand in his afterwards. Lily, he thought. Lily. Over and over again.

Chapter XXIV

28ᵗʰ January 1941

Whenever Khalid closed his palm, he felt Lily's hand in it just like the day they had made love. He could not believe he had slept with her. He had been wrestling with guilt since that day. But there was no one he could turn to for advice.

Who could I confess to? Khalid thought, whenever guilt pricked him hard. It's okay, we're getting married, his next thought usually was. But the certainty and clarity of that night, sparkling like a diamond in his memory, had faded away as the weeks passed. He had not heard from Lily at all. He worried all the time if she was alright or if she hated him now for taking away her virginity. The virginity of a nyonya woman was prized much more than that of a baba man. Khalid frowned at the double standard as he filed notes in one by one, sitting at his desk at work. This week was his last week at Braddell Brothers. He did not have another job lined up. 'It's okay,' Pak Ambi had assured him. Ibrahim, visiting one night, had echoed Pak Ambi's words. 'With a Grade I certificate, of course, you can find a job, K,' Ibrahim said, smiling in encouragement. He seemed to be adjusting just fine to married life. His wife, he confided in Ibrahim, was kind and she cooked well. 'She knows what to do to please me,' he had said, winking at Khalid. He seemed older to Khalid, like he had aged a year in a little over a month. 'I'm married now,' his demeanour seemed to say whenever he visited. 'I'm a responsible husband and soon I will be a devoted father.'

Khalid put the hole puncher down. Was he ready to be a husband and a father? He did not know the answer at all. He would turn twenty-one in June; he would officially be a man. A man should be ready for marriage and children. Khalid sighed inwardly. He had not dared to look for Lily since that night but at that moment, a sudden thought came to him. What if Lily was pregnant? What would she do? What would he do? He closed the file as his heart pounded wildly with trepidation. Khalid decided that he would have to talk to his father and confess first of all, that he wanted to marry Lily and second of all, that he had slept with her. He could not predict how Pak Ambi would react. Very angry, he thought. He would be disappointed I didn't listen to his advice.

Khalid turned his head as he heard the clicking sound of the typewriter. He took a sip of water from his cup. Then he exhaled and got up from his desk to hand the file to Mr Ong.

As the hours passed on the clock, Khalid sat at his desk, doing his work as best he could though his mind kept wandering elsewhere. He could not wait for the workday to be over.

As Khalid cycled home, he silently rehearsed what he was going to say to Pak Ambi. After he had locked his bicycle, he looked up and saw a familiar dark-haired and tall friend in front of him.

'Edmund!' Khalid called out. He beamed as Barker spun his head around.

'Khalid! Since when do you call me Edmund?' Barker asked, laughing.

'How are you, Barker, old friend?' Khalid asked. 'What are you doing on my street?'

Barker smiled warmly as he approached Khalid. 'Visiting a friend. He stays in the next street I think.'

'Schoolmate?' Khalid asked, wondering about this friend of Barker's who stayed near him.

'Yes,' Barker said with a nod. 'He's sick so I'm passing him notes to peruse while he recovers.'

So, there is someone in my neighbourhood who attends Raffles College, Khalid thought with an unwelcome pang of envy.

'How's work at Braddell Brothers?' Barker asked.

'Okay,' Khalid said with a tilt of his head. 'I have to look for a new job soon. This Friday is my last day with the company.'

'Ah okay,' Barker said, concern creeping over his features. 'Hope you find one soon!'

Khalid thanked him warmly as Barker scratched his right temple and looked around.

'Can you help me find this address, K?' Barker asked, handing Khalid a scrap piece of paper.

'Oh yes, this is nearby,' Khalid said. 'But not on the next street.'

Khalid checked that his bicycle was securely locked before smiling at Barker and gesturing down the street. The two friends chatted casually as they walked in step towards Barker's friend's house. Khalid felt like they might have been sauntering together in school towards the soccer pitch. By the time they reached Barker's friend's house, Khalid felt a sense of nostalgia. Barker gave him a quick brotherly hug before promising they would catch up soon with the other soccer boys. Khalid stood on the street, waiting, till the door opened and Barker went inside the house. Barker did not look back at Khalid but Khalid stood there a little while longer and stared at the house.

As he walked home alone slowly, Khalid wondered when and if Barker would settle down. He expected that it would be some years before the thought would even cross Barker's mind. Maybe Barker would win the Queen's Scholarship to Cambridge University to further his studies. He imagined Harry would also be a candidate for the Queen's Scholarship.

Our lives are so different now, Khalid thought sadly. Maybe by the next time I see Barker, we won't have much in common anymore. Khalid supposed this was what happened in life; friends' paths diverged after a point and they would either stay in touch or grow apart.

It seemed like common sense but it was hard to accept. He longed for the most ordinary of school days that would rise to his conscious mind once in a while, idyllic days of attending lesson after lesson in their class, laughing in the canteen as they mimicked their teachers and playing soccer with as much ardent fervour with his teammates. Khalid thought that the most ordinary days tended to meld together over time, with nothing remarkable to distinguish one from another in a person's memory, until they grew to become a part of the person. He thought that years from now, he would still remember every single detail of these memories which lived in his skin and soul.

* * *

In the toilet, Lily pulled down her underwear and stared at her sanitary napkin. Still no blood, Lily thought, her heart sinking into her stomach. She scratched her nose as she thought of how she might grow sick with worry. There was nothing wrong, she assured herself. But as she leaned against the sink, snatches of what she had done with Khalid in his room came to her mind. She knew she had been wrong to sleep with him. Sex was meant for a husband, after marriage. Even though she had agreed to marry him, she should not have slept with him. Lily had been chastising herself in the hardest way possible for weeks now. I just keep doing the wrong thing, she had thought. What's wrong with me? Is it just love? Love makes people do wrong things. Lily did not have an easy answer.

She left the toilet and took a deep breath. Mak Kong was sitting in her chair in the main hall, fanning herself with a turquoise paper fan. Later that day, Lily knew that the family masseuse would be coming to the house to give Mak Kong a good rub-down with balms. If only I could get a massage too, Lily thought as she pictured the masseuse with her strong fingers massaging her body.

I'm not marrying Teck Soon, Lily thought next. Not marrying him.

Mak Kong did not notice Lily as she continued to fan herself. Lily took another breath and exhaled slowly.

'Mak Kong,' Lily said in a quiet voice that she hoped Mak Kong would hear anyway. Mak Kong tilted her head slightly with a questioning glance at Lily.

'Maaf, Mak Kong,' Lily said. What am I apologising for? Lily thought. A marriage shouldn't be forced.

Mak Kong furrowed her brow, as annoyance crossed her features. 'Kenapa?' she asked with a sniff.

The words felt stuck in Lily's throat, caught under layers of guilt.

'Are you starting embroidery soon, Lily?' Mak Kong continued.

'Yes,' Lily said. She frowned, feeling like she might burst.

'I cannot marry Teck Soon,' Lily said finally in a tone that sounded a lot stronger than she intended.

Mak Kong raised her eyebrows and waved her hand dismissively with her fan.

'Normal to be nervous,' Mak Kong said. She got up and nodded in the direction of the stairs as she frowned at Lily. Lily understood then that the conversation was over. I'll try again later or another day, she thought. She would try her utmost best to make Mak Kong truly hear what she had to say.

That night after dinner, when Mak Kong and Pak Kong were sitting in the main hall and talking to each other, Lily mustered all the courage she had within her and asked to speak to them. Mak Kong sniffed and folded her hands on her sarong while Pak Kong raised both his eyebrows at her.

'I don't want to marry Teck Soon,' Lily said in her most pleading and passionate voice.

Pak Kong frowned and shook his head. Mak Kong shook her head too but neither said anything. Lily took a breath and continued again, 'I want to marry Khalid. Please.'

'No,' Pak Kong said, as he reclined in his chair. 'You marry Teck Soon.'

'Khalid is not Chinese,' Mak Kong said as if that settled everything. She glanced over at Lily and shook her head again, sniffing as she examined her fingernails.

'Nothing more to talk about,' Pak Kong said, without looking at Lily. He folded his arms across his chest and turned to face Mak Kong.

Lily felt as if she had been hit hard on the face. She thought of saying something more but decided against it. With her head bowed in a manner that disgusted herself, she left the main hall, as she hated herself for her silent acquiescence. When she reached her room, she threw open her cabinet with a flourish and pulled some clothes out one by one. She grabbed her bra and underwear; she did not notice how few or many she was taking. Lily threw all her clothes in a bag. Then she waited till she heard Pak Kong and Mak Kong's footsteps going up the stairs. She waited and waited till there was silence and she was sure they were in their room.

Hot anger and fear churned together in her chest in a mixture that made her head spin. She would go to Mak Wee's place tonight. Lily repeated that to herself a few times till she calmed down. She took one deep breath after another. She would run there once all was still in the house, she promised herself.

About half an hour later, when Lily was sure everyone was in their rooms, she peeked out of her room, almost jumping when she thought she heard a sound near her. She turned her head slightly to listen. It's Ivy in her room, she thought, assuring herself. Then Lily grabbed her bag and fled.

Before she knew it, Lily stood outside the door of Mak Wee's shophouse, trembling. The pintu pagar was closed as were the main doors behind them. Visiting Mak Wee once a month was not enough for her to feel like she belonged here. But where else could she go? Visiting Khalid is risky, she worried. She did not want to be alone with him until they could get married. She had a deep fear that they would end up sleeping together again and she knew that the guilt would destroy her or worse, both of them.

Lily curled her hand into a fist and reached out to knock the door. She had forgotten about the lion door knocker and paused as she saw it. Then she saw a crouched figure moving in the window. She recognised it as Wen Jie, one of the family's majies.

'Wen Jie!' she called out.

Wen Jie stopped and stared out the window at Lily. As the door opened, they came face to face. Wen Jie's heart-shaped face, tired after a long day of work, frowned at Lily's watery and pained gaze.

'What happen?' Wen Jie asked, looking warily at Lily. 'Someone die?'

'No,' Lily said quickly. 'No one died.'

'Oh?' Wen Jie asked, lines of perplexity working their way into her forehead.

'I need to talk to my mother,' Lily said.

Wen Jie's brows furrowed as she held her hands firmly on the door. 'She sleeping,' Wen Jie said. 'Go home.'

'But—I,' Lily began.

'Come tomorrow,' Wen Jie said, closing the door.

'Please, Wen Jie,' Lily said, pleading as she placed her right hand on the door.

Wen Jie sighed then opened the door reluctantly. Lily stepped in and looked around the main hall tentatively. Where would she sleep? Her eyes moved from the teakwood three-seater sofa in front of her to the two chairs that made up a complete set.

Wen Jie stared at her blankly and frowned. 'You wait here till morning?' she asked.

Lily did not respond. Wen Jie shrugged as if to say 'suit yourself' and disappeared into the house. Lily sank down into the long sofa, feeling tiredness in every crevice of her body. The next thing she knew, someone's hands were patting her on the shoulder and trying to wake her up.

As Lily awoke, for a moment, she could not remember where she was. She looked into Mak Wee's face. Was she dreaming? Then last night came flooding back to her.

'Mak,' she said, her voice shaky with fear.

'What happened?' Mak Wee asked, her long face taut with solemn concern. 'Are you okay?'

'No,' Lily said, shaking her head as vigorously as she could. 'I don't want to marry Teck Soon.'

Mak Wee's face looked heavy with disappointment and she did not speak for a while. 'How?' she asked finally. 'What to do?'

'I don't know,' Lily said, looking down at a spot on the floor.

At that moment, Lily heard quick footsteps coming their way but she did not look up.

'Hello,' Irene said, peering at Lily with mild curiosity as if she was a new piece of furniture that had suddenly appeared in the house.

'Go and eat breakfast,' Mak Wee said in a gentle voice.

Irene hung around, still staring at Lily, wearing an obstinate frown on her face. Lily did not meet Irene's gaze. She frowned as she pretended to be busy searching for something in her bag which she picked up from the floor. She was not in the mood to talk to anyone who could not offer a solution to her unfortunate predicament, especially someone who was being cared for by her biological mother. She's my biological mother, Lily thought possessively. Not yours.

After some coaxing and assurance from Mak Wee, Irene slunk away, with a sulky expression she wore on her lips. Lily looked up from her bag and placed it next to her.

'I'm not marrying Teck Soon,' Lily said as she dug her fingernails into her palm. 'I know who I want to marry.'

'Who?' Mak Wee asked. Lily looked up into Mak Wee's face.

'His name is Khalid. He is a good man. He is Charles' tutor,' Lily said, the words about the man she loved tumbling easily out of her mouth.

Mak Wee's thin eyebrows moved closer together as they questioned what Lily meant. Lily glanced at the long and thin fingers of Mak Wee's hand. She could see the bluish-green veins on the hand spreading out like a spider's web.

'Then I will tell Mak Kong and Pak Kong,' Mak Wee said after a long pause.

Lily felt the knot around her heart loosen instantly. 'Really, Mak?' she asked, not daring to believe it could be so.

'If you don't want to marry Teck Soon, we cannot force you,' Mak Wee said. 'Won't be happy.'

Feeling relieved, the knot in her heart truly released, and wanting to believe what Mak Wee said was true, Lily flung her arms around Mak Wee's shoulders. Mak Wee tensed for a moment at the touch. When Lily did not let go, Mak Wee patted Lily awkwardly and slowly on the back as if to say everything would turn out fine.

'Thank you, Mak,' Lily said as she exhaled.

Mak Wee did not reply. There was a sadness in her downturned eyes Lily could not understand. Finally, she said, enunciating each word slowly, 'Follow . . . your . . . heart.'

Lily raised her eyebrows in surprise. She would have expected to hear such words of encouragement from Chek Chuan but not Mak Wee.

'I wish my father had not died,' Lily said, words rushing out of her with passion. 'I wish I had stayed with you and him.'

Mak Wee's eyes rimmed with sudden tears, weighed down by regret. 'I'm sorry,' she said finally. 'I don't know what to say.'

Lily put her head down and her hands around her stomach to hug herself and to will herself to be strong.

Mak Wee looked at her carefully and after a beat, she asked, 'Are you pregnant, Lily?'

Lily felt her breath catch in her throat as she saw Mama sidling slowly down the stairs. She looked thinner than the last time Lily saw her.

'Selamat pagi, Mama,' she said.

Mama stopped on the step, holding onto the railing. 'Lily?' she asked as if she thought she was seeing things.

'Ya,' Lily said. 'Lily.'

'Kenapa datang?' Mama asked.

'Datang melawat, Nya,' Mak Wee answered for her.

Lily felt her body sigh. She did not like lying even if someone else was doing it on her behalf. She was not here to visit Mama.

Mama's mouth broadened into a toothy smile. 'Ah,' she said. 'Bagus.'

Lily supposed it was a lie that needed to be told so as not to worry Mama. She would not be telling anyone in the Kong household, even Zhu Jie, that she was pregnant. Was the omission of truth a lie too? She did not know the answer. But she knew she had to tell Khalid although she did not want him to marry her because she was pregnant. Could she tell him after the wedding? Mama was by her side now, patting her on the hand. With her head turned slightly to Mak Wee, she nodded once. Mak Wee's forehead creased with lines of worry. After a while, she put her arm around Lily. The three generations of women sat there for a few minutes in a silence that was strangely comfortable.

Chapter XXV

27th April to 30th April 1941

When you had a secret, you did not look different to the outside world. But you felt different, carrying the secret with you and letting it live in your mind and body. That was how Lily felt about being pregnant. It was her secret that grew bigger each day. Only Mak Wee and Khalid knew. She could imagine what Mak Kong would think if she found out. Probably chase me out of the house, Lily thought. After a lengthy discussion between Mak Kong, Pak Kong and Mak Wee that Lily was not privy to, it was decided that Lily would remain with the Kongs until she married Khalid. The wedding to Teck Soon was cancelled, which caused tension within the Kong household, and between them and the Chongs. She shook her head and splashed water on her face. *Sian pukol tambor lagik ada salah, amcham lagik gua,* she thought. Even the deities make mistakes drumming, much less me. Too err is human. She would stop punishing herself for the cancelled wedding and the unpleasantness it caused.

As she dressed herself in her nightgown, there was a knock on the door. To her surprise, it was Ivy. Ivy had just turned twelve a few days ago and had been greeted by blood spots on her underwear. She screamed and ran out of the toilet, much to Charles' amusement and Mak Kong's concern and worry. Later, watching her sob on Mak Kong's

211

lap, she wondered if Ivy was grieving the loss of her girlhood or the start
of her womanhood, both of which meant being confined to the house.
She figured it was everything coming together.

'Hello,' Ivy said softly.

'Hello,' Lily echoed.

'Can I come in?' Ivy asked. She bit the side of her lip.

Lily hesitated for a few moments. In a few days, she would be
marrying Khalid and moving out of the Kongs' home. Mak Kong had
hardly spoken to her since the wedding was cancelled. Ivy and Charles
did not seem to treat her any differently but still she had wondered if
Mak Kong had told them she was a bad nyonya. But here Ivy was asking
to come into her room.

'Okay,' Lily said.

Ivy came in and stood in the middle of the room, looking around.
Lily tried to remember the last time Ivy was in her room but she
could not.

'Are you really leaving?' Ivy asked as if she had been bursting
to ask it.

'I—I'm not leaving,' Lily replied.

Ivy edged closer to Lily. 'I thought you're moving out . . .
getting married.'

'Oh,' Lily said. 'Yes, I'm moving out.'

'Are you scared?' Ivy asked, her eyes wide.

'Yes,' Lily admitted.

'Why not Teck Soon?' Ivy asked.

Lily shrugged. She did not feel like relieving the pain and guilt of the
cancelled wedding again in her mind.

'If I'm matchmade, I'll run away too,' Ivy said.

Lily swallowed her saliva as she stared at Ivy. She thought she
should say something that a big sister might say but she did not know
what that would be. It had never seemed to her like she was Charles'
and Ivy's sibling.

'I'm not running away,' Lily said after a while.

Ivy did not seem to hear her. She noticed the heart-shaped cockle
on Lily's dresser.

'The shell,' she said. Lily brightened a little. She remembered going to the beach that day and picking up shells with Ivy.

'You won't go to the beach with us again?' Ivy asked.

Probably not, Lily thought. But instead she said, 'Tak tahu' because who knew what would happen in future.

Ivy seemed to accept this answer and fell silent. She sat on Lily's bed and turned to face the dark sky. Feeling awkward, Lily stood until Ivy felt sleepy and left her room.

The next morning, Ivy slipped into the kitchen after lunch and passed Lily a shell. Lily recognised it as the spiral snail shell that had collected together on the beach.

'So, you can remember me,' Ivy said shyly.

Lily was moved by Ivy's sweet gesture but did not know how to say it. Ivy put her arms around Lily's waist, giving her a quick hug, and then rushed out of the kitchen. Zhu Jie looked up from washing the dishes as Lily turned the shell over in her palm. She had not thought of what she should give the Kongs as parting gifts; she thought they would not want to be reminded of her. But maybe she should give Ivy something, Lily thought at that moment. She racked her brains as she tried to think of something. She had an old doll that Mak Wee had bought for her when she was ten. Maybe she would find something when she was out of the house later. Lily made a mental note to ask Khalid where she could buy something for Ivy.

Lily headed to her room and placed the spiral shell next to the heart-shaped one on her dresser. She picked up the embroidered handkerchief she had secretly sewn for Zhu Jie using cloth from her old baju panjang. She wanted to wait until her last night to give it to her but decided it would not hurt to give it to her earlier. Back in the kitchen, Zhu Jie and Leng Jie were done with washing the dishes. Lily poked her head in and waved Zhu Jie over.

'For you,' Lily said.

Overwhelmed with emotion, Zhu Jie's face crumpled. She embraced Lily. Lily knew that while she was not sad about moving out, Zhu Jie was. She had been teasing Lily about marrying Khalid, which Lily supposed she did to hide her sadness. Lily worried that Mak Kong would treat Zhu Jie badly while Lily was away but maybe that fear was unfounded. She did not seem to treat Zhu Jie any differently than before she found out about Zhu Jie's role in helping Lily and Khalid. Zhu Jie had insisted to Lily that Mak Kong did not give her any punishment. Lily knew, though, that even if Zhu Jie's pay had been cut or her employment with the Kongs prematurely terminated, Zhu Jie would never admit to it. She held on to Zhu Jie tightly; Zhu Jie would always be her true friend.

So, this is a mosque, Lily thought with wonderment that afternoon as she stood nervously inside a mosque along Upper East Coast Road for her conversion ceremony. Masjid Kampong Hajijah. It was beautiful with its rusty red roof. The mosque seemed bigger on the inside than it looked on the outside. Lily was struck by how clean and white everything appeared to look like a new piece of cloth. She was wearing her favourite light grey baju panjang and a loose pink scarf wrapped around her head.

Khalid and Ibrahim were there with her as the male witnesses to her conversion to Islam. They stood near the ustaz, more than an arm's length away from Lily, both wearing solemn expressions on their faces. With a booming voice, the ustaz recited the Shahadah, the Muslim declaration of faith, and Lily repeated after him. All the while, she stared at the white cap he wore on his head. Just like that, Lily became a Muslim. She had no idea what that meant; she only knew that to marry Khalid, she had to be a Muslim too. Some Muslim women, Lily knew, wore a head scarf called a tudung around their head. But there were some who did not. It confused her but she did not ask Khalid. She would have to assimilate into the Muslim community. She would learn slowly and observe carefully how to best do that on her own.

Ibrahim smiled tentatively at her. Lily sometimes thought she saw a guilty look in Ibrahim's eyes. She supposed that he knew that she was aware he had reported her clandestine dating to Mak Kong. But neither broached the subject, letting the awkwardness hang in the air between them as they tiptoed around each other.

'Do you have to go home now?' Khalid asked when they were outside the mosque. Lily was looking at the silver crescent moon at the top of the blue minaret, wondering what it symbolised.

'I don't know,' Lily said. 'I don't want to go home.' It was the truth. A few months ago, the answer would have been 'Yes'. But now Mak Kong acted like she did not exist. What difference does it make, Lily thought, whether I go home early or not?

'I want to buy something for Ivy,' Lily said.

'Okay,' Khalid said.

'I have to go home,' Ibrahim said.

'Okay,' Khalid replied. 'Thanks for coming.'

Ibrahim smiled a little. 'Take care.'

'Bye,' Lily said softly. 'Thank you.' As Ibrahim walked away, she moved closer to Khalid.

'Where can I buy something for Ivy?' she asked.

Khalid thought about it for a moment. 'Depends on what you want to get. A toy?'

'I think maybe Ivy is too old for toys,' Lily said, turning her face away from the sun.

Khalid smiled at a man who glanced at them as he strode into the mosque before asking, 'How old is she?'

'Twelve!' Lily said.

'Oh,' Khalid replied. 'She's quite small-sized for twelve. I thought she was ten.'

'Is there a shop selling hair clips?' Lily wondered.

'I don't think there are any nearby,' Khalid said.

Lily considered for a passing second that they could take a bus but then she worried all over again that Mak Kong would get upset if she stayed out too long.

'Maybe I better go home,' she said.

'Are you sure?' Khalid looked concerned.

Lily stared down the end of the street before she met his eye. 'Yes. But we'll see each other again soon.'

Khalid smiled. 'It's a promise,' he said as he reached out to hold Lily's hand. He walked her home, feeling safer and happier than he could ever remember.

At home, Khalid worried about his lack of employment. He was getting married in three days and still had no job. Pak Ambi told him he would get one soon but still Khalid felt uncomfortable. He had only gone for two interviews; one with the Singapore Post Office and the other with the *Straits Times*. It would be a dream, Khalid thought, to get a position with the *Straits Times* as a junior reporter, the position he had interviewed for. But he knew that he had no experience with journalism; he had not even worked on his school newsletter. He was sure that there would be others who were more qualified. The Singapore Post Office position was that of a temporary clerk; the interviewer had promised him that if he performed well, he could get a permanent position. This was what Khalid coveted most for a permanent position meant job security.

On a lark, he had even applied to Raffles College last month and received a letter of admission a few weeks later, welcoming him for the next school year. 1942, Khalid thought. He did not know if Lily and him would have a child by then. Imagining a chubby baby with olive skin, gurgling at him, made him smile. Maybe his hopes for his life were smaller than what they had the potential to be. Maybe a person's life grew bigger if they decided to dream bigger. He had just planned to find a job; he had not planned on looking for true love. But yet it had come his way. How many people get to experience that even once in their life? Khalid thought. Ibrahim seemed to like his wife well enough, but Khalid did not know if it was love. He was sure his parents had not loved each other. He did not know if Pak Ambi loved Mak Jah or just felt like he had to take another wife.

I love Lily and Lily loves me, Khalid thought. How lucky we both are.

He got up from his bed and headed to his desk. Slowly, he ran his index finger down the spine of a slim book Samad had given him for his birthday. 'From my Ayah,' Samad had said. The spine of the book read *Islamic Faith*. Faith demanded a lot of a person; it required them to believe in things they could not see. God was invisible. So was the future and a person's dreams for it. One could imagine it but not be sure it existed.

Lily gave me faith to find my dream, Khalid thought as he put the book back on the table. What neither of us knew at the time was, my dream was her.

Days later, Lily glanced around the main hall of the Kongs' home, wondering whether Mak Kong would say anything to her. Little was yelping at her heels as if he knew she was leaving. Lily bent down and scooped him up with her hands. She buried her face into his fur as he whimpered. 'Bye Little,' she said, breathing in his scent.

Lily had already said goodbye to everyone she could last night. Lily had given Ivy one of her kebayas. Charles had wished her all the best; Chek Chuan had asked her to come back and visit. Leng Jie muttered a simple 'Bye' that morning over the kitchen sink, so softly that Lily might have missed it if she had not been right next to her, rubbing soap into her palms. Lily did not expect Pak Kong to say a word to her, but she still hoped Mak Kong might. After all, today was her wedding day.

Mak Kong emerged from the kitchen just then.

'Still here?' she asked.

Lily's face fell a little. 'Leaving now.'

Mak Kong's lips pursed. As Lily wondered what she should say, Mak Kong sighed and then said, 'Tunggu.'

Lily waited, holding her breath. Mak Kong pointed to the cabinet where several kamcheng were displayed. 'You can pick one,' Mak Kong said.

Lily understood this to mean it was a wedding gift. 'Terima kasih, Mak Kong,' she said when she found her voice. She put Little down and he darted away into the house. She watched him go, wondering when the next time would be she would see him.

Lily felt moved but she did not know how to say so. She walked to the cabinet and her eyes fell on the smallest kamcheng. It was a soothing jade green with orange handles and yellow trimming at the top. In the middle, in a white clover shape sat a small magpie on a branch of pink peony blossoms. She picked it up and held it up to Mak Kong silently, asking for permission to take it.

'Okay,' Mak Kong said.

Lily clutched the kamcheng tightly in her hands. 'Terima kasih, Mak Kong.'

'Jaga diri,' Mak Kong said. With that, she turned to leave.

Lily bit her lip. Take care too, Mak Kong, she thought. She wanted to run into the kitchen and embrace Zhu Jie for one last time. Instead, she picked up her luggage bag, safely wrapped her newest possession in a cotton bedsheet and headed towards the door.

'Bye everyone,' she whispered. She had expected to feel some sadness when she left but not this deep pain that was slowly taking root in her heart. This house had been more of a home than she thought. Was it at the point of leaving somewhere that someone finally understood what their life there had been? Lily stopped for a moment, placing her palm on the pintu pagar, to steady herself. I'll be back one day, she promised. I'll see Zhu Jie again.

She pushed the pintu pagar outwards and stepped outside into the open air, her feet on the five-foot way. Across the street, Lily saw Khalid waiting for her with an expectant smile on his handsome face. Lily could see a shadow of nerves cloud his face just then. Somehow that made her feel better. She was not alone in her anxiety or sorrow now. Neither would she be alone in her excitement or joy. Khalid would be there with her always.

My new life awaits, Lily thought. As she walked across the street, Khalid held out his hand. And soon Lily was running to reach him.

Chapter XXVI

8th December 1941 to 13th June 1942

Khalid woke up with a start, his face beaded with sweat. He had just had another nightmare about war. He turned around to see Lily sleeping soundly on her right side next to him. She was curled up around her pillow, a picture of peace. He had been worried about how he and Lily would cope with taking care of their baby son Ihsan. Ihsan was two months old now. There were many times Khalid felt so grateful that his love for Lily had deepened and strengthened with Ihsan's arrival. She was the mother of his child now. In their new rented room at a shophouse at Beach Road, their little family of three lived together. He placed his ear to the wall and through it, he could hear the muffled sounds of Pak Ambi's snores.

Khalid padded to the crib where his son lay sleeping. When he was born, Pak Ambi had laughed and joked, 'You sure your son or not? Look like Chinese baby.' But the moment Khalid held Ihsan in his arms, he knew Ihsan was his flesh and blood, his beautiful child and Lily's. Ihsan was perfect, Khalid thought. Ten little fingers and ten wriggly toes. His heart burst open with so much love, something he had only felt once before the day he married Lily.

He had gotten used to the stares people on the street gave when he and Lily were out together. Some people would point and whisper to each other; others would avert their eyes immediately as if the sight of an inter-racial couple together, the warm brown next to light yellow skin, was an offensive sight. He supposed it was normal but he knew Lily did not like it. He had promised Lily when they moved to Beach Road that a new neighbourhood meant a new start. She would not have to bump into the Kongs or Teck Soon nor endure the gossip of the neighbours. But his promise had not come true; no one knew them here but their marriage was still regarded with wariness and suspicion among the neighbours. Khalid could feel neighbours' looks trained on his back whenever he and Lily walked side by side, taking turns to strap Ihsan to their body with the baby wrap. He did not care to know what they were saying but he could tell it bothered and angered Lily even as she tried to hide it. Khalid was starting to pick up on little cues that hinted at his wife being upset. How her body would tense up next to him if they passed by Mrs Ng in the hallway or the way annoyance flickered over her face when she felt other neighbours were gossiping about them, her face turning away from theirs and towards his. In their room, Khalid liked it when Lily sought comfort in him, leaning her body against his or curling up beside him to sleep. It did not matter what life was like outside. In their little world, life went on.

Khalid expected Ihsan would wake up soon and wail for milk or to be held. All of a sudden, he heard the sound of explosions bursting through the still of night. He froze. Was he imagining it? The Governor had repeatedly assured Singaporeans that no Japanese bombs would fall on Singapore. Maybe it's a test, Khalid thought. A practice. His heart lurched forward in his chest. He ran to the window; all the streetlights were still switched on. Nothing looked any different. The sky was cloudy but bright, lit up by moonlight. It's a test, Khalid thought. But what if it's not? Instantly, he picked Ihsan up. He looked up and saw Lily moving towards him in the dark, groggy with sleep. She looked stricken with fear. He passed Ihsan, who was still peacefully asleep, to Lily.

'Go,' he said, trying to stay calm and keep the fear out of his voice even as his hands trembled. Lily nodded and ran out of the room with Khalid close behind. There was no time to take any of their belongings. Khalid threw Pak Ambi's door open and dashed to his bed. He shook his father's shoulder. But still Pak Ambi lay fast asleep, his belly rising and falling. Frantic, Khalid hurried to the toilet, grabbing a cup on his way there. He filled it with water and ran back to the room. He splashed the water on Pak Ambi's face. Pak Ambi stirred then sputtered, 'Wh-what?'

'Bombs!' Khalid shouted as he heard another explosion. Pak Ambi jolted awake and grabbed Khalid's hand. They bumped into a neighbour running down the stairs, the sarong around the neighbour's waist slipping off as he ran. Khalid did not look into anyone's face but he could feel their fear, so palpable was the tension in the house. Pak Ambi pushed Khalid into the space under the stairs where all eleven occupants of the shophouse were huddled together. Ihsan was wailing loudly now. Khalid thought about how suffocated and confused Ihsan must feel, stripped from his comfortable crib and brought to a dusty and dry space. Each explosion Khalid heard shook him as it echoed through the house. After what felt like hours but might have been minutes, he heard the sound of the sirens' call. They seemed to be screaming. The sirens felt far away then closer and closer. Why did the sirens sound after the bombs? Khalid wondered. He dreaded leaving the house later to assess the damage done to their neighbourhood.

Later, while Lily nursed a colicky Ihsan, Khalid got dressed for work and walked out, bracing himself for a sight that would break his spirit. But everything looked more or less the same, unscathed from the bombing. Khalid realised that the Japanese must have bombed selected areas and Beach Road was not one of them. He would later learn that these areas were Sembawang Naval Base, Keppel Harbour, Tengah Air Base, Seletar Airbase, Chinatown, Raffles Place and Keppel Harbour. The bombing would have been much heavier had 48 Japanese bombers not abandoned their attack due to bad weather. He walked as fast as he could to the post office, relieved that it was nearby. He had been working there since the start of May as a temporary clerk. He had thought it was a stroke of luck. The job offer arrived in the mail the day before his wedding, putting his mind at ease. 'Very lucky!' Pak Ambi had shouted. 'I told you job will come!' When Khalid reached the post office, his colleagues were buzzing about the bombing. No one greeted him so he stood listening as they exchanged stories about their experience. After a while, their boss emerged from his office and instructed them to get to work.

'We're lucky that it's not this area,' Khalid's colleague muttered as he stirred his cup of coffee. There were murmurs of agreement from other colleagues.

'Yes,' Khalid said though he did not completely agree. He wondered how many people had been injured and how many others killed. It did not feel fortunate at all that his neighbourhood had not been bombed when other parts of Singapore had been struck. Khalid thought everything about the war was disastrous; what affected one Singaporean surely had an effect on others. He wanted to go back to bed and pretend this day never happened, like it was a bad dream he could wake up from.

It was almost nine in the morning when Lily had finally put Ihsan back to sleep. After breakfast, she crawled into bed herself and wondered about Zhu Jie, the Kongs, and Mak Wee. Were they okay? She was sure that there were those who had been injured, or worse, killed. She had tried to persuade Khalid not to go into work today but he had insisted. Lily had only relented because he said he could not afford to lose his job. Pak Ambi had gone to check on Ibrahim who lived on the same street. He had not returned home yet, which concerned Lily.

What if the bombing started again? Lily thought. She shuddered and lay in bed. Allah, she whispered. Help us. For what felt like a long time, she stayed awake, sick with fear and rousing only to check on Ihsan. Lily realised suddenly that if she gave into terror, the Japanese would win. She got up and looked at the sky. It was the lightest blue and fluffed up with chiffon clouds. I will not be afraid, Lily thought as she stared into the clouds. She grabbed the basket of dirty clothes from the day before and headed down the stairs.

Her neighbour, Mrs Ng, was pinning her freshly washed clothes to the clothesline. She turned to Lily and waved, though her face was set in a frown. Lily waved back. When she was done with hanging clothes, she came to stand over Lily with her arms on her hips.

'Stupid Japanese,' Mrs Ng muttered.

Lily did not look up from the washing board. She was scrubbing Khalid's shirt.

'Yes,' Lily said.

'Men know only how to fight,' Mrs Ng said. 'It's women who know better.'

Lily did not reply.

'Right?' Mrs Ng asked.

'Yes, Mrs Ng,' Lily said, wishing she would go away. She did not appreciate the way Mrs Ng stared at her and Khalid when they met her in the hallway.

'Khalid at work, is it?' Mrs Ng asked, seemingly not noticing that Lily did not really want to talk.

'Yes,' Lily replied, as she took another shirt and soaked it in the sud-filled basin.

'Today don't need to go work,' Mrs Ng said. 'Mr Ng didn't.'

Lily jerked her head slightly which Mrs Ng mistakenly interpreted as acquiescence. After a few moments, Mrs Ng spoke again.

'How did he get you to marry him?' she asked.

'What?' Lily asked, looking up from the basin. She thought by now that such questions would not faze her but they still did.

'He's Indian,' Mrs Ng said. 'Muslim too, right?'

Lily felt her heart shrink and wilt in response. She turned back to the basin, picking up the shirt and rinsing it in a basin filled with water.

'Nyonyas are matchmade?' Mrs Ng asked.

Lily did not know if that was a question or a statement.

Mind your own business, she wanted to say.

She bit her lip and picked up Khalid's sarong to wash next.

'It's a long story,' she said, feeling Mrs Ng's gaze on her back.

Mrs Ng shrugged and sighed. 'Your parents must be angry with you,' she said before walking away.

Lily felt her cheeks turn warm as anger rose within her.

You don't know anything! she screamed in her mind.

She wrung the sarong hard then threw it on the ground, her body shaking with the force of her anger. It took her a while to compose herself before she continued washing her clothes. Lily breathed in and out slowly.

When she was done with hanging the clothes out to dry, she hurried to check on Ihsan. He was awake and stretching out his little bracelet arms in his crib. She picked him up, breathing in the scent of his baby-soft skin and whispered, her cheek touching his, 'You are safe. You are loved.' I will do my best not to let the war hurt you, she promised in her mind. My dearest, my Ihsan.

Ihsan was eight months old now; he was crawling around their room and babbling to himself. Sitting on the floor, Lily beckoned Ihsan towards her.

'Baba,' Ihsan said, grinning away, a spot of drool near his mouth. Lily had tried to teach him how to say 'Nya Nya' for Mother but to no avail. Inside their room, it was possible to pretend life was normal, part of pre-war days perhaps. Once they stepped outside though, the sight of the tanned, hardened faces of the Kempetai, the Japanese military police, was hard to ignore. They seemed to tower over everyone with their intimidating presence. Everyone had to bow to them or risk being slapped, beaten or taken away. Every time Lily walked past them on the way to the market, she held her breath in fear as if a policeman might reach out and hit her for daring to walk in front of him.

'Bababa,' Ihsan babbled as he reached Lily. Lily giggled and picked him up, kissing his chubby cheek. She was glad she had Ihsan and Khalid; they helped her stay sane. She tried to visit Mak Wee once a week now and felt closer to her than before the war had started. Mak Kong seemed to have forgiven her; the terror of war had pushed the ignominy of Lily's cancelled wedding to the back of her mind. Whenever she visited the Kongs, Mak Kong tried to give her a drink at the very least and though she never enquired about Khalid, she asked her how Ihsan was doing. Zhu Jie was still working with the Kongs. Her face would brighten whenever she saw Lily in the kitchen again.

Lily placed Ihsan back in his crib so she could do her chores. Before she headed down the stairs, she looked out the window for a moment. The sky was a blue so clear that in the not-so-distant past, it would have made Lily's heart ache in a good way. Lily moved her hand to her stomach. She had a feeling that the baby she was carrying was another son, a younger brother for Ihsan. She was two months pregnant and it was four months into the Japanese Occupation. Scarcity, loss, uncertainty and hardship weighed heavily on her mind and heart. Singapore was now called Syonan-to. The flag fluttering high on a pole above Cathay Cinema, the tallest building in the country, was the Japanese flag, white with a red circle in the centre. The flag had been there ever since the end of a long week of fighting between the British and the Japanese when the British had chosen to surrender. At the time, Khalid could not believe it. How could the British give up? he had thought, filled with disappointment. Cathay Cinema was now used to exhibit the consequences of disobedience. Occasionally, the Japanese military displayed the severed heads of looters and other criminals outside the building. Flies swirled around the unfortunate heads, feeding on the dead cells and open wounds.

Three days after the fall of Singapore to the Japanese, the Japanese military began mass killings of people they deemed 'undesirable', mostly ethnic Chinese men. Khalid was weighed down with worry that his classmates and friends had been murdered in the Sook Ching massacre. Mostly it was Roy, running lightly across the soccer field, who would flash through his mind. Was Roy okay? Khalid had no idea. Food grew scarce and was rationed out. The Japanese encouraged people to find substitutes for rice like tapioca and sweet potato. Khalid and Lily felt hungry every day and worried about the next day and the next week if they would have enough to feed Ihsan.

Khalid tried to do the best he could at work though he hated the idea of working for the Japanese. After the British surrender, the post office had closed for a month before it reopened under Japanese rule. The Japanese recalled existing stamps throughout the country and printed over them in Japanese characters to deface the British sovereign head on the stamps. Every time Khalid looked at a stamp, he felt sick to his stomach.

One day, his boss, who had been outspoken about his disdain for the Japanese, did not report to work. Khalid knew that as a Chinese male aged below fifty, he had probably been arrested. The best-case scenario was imprisonment, but they feared that he had been packed into a truck and sent to a killing site. Khalid thought of how his boss' family must be coping without him. Together with a few other colleagues, they wanted to pay the family a visit but did not do so in the end out of sheer fear that they might be targeted next. Khalid felt like fear dictated what he did and did not do. He hated feeling weak and afraid, but he wanted to be careful. He did not want Lily or Ihsan to have to survive without him.

Lily's days were marked by uncertainty. Every day that Khalid went out to work, she did not know if he would return. She tried to stay at home as much as she could. There were months where she did not try to visit Mak Wee or the Kongs. She let morning, afternoon and night pass by doing her chores and taking care of Ihsan. The best way to occupy herself she realised was by cooking. It was not the same as cooking with Zhu Jie, Leng Jie and Ah Huat. There were moments of loneliness as she huddled in the kitchen, pounding spices in the mortar. Besides the family before her eyes that she could see and hold onto each night, everything seemed unknown. However, Lily felt sure of one thing: no matter the terror Man could wreak, Nature stood its ground. The sun still rose in the east and set in the west. The moon shone every night and the sky brought the memory of comfort to Lily. She did not know then how long the war would last but she knew the skies would darken to a deep grey and bring more showers of luck.

Epilogue

17th June 2021

Khalid stares at the blank television screen in his room. Today is his 101st birthday. He cannot believe he has lived so long. Lily passed away twenty-one years, nine months and eight days ago. 9th September 1999. Life since has not been the same. Some of his dearest children have departed the earth. He counts them on his fingers. Four dead, five alive.

His granddaughter, Naima, walks in and says it is time to go downstairs. Everyone is waiting. Khalid cannot really hear her; he adjusts the hearing aid in his ear. He peers at Naima and wonders why she is still not married. His smart and adorable Naima. Every year he has been asking her to get married so he can witness her wedding before he passes on. He sighs, wondering when that day will ever come. Naima sighs too because she knows her grandfather can't hear a word she is saying. She grabs a piece of paper and pen from the table next to his bed and scribbles on it in big letters.

Khalid puts on his glasses and reads the note, 'Birthday party for you downstairs.'

'I told you not to throw a party for me,' he complains.

Naima smiles wryly; she knows her grandfather probably does not fully mean what he says. She takes his arm and escorts him downstairs where his fifth son Baqil hands him the newspaper. Life! Khalid thinks.

He sees a photograph of an old man with white hair on the front page. Is it me? he wonders. After all, his hair is white; it had turned all-white more than three decades ago when his body was still fit and strong. Khalid decides Naima must have written an article about him, in celebration of his 101st birthday. He does not realise the featured centenarian is not him but a famous local artist.

'You write about me?' he beams at Naima and presses his soft lips to her cheek.

He is delighted. Then all of a sudden, he sees his second daughter Noora with a round cake with ten big candles in front of him. Khalid wonders what flavour the cake is. Maybe marble cake, he thinks. That is his favourite. This cake looks different though. He peers at it. There seems to be mango, kiwi and strawberry on the top of the cake.

Oh, he thinks. Must be a sponge cake with fresh fruit and cream. That would be delicious too.

'Why did you do all this?' he says to Naima but she just smiles at him in response. Everyone starts singing the birthday song loudly. Khalid hears it at a muted volume. He looks up at Naima's mobile phone, wondering if she is taking a photo or video. He had finally obtained a mobile phone from Baqil two years ago but is struggling to learn how to use it. He looks up at Naima again. Her eyes seem like pools of adoration and reverence.

This girl, he thinks. She loves me so much. Will she be okay after I'm gone? He tries to let the thought leave his mind peacefully. He has been preparing her for his death ever since Lily passed away. When Lily was ill with lung cancer and preparing for her death, he remembers Lily asking him to 'Take good care of Naima.'

'Your grandmother loved you so much,' he remembers telling Naima two years ago. 'She didn't want you to be alone after she died.'

Khalid blows out the candles. Ten candles feel like a lot of effort to blow out. It takes him four attempts to blow them all out. Next to him, Baqil helps him cut the cake. As the cake is passed around, Khalid looks around at everyone gathered around him today. His fourth son Hamza and his wife Jamila are here. Hamza is standing right next to him, looking deep in thought. He wants to reach out to hold Hamza's hand but he does not. Khalid feels a rush of gratitude for his children that are with him today. He thinks of his youngest son Iskandar and his first daughter Mariam who are both overseas. How he misses them and longs to see them again. What about Ihsan, Ibrahim, Omar and Nadira? His beloved children. Soon he will be with them again.

Khalid feels tired as he lifts a spoonful of cake to his mouth. He hopes that he can take a nap soon. He closes his eyes to rest. He is a young boy, running barefoot on the sandy beach. He's running forward then he spins on his heel and runs backwards, laughing lightly. Ibrahim is chasing after him. There is so much light Khalid has to squint his eyes. Now he has just scored a goal. Roy, Zaid, Noor and Barker run up to him, yelping and cheering. He pumps his fist into the air as Mak Aisha waves her hand at him. Then he is on his first date with Lily. She smiles and he feels instantly at ease. Now he is older and married, carrying Ihsan in his arms. It is 1944, the midst of wartime. Everything feels heavy. Pak Ambi's voice booms through the house as he calls out Khalid's and Lily's names.

After an air raid, Khalid sees a bleeding man lying on the street. He feels the man's pain so acutely as if it is his own. He cannot look away. His throat is parched, his eyes are swollen from crying, and his body is aching for rest. He joins the winding queue for rations. He is so hungry for rice and meat. Everyone celebrates with impassioned relief when the war is finally over. He does not know who is hugging him; body upon body are piled together. Khalid has never felt so grateful to be alive. He opens his eyes. He sees Baqil, his devoted son, in front of him. When he closes his eyes again, he sees his beloved Lily. Lily in the morning, preparing breakfast as their children chatter on. Lily in the afternoon, planting tapioca in the garden and wiping sweat from her brow. Lily at night, curling up to sleep with a pillow, her hand in his. Lily at the door, her arms open and her heart filled with love, welcoming him home.

Letter to the Reader

Dear Reader:

Thank you so much for reading. I feel honoured and privileged that you chose to read this book.

This work of fiction is inspired by the true love story of how my maternal grandparents met and fell in love. I believe my late grandfather was a great man and he experienced a great love. An unlikely love that existed before either him or my grandmother knew it. Without my grandparents' courage and strength to fight to be together, I wouldn't be here today to share this story with you.

If you're like me, then you believe in love that endures all. Since I was a little girl, I've dreamt of being a writer, a wife and a mother. Perhaps I can consider myself a writer now. But the other two dreams sometimes feel like they might never come true especially as I approach the age of thirty-five. Yet I continue to dream them anyway. Through times of doubt and struggle, it is my grandparents' love for each other and for me that has kept me going. One day, I hope to experience a love like theirs that will create a family of my very own.

At whichever stage in life you're currently at, I hope that this story gives you a bit of comfort, courage and perhaps even clarity to find and pursue your own path in life. Have faith. Be brave. Love deeply. The world is yours to explore. Your journey is yours to take.

With love,
Nadia

Historical Note

Place

This story is set against a backdrop of a world about to go to war. On 1 September 1939, Hitler invaded Poland from the west. German forces broke through Polish defenses and advanced on the Polish capital of Warsaw. Hundreds of thousands of refugees fled the German advance. Two days later, France and Britain, standing by their guarantee of Poland's border, declared war on Germany, beginning World War II.

In colonial Singapore, war came first with the bombing of Singapore on 8 December 1941. The attack began before dawn shortly after the Japanese forces landed on Kota Bharu, Malaya. It was the first knowledge the Singapore population had that war had broken out in the Far East. The streets were still brightly lit despite air raid sirens going off at 4 a.m., allowing pilot navigators to locate their targets without difficulty.

When the bombers began their attack at 4.30 a.m., Allied anti-aircraft guns immediately opened fire. The battleship *Prince of Wales* and battlecruiser *Repulse* responded but no aircraft was shot down. A formation of nine bombers flew over without releasing their bombs to draw the searchlights and anti-aircraft guns away from the other group. The bombers succeeded in bombing the airfields at Seletar and Tengah, damaging three Bristol Blenheim bombers of No. 34 Squadron RAF. Bombs fell on Raffles Place. 61 people were killed and over 700 were injured.

On 15 February 1942, Singapore fell to the Japanese. The Japanese moved quickly across the island. With one million citizens trapped in the city and water supplies at critical levels, British commander Lieutenant-General Arthur Percival surrendered on 15 February 1942. More than 130,000 Allied troops were taken as prisoners. In London, Prime Minister Winston Churchill announced that the fall of Singapore was the 'worst disaster and largest capitulation in British history'. For Australia too, the fall of Singapore was a disaster. More than 15,000 Australian soldiers were captured, more than 7,000 of whom would die as prisoners of war.

Characters

The character of Lily is inspired by my late maternal grandmother, Asmah Binte Abdullah nee Rose Wee. The character of Khalid is inspired by my late maternal grandfather, Kassim Bin Tambi. Although most of this book is in English, do note that the dialogue in the Kong household is actually a mixture of Baba Malay, English, and Hokkien, which is the dialect spoken by the majies Zhu Jie and Leng Jie. In Khalid's world, his family converses in English and Malay.

The character of Harry Lee is inspired by the late Harry Lee Kuan Yew, widely recognised as Singapore's founding father. The character of Kwa Geok Choo is inspired by the late Kwa Geok Choo, who would become the wife of Lee Kuan Yew. She was a lawyer, co-founder and partner of law firm Lee & Lee. The character of Barker is inspired by the late E. W. Barker, a Singaporean politician and lawyer, who authored the Proclamation of Singapore. Barker was a Head Prefect, a champion athlete and soccer team captain in 1938 at Raffles Institution.

My grandfather Kassim Bin Tambi in the 1940s

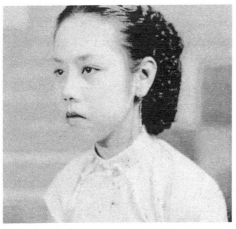

My grandmother Asmah Bte Abdullah nee Rose Wee
on 15 February 1941

Cultural Note

Peranakan is a conjugated word adopted from Indonesian or Malay. It means 'keturunan anak negeri dengan orang asing', the descendants of the intermarriage between indigenous people with foreigners. Peranakan culture and identity is both maternal and paternal, meaning that you are considered a Peranakan if one of your parents is of Peranakan extraction.

The Peranakan groups covered in this book are the Straits Chinese, a subgroup of Chinese Peranakans, and the Jawi Peranakans. The Straits Chinese, defined as those born or living in the Straits Settlements, the British colony consisting of Penang, Malacca and Singapore established in 1826. Straits Chinese were not considered Baba Nyonya unless they displayed certain Sino-Malay syncretic attributes, in terms of attire worn, food, spoken language, and choice of education. Peranakan men are known as 'baba' while the women are known as 'nyonya'.

The Jawi Peranakans comprises Straits-born Muslims of mixed Indian (especially Tamil) and Malay parentage. They were an elite group within the British Malayan community in mid-19th century Malaya. In addition, to their wealth and social standing, they are remembered for setting up the first Malay newspaper in the region and their influences on Malay culture.

Acknowledgements

This book came together piece by piece, scene by scene, in my mind. There were many times when I stopped researching and writing, took breaks and then started again. It was a long journey which sometimes felt smooth and easy but other times, bumpy and arduous. Sometimes I walked alone but many times, people were there to support me and cheer me on. The following are people that I feel gratitude towards for *Showers of Luck*.

Deep thanks to the Penguin SEA Team: publisher Nora Nazerene Abu Bakar for believing in this story, editor Amberdawn Manaois for your valuable feedback, executive Chaitanya Srivastava from the publicity team, and the PR and digital media team of Pallavi Narayan and Garima Bhatt.

The Pink Pangea Switzerland writing and hiking retreat ladies for the much-needed fellowship in 2019. In particular, Jaclyn Mishal for leading the retreat, Rebecca Noel for your poetry that moved me (keep writing), Kristin Waites for our comfortable sharing of pieces we wrote, Jaclyn Goldis for sharing your knowledge on publishing, Gail Weber for your warmth and wit, Amy Eyler for my birthday dinner together after everyone else had left and Linda Mims for seeing me as I am.

My MA Creative Writing professors: Dr Daryl Whetter, thank you for your detailed feedback in the CNF module. It was a privilege to have been taught by you. Dr Rosslyn Prosser, thank you so much for your support, guidance and feedback in the poetry and fiction modules. Your warm, nurturing nature is a balm for me.

My LASALLE classmates: Subhransu Behera for always encouraging me to write what I experience, Gabriel Oh for your quiet and steady presence that calms me, Hanis Husin for the writing workshops you've suggested and for the space you gave me at QUIET. And Hazel Huang, I'll always remember the MRT ride when we shared our hopes and dreams.

The WR!TERS @ WORK team. Firstly, my bosses Agnes Ng, Jemmies Siew, Kym Ng, Ang Kai Ning for the opportunity to learn and grow as an enrichment teacher. To Yashini Devi, always thankful for you. Hazimah Saini, my fellow writer, thanks for the encouragement. Keep sharing your work; it matters. Sharon Ellesia, I'll always remember the heart-to-heart talk we shared. To my MP team: James Nayar for being my sweet Sunday buddy, Iffah Syahirah for your cheerfulness and wit, Fatima Nushrath for being my dear art and book friend, Mitsuko Cabillada for your warmth and honesty, and Vanessa Wee for your helpful ways. Thank you so much for the camaraderie.

The entire KKH KIDS 0-3 team for the work you do to benefit mothers and children. It was a privilege to work with you. Special thanks to Team I - Rachel Yeo, Dr Abiramy, Dr Tan, Low Tok Cheng, Yan Zhen Ying and Kak Rina for the safe harbour that was our meetings. Rajni Ram for your guidance and belief in my life goals. Nurse Yuan Yuan, thank you for the chats and time we spent working together for our client. To colleagues who stayed in touch, Ina Ow, Loo Soh Teng, and Yasotha Narendran. Thank you for the friendship.

Adeline Lee, I hope you know how strong and kind you are. Paul Lee, you are an inspiration. Always grateful for the both of you.

Jillian Terese Teo, I've enjoyed all our chats, especially the grandparent ones. Grateful for our connection. You'll Never Walk Alone.

Josephine Ng, good things will come into your life.

Caryl-Anne Linderson, I remember the first time we had lunch together and we clicked instantly. Grateful for our friendship that continues to this day.

My grassroots advisor, Tan Chuan-Jin, I am deeply grateful to you for coming over and listening to my grandfather's stories in April 2021.

I believe he will never forget that day. Thank you for being such a down-to-earth Speaker of Parliament, someone I've been able to talk to about our shared love for Liverpool FC. YNWA, Sir.

To my neighbours:

The Ho family, we've stayed side by side for more than three decades. Thank you for being wonderful neighbours.

The Oh family, thank you for being lovely. I remember the hamsters you gave me when I was fourteen. Thank you, Osbourne and Jacqueline, too for the supper we had. It was fun!

To all my friends, near and far in particular:

Esther Ng, thank you for being my mentor and believing in my every dream. You helped me realise so much about my inner child, the girl who loved to share stories, play and explore.

My LJ and beyond friend, Jess Bonsell, I've enjoyed all the talks we've had over the years about everything life and love has the potential to be. You're someone who sees me as I truly am. I look forward to reading your books one day.

Bernadette Bonsell, for the love and acceptance I've felt from you since the day we met. Your warmth has stayed with me though it's been a while since we've met.

Nadiah Isa, thank you for being you and spending quality time with me.

Shreya Gopi, your kindness always astounds me. Thank you for lending me some insight into the publishing process at the initial stage of this journey.

Pavithra Raja, thank you for letting me into your world a little bit and for your quiet, gentle ways.

Baona Teo, where do I begin? Maybe with: I'm so glad we met all those years ago through PAYM HK and that we stayed in touch.

Shirin Chua, your work with migrant workers is inspiring. You're going to do good things with your life, I know it.

Juliana Ajis, my fellow Liverpool fan. I believe your faith can move mountains.

Farah Izzah, thank you for your generosity of spirit and warmth.

My KKAdventurers co-founder Wan Nazurah, all we have ever shared has meant so much to me. Like you said, it was fate that we met.

Yang Jin Jie for the spirit of adventure that will always bind us. Climb on.

Andy Ng, for all your astute and wacky observations about life.

Paula Loh, I just adore you. Thank you for being a great friend.

Samantha Fong, for the study you conducted and the quality time.

Eric Ma, you never gave up on your goal of becoming a doctor and now you're living the life you planned. Thank you for believing in my dreams too.

Carol Calpan, I remember the day you were sitting on the grassy patch surrounded by pink trumpet flowers with the dog you care for, Tata. I was moved to approach you to chat with you. Since then, we've kept bumping into each other in our neighbourhood. I'm grateful for you.

Paolo, thank you for the fun quality time we spent together. I cherish those memories. Thank you too for being there for me when my grandfather was dying and in the aftermath of his death.

Mia, I miss your cuddles and companionship. Thank you for being the cat I never had. Although it was only for a short while, I will always remember you.

My KCC girls, Nurrasyidah Aris and Nurul Akhyar, thank you for the sisterhood. Love you both!

Yuko, thank you for the talks we shared and the encouragement to pursue my goals.

Susana, thank you for the friendship. 'We will never know the outcome of the paths we did not take,' you told me one night. I appreciate your wisdom.

Amélie, thank you for being a good floormate and an even better friend.

Eve, thank you for being my birthday twin. I appreciate the fun and laughter we share.

Rupert, I appreciate your kindness and humour. You helped me in my grief process and your presence makes a difference. Thank you for being you.

To all my paternal family members, thank you for being my family.

Susanti Binte Subakri Daimin, thank you for taking care of Datuk so patiently and for the delicious food you prepare. Your kind and unselfish disposition has been a true blessing to our family.

Ilya Haider, thank you for being my nephew and a friend I can talk to about life.

My cousins in particular: Shirin for being the first person to suggest I write this book. I carried our favourite story within me all these years. But it was not until you gave me the gentle nudge and stars aligned that I found the courage to start. Teja Salehuddin Tan for sharing your interesting insights on life and the quality time I've spent with your lovable children, Isa, Darius and Rumi. Tan U-Jiun for your awesome sense of humour and kindness. Shazwani Babjee for being one of the first readers of my first draft. Farah Kools, my memories of us from our halcyon childhood days spring to my mind as I type this. Looking forward to seeing you again.

My strong aunts, Aunty Norma and my late Aunty Noraini, thank you for your love, courage and wisdom.

My Aunt Zahara, thank you so much for the talk and hug we shared on Eid and for being there with Datuk when he passed.

To my amazing uncles:

My late Uncle Ismail, the journalist, writer and dreamer. I try to remember all the things you've tried to teach me over the years. I will never forget the last words you said to me. Your qi lives on and wherever you are now, I know you're seeking peace. I love you so much, Uncle Mail.

Uncle Babjee, my mutton briyani friend. Thank you for being with me in the ward when Datuk was hospitalised. I will never forget the time we shared. Your care and devotion towards Datuk is something I truly admire. Fist bump!

My late Uncle Mohd, thank you for being a good son to my grandparents.

Uncle Shariff, thank you for your devotion to our family and your wonderful sense of humour.

To my family:

Dear Mama (Noor Bee Binte Kassim), you filled our home with a myriad of books, classical music and old movies, determined in your efforts to give your only child some companions. When I would look out the window and long for my sibling, I always looked back and found a friend in a book you had left for me. Know that I am who I am because of you. Love, your Mimi.

Dear Papa (Mohamad Anwar Bin Yunus), my happiest memories of us come from early childhood: pak pak, warm and steady, to lull me to sleep, how you used to carry me out to the little farm diagonally opposite our street to pet the animals and feed the goat, and how I learnt to toddle on your feet. Now my favourite times are when we eat prata or nasi padang together and when you tease me about LFC's match results. Thank you for your patience with me. I love and admire you so much.

My beloved grandmother, Rose Wee nee Asmah Binte Abdullah. Your children called you Nya Nya (Mother). I was taught to call you Nenek (Grandmother). But you were more than my Nenek; you were Nya Nya to me too. I have your impulsivity and temper, but I also have your bravery and loyalty. There isn't anything you wouldn't have done for me and by that same measure, there isn't anything I wouldn't do for you. Once in a while, I sleep with the patchwork quilt you sewed for me, clutching the inner emerald layer to my chest. When I eat pineapple tarts or chicken soup or watch a Channel 8 drama, I feel your presence with me. I can't wait to see you again, Nya.

My dearly departed grandfather, Kassim Bin Tambi. You used to tease me with this rhyme: 'Nadia Ayesha seperti telur ayam pecah' as I skipped lightly through your home. You passed away on my birthday, leaving behind treasured memories of thirty-four years of doting on me. Remember the pink and white bedroom furniture you bought for me? I kept it in my room till I was twenty-nine because it was from you. Those colour pencils you had my name printed on? I coloured many drawings with them. But more than those presents, what I remember more is the quality time: the countless soccer matches, trips to the hospital and the bank, quiet moments in your room, organising your appointment cards and listening to all your stories, fantastically and passionately retold. Thank you for believing in me all my life, Datuk. I love you endlessly.